INTRODUCTION

Spring in Paris by Peggy Darty
Melanie Roberts is fulfilling her dying grandmother's wish that she visit Paris. Melanie is prepared to see the sights alone, but a chance encounter with fellow American, Dave Browning, makes the city of romance come to life. Can a brief holiday romance have a future?

Wall of Stone by Nancy J. Farrier
As the first anniversary of her parents' murder approaches, Chandra Kirby realizes she needs to get away from familiar places in order to deal with her pain. She arrives in England to take a bike tour, only to discover that she will be reunited with one man she has ever loved, Pierce Stillwell—and with his girlfriend.

River Runners by Marilou H. Flinkman
One year shy of completing her training as a veterinarian, Anthea Hoyt is spending part of her summer as she has every year since she was a child: rafting the mighty Colorado River. Paid to be a tour guide, she usually stays aloof from male passengers. But this year is different. And so is John Briggs.

Sudden Showers by Gail Sattler
With no car and no money, Sharmane Winters' vacation seems to have ended before it even began. Resigned to spending the week at home, a sudden downpour throws her into the company of Alex Brunnel who is long overdue for a vacation. Partnered to see the sights of their hometown, Vancouver, British Columbia, together, will they find a common bond to unite them when the routine of everyday life takes over?

Summer Getaways

Spring in Paris © 2000 by Peggy Darty.
Wall of Stone © 2000 by Nancy J. Farrier.
River Runners © 2000 by Marilou H. Flinkman.
Sudden Showers © 2000 by Gail Sattler.

Cover art by Julie Sawyer and Image Zoo

Illustrations by Mari Goering

ISBN 1-59310-834-6

Scripture verses are taken from the King James Version of the Bible unless otherwise noted.

Published by Barbour Publishing, Inc., P.O. Box 719, Uhrichsville, Ohio 44683, www.barbourbooks.com

Our mission is to publish and distribute inspirational products offering exceptional value and biblical encouragement to the masses.

ecpa   Member of the
Evangelical Christian
Publishers Association

Printed in the United States of America.

Summer Getaways

*4 unforgettabe stories that will sweep you
away on romantic excursions*

Peggy Darty
Nancy J. Farrier
Marilou H. Flinkman
Gail Sattler

BARBOUR
PUBLISHING

Spring in Paris

by Peggy Darty

Chapter 1

It was five A.M. in Paris when Melanie Roberts' plane touched down at Charles de Gaulle airport. Melanie felt every mile of the journey. Her clothes were rumpled, and she had reverted back to her thick lenses because she was still adjusting to her new contacts. Her shoulder-length, glossy hair had now been whisked back from her face and secured with a rubber band.

Her shoulder bag tugged hard on her shoulder and she gave over to the slump. Despite aspirin, soothing music, and earphones, she hadn't slept more than an hour. She kept thinking about all that water underneath the plane.

Glancing around her, she noted the other passengers looked as bedraggled as she did. They were businessmen, or women who were probably visiting family, and a few stray singles like her.

She sighed and took a firmer grip on her bulging shoulder bag, but not before it had slammed into the passenger behind her.

"Sorry," she called over her shoulder to the man who looked far too crisp at this hour in his expensive suit.

"No problem," he answered in a slurred voice, but she could tell from his expression that he considered the jab of her shoulder bag a big problem.

She turned back around, shuffling with the line, realizing why the Ivy League types never appealed to her. Too arrogant.

She was herded into the long customs line, proof that at last she was in Paris.

"Business or holiday?" the customs officer asked.

"Holiday."

His eyes lingered on her passport then returned to her. She looked down at the passport picture, recalling it was made before she got a different hairstyle, but at least she was wearing the same glasses. His eyes swept her five-foot-seven-inch frame, all one hundred thirty-five pounds of it; then he stamped the passport and handed it back.

She fought her way to the luggage carousel where she spotted the Ivy Leaguer again. There was the usual wait for the luggage to arrive, so she sank into a hard chair and closed her eyes. Her second graders flashed through her mind, and she wondered how they were spending their spring break. Then she thought of her wonderful grandmother, who had passed away in January. The money she had left Melanie had been earmarked in a special note. "Go see Paris for me. . . ."

Paris was a long way from little Milton, Ohio. *Thank You, God.*

A flurry around her jolted her back to her senses and she struggled to her feet as a jumble of luggage rolled around the carousel. She spotted Ivy League again.

Watching him hassle his sleek luggage gave her a bit of satisfaction so that she almost missed her maroon canvas bags.

After another tussle, she ended up out on the street, her mind suddenly blank. She reached into her jeans pocket, fumbling around for the engraved card with the address of the Ritz. She had told herself she was going first class, especially with the hotel, and by the price, she knew she had.

The limos were disappearing, along with the taxis as the crowd elbowed ahead. She hesitated, wondering what to do. Then suddenly a taxi screeched to the curb before her. A little Frenchman hopped out and tossed off some words that didn't seem to match anything in her French-English dictionary.

"Want to share a taxi?" Ivy League suddenly appeared. "Where are you headed?"

"The Ritz," she informed him with pride.

He nodded. "I'm staying near there."

He related all of this to the driver who was loading their luggage into the trunk. Ivy League opened the back door and glanced over his shoulder at her. "Well, do you or don't you want a ride?" The slur was actually a southern accent, because the lazy drawl had been sharpened with crisp consonants. He was clearly irritated.

"I do," she snapped back, piling into the backseat and staring pointedly out the window. As she gazed, she quickly forgot about her grouchy traveling companion. It was still early morning in Paris, and the taxi zipped right along. Melanie watched with delight as they approached the famous landmarks she had studied about in the travel books. She knew exactly where she was. She didn't need to speak French!

They had passed the Champs-Elysées and were heading toward the Arc de Triomphe. Melanie pressed her face closer to the window, pushed her glasses securely in place, and peered at the French flag from inside the Arc. Soon the taxi was pulling into the Place Vendome.

She bit her tongue to keep from saying, *There it is*. She glanced quickly at Ivy League who was fast asleep, even snoring! How could one sleep when the statue of Napoleon crowned the middle of the square?

She turned in her seat as they swept past it, and now the driver was pulling to the curb where a green canopy overhung the entrance to a hotel. It took a moment for her to realize this was the Ritz. It was obviously understated elegance, so typical of Paris class.

The driver had announced their arrival as he swung to the curb, and Melanie gripped her shoulder bag and glanced again at her sleeping traveling companion. *So long, Ivy League.*

She stepped out onto the curb and discovered her driver knew English for his fares; he briskly told her exactly what she owed him. She added a generous tip, and then he led the way through the revolving doors where a smartly dressed concierge took charge, escorting her up to the reception desk.

There was no line here, and the concierge at the desk spoke English. She listened carefully as he handed her a registration form while explaining the amenities of the hotel. She went through the process, nodding gratefully while handing over her passport and credit card. She had pre-registered by mail weeks ago, so the paperwork went swiftly, and soon he was handing back her passport and credit card, motioning for one of many fast-paced bellboys.

She was ushered down a couple of steps and across the lobby, where several distinguished-looking men wearing business clothes and reading newspapers glanced disinterestedly at her.

Melanie ran a hand self-consciously over her hair, realizing she hadn't put on any lip gloss in hours or even brushed her hair. It was no wonder she was not attracting any attention. On they went, down a long hall flanked by impressive little boutiques.

"Is this your first trip to Paris?" the concierge asked as they reached the elevator. She wondered if it was that obvious.

"Yes, it is," she replied as the elevator door slid open and they stepped inside.

He glanced at her once again as he led the way down the hall and unlocked a door. He seemed to sense how tired she was and didn't attempt to continue polite conversation. She reached for her billfold to tip him as he opened the door and placed her luggage inside.

"If you need anything—"

"I'll be fine," she smiled as he walked out, softly closing the door.

Her eyes widened as she surveyed her new home for the next six days. The room was filled with antiques, which would bring a rare gulp of enthusiasm from her mother, but which held little fascination for her. What she did like was the gorgeous soft pink brocades and marble fireplace. Her bedroom was a gracious blend of more pale pink in the satin coverlet of the bed with its matching pink chair. She peered into the bathroom and spotted the same marble elegance there.

She quickly opened her canvas bags, shook out the new clothes, and proudly hung each treasured garment on a padded hanger. Then after she had luxuriated in the beaded-oil bath water of the huge tub, she pulled on a loose gown and sank into the pink satin bed. She felt as though she had just melted into a pink cloud.

When she awoke and glanced at the ornate clock on her bedside table, she had slept until noon! She stirred lazily, enjoying the comfort and luxury.

"Oh, Granny," she said, hugging the companion pillow, "thank you for making a dream come true!"

Melanie had dressed in her least-wrinkled outfit, a floral silk skirt that swirled about her ankles and a yellow silk blouse that matched the delicate buttercups in her skirt. She had found some comfortable yet attractive sandals.

She took more care with her hair and makeup today, then sauntered down to the lobby. There were people everywhere and she quickly hurried out to the sidewalk. A warm sun greeted her, and just ahead, the aroma of coffee and freshly baked bread lured passersby to a cozy sidewalk café.

Since she was not a coffee drinker, she bypassed the espresso in favor of a morning tea. She watched with delight as the tea was delivered to her in a beautiful little floral teapot and a proper-looking English china cup. She poured the steaming tea and added honey. Ah, this was living!

Sipping her tea, she studied the entertaining array of people passing the café. Men in lightweight suits, stepping quickly along. Women of all ages and sizes wore flowing dresses or skirts, looking chic, fashionable, and *thin*.

But she took a deep breath and reminded herself that she was no longer overweight with mousy brown hair and simple clothes. To reaffirm her thoughts, she ran her slender, manicured fingers over her silk skirt and enjoyed the idea of feeling pretty and moving at her own pace, for a change. She had chosen not to sign up for any tours, preferring instead to roam around at her own leisure.

The man from last night—Ivy League—had just come in and was looking for a seat. Suddenly, his eyes landed on her and widened in recognition. She stared back. He looked so different today. Khakis and a green golf shirt had replaced the well-tailored business suit and flashy tie. Somehow seeing him more relaxed made her take notice of him in a way she hadn't during their first meeting. For example, she hadn't noticed what a nice tan he had.

He had smooth dark brown hair, worn short with a side part on the left, a rather long jawline, offset by a nose that just missed being too short, and wide-set blue eyes. Actually, he was quite handsome until she remembered his attitude.

Then she dropped her eyes to her cup, not acknowledging him; after all, he had been downright rude. Almost. But then so had she. As she concentrated on placing her cup on the table and looking out at the crowd, she saw from the corner of her eye that he was slowly approaching her.

"I almost didn't recognize you," he said, standing uninvited at her table. The southern drawl floated smoothly on the balmy spring morning, sounding both interesting and appealing. "You. . .look so different from last night."

Since she had recently checked her image in the mirror of her compact, she knew what he was seeing. Gray eyes with the contacts in place and the caramel highlights in her brown hair gleaming in the sun.

"You look different too," she said with that edge to her voice that had emerged during her adolescence. For her, it had been a wall of defense against being fat, but her father termed her defense an "attitude."

She smiled to soften any trace of sarcasm as she looked into the blue—very blue—eyes.

An awkward moment of silence followed, and she realized he was lingering because he wanted her to invite him to sit down, so she did.

"I'm Dave Browning," he said, settling into the seat.

"Melanie Roberts," she said, not offering her hand.

"*Bonjour.*" Her waiter had returned and was looking interestedly at Dave.

He ordered one of the strong espressos like everyone else was drinking then turned back to her. "So did you sleep well at the Ritz?" he asked politely.

"Very well," she replied, touching a linen napkin to her mouth. "And you?"

He leaned back in the chair and stretched, showing off nice shoulders and muscled tan biceps. He either was a sportsman or he pumped iron.

"Everything was fine," he replied as the waiter delivered coffee. "I was so tired I think I could have slept on a park bench." He paused and frowned. "In fact, you were already out of the taxi and the driver was shaking me awake before I knew what had happened."

"You fell asleep; in fact, you were snoring when I got out."

He chuckled, a nice rich sound that the southern drawl somehow complemented. "The perfect traveling companion, right?"

She smiled, and he was staring into her eyes and smiling back. She hoped he liked what he saw. "I was envious because I was so exhausted I could hardly think," she replied honestly. "But I've never been able to sleep in a moving vehicle."

"Didn't you sleep on the plane?"

"Not really."

He shook his head, taking a sip of the strong coffee. "I guess I snored all the way to Paris."

"I wish I could have! We've been busy at school and there's never any time to rest before a vacation."

"School? Grad school?"

She smiled. "No, I teach second grade."

"My mom's a teacher," he said, taking another deep sip of his espresso.

"What grade?"

"Ninth and tenth. Mostly English."

"Mine too! Her field is history. Thank God she's at the high school or she'd be strolling down to my second grade class to observe my method of teaching."

"Or reminding you about your passport?"

She had to laugh. "How did you know?"

"Well," he said, giving her a long look, "we have more in common than I thought."

She picked up a spoon to stir the honey from the bottom of her cup. It was merely an action to cover a moment of embarrassment. He must have thought of her in much the same way she had judged him: *Not my type.*

"Where are you from, Melanie?"

"Milton, Ohio. Small town you've probably never heard of. And where in Dixie do you call home?" she asked, suddenly very interested in him. Her mind seemed to produce questions and supply answers more easily now. Perhaps it was because she was in Paris and had left the old Melanie Roberts back in Milton.

His lips spread over even white teeth into an amused little smile. "Atlanta. Deep in the heart of Dixie."

She didn't have to ask which state, for there was only one Atlanta that people talked about.

"I've never been to Atlanta," she admitted. "We took a family vacation in Florida when I was in high school. The area was pretty and I liked it, but that's the only part of the South I've visited."

"Really?" He seemed amazed. "Then you should come in the spring. If you like beautiful flowers and the flavor of the Old South, there are lots of tours of historical homes and beautiful gardens."

"Oh? Then I'd either have to come south soon or wait until next spring." Her words flowed easily, because it seemed so natural to be sitting here in Paris, France, on a weekday morning, talking to a complete stranger yet feeling incredibly comfortable with. . .*Dave Browning*. She even liked the name as she repeated it again in her mind.

"Well, you could come in the fall. We have lots of hardwoods that turn beautiful colors—and there are always tours then," he added, grinning.

"Maybe I will," she said lightly, as the waiter stopped to lift her pitcher and pour more tea. "*Merci beaucoup.*" There, the phrase from her book sounded okay after listening to Dave.

"What are you doing in Paris?" he asked as he sipped his coffee.

"I'm on spring break. What about you?"

"Not on holiday," he said, and for the first time a slight frown rumpled his tanned forehead. His dark hair gleamed in the sunlight as though he had just shampooed it.

"I'm here on business. My company is having one of its international meetings." When he named the company, she recognized it immediately as one of the top dogs in the computer industry.

"And what precisely do you do for your company?" she asked, trying not to sound too impressed, although she was.

"I work with a development team designing software programs." His blue eyes grew serious as he spoke of his job. "We're trying to work the kinks out of a new program that will be a major breakthrough in the world of computer programming."

"That sounds exciting," she said, trying to imagine

him behind a desk, staring at a computer screen, his mind conjuring up new techniques to keep abreast of the expanding world of technology.

He tilted his head slightly and looked at her. "Well, my job interests me but—"

"But what?" she leaned forward, placing her elbows on the table and cupping her hands under her chin. She was aware that her French manicure complimented her long slender fingers, and she was glad that she had added a few rings to her fingers, other than the usual birthstone.

"But. . .I guess it sounds dull to other people," he continued. "At least, most women I talk with frown and change the subject when I mention computers. Or they launch into something negative about their experiences with computers."

"My second graders are already learning the basics." She thought about that for a moment and decided to voice her feelings. "It's remarkable how quickly their young minds pick up on computer knowledge, and I'm always amazed at how their little hands handle the mouse. . . ." She stopped herself before adding *better than I do.*

She was by no means computer illiterate, but she had never bothered to get E-mail or browse the Internet, as most of her friends had. She spent her spare time curled up on the sofa, reading a new book. Taylor, on the other hand, was constantly zipping out E-mails from Cincinnati to her mom and all of her friends.

Dave was saying nothing, sipping his coffee and she realized her mind had dashed off again. "How long will you be here?" she asked quickly, noticing that his coffee was almost gone and he was refusing another serving from the waiter.

"Just until Friday," he replied. "And you?"

"Until Saturday."

"So what are you planning to do and see?" he asked.

"As much as I can," she admitted honestly, glancing toward the busy boulevard and wondering where to start.

"You were alone on the plane," he recalled suddenly. "Do you have friends here?"

"No. But then I'm a bit of a loner."

He nodded. "So am I." He looked at his watch but he didn't stand as she had expected. She knew the noon hour was over, and he was probably due somewhere.

"Do you have plans for tonight?" he asked suddenly.

"I. . .well, no. Not yet."

"Would you like to go to dinner? One of the advantages of my job is that I do get to come here twice a year. I know a few places to dine, and I've seen the major landmarks."

"Then maybe you can give me some advice. I have certain places in mind, but I'm not sure about the best times to visit." It was something she had been worrying about as she left the hotel this morning.

"My pleasure," he said, the southern accent dripping with charm. And she really liked the smile. It all fit together just right. She was aware that her heart was beating a bit faster, as though she had just climbed a flight of steps.

"In fact, I'd like to skip out of the afternoon meetings and go with you today," he said, his soft voice holding a tone of regret, "but I have to be at this particular meeting."

"Oh, I wouldn't want you to miss it," she replied, a bit too quickly, and she wondered if her "attitude" had surfaced. *Dinner*, she remembered. "I'd love to have dinner with you," she smiled up at him, hoping, if there had been any sarcasm in her tone, she had just erased it.

"Great! How about if I pick you up in the lobby of the Ritz at eight? Nightlife starts late here. But then it does in Atlanta, as well."

Nightlife never starts in Milton, she could have added. Instead, she replied casually, "Eight will be fine."

"Okay." The waiter had magically appeared with both checks and Dave took hers as well.

"You don't have to do that," she said, but then shut her mouth. She realized he was doing something nice for her, and she had to learn how to accept compliments, another failing of hers. "But thanks," she added sweetly. Not saccharine sweet, like Taylor, but the kind of sweet she used when her students brought her little gifts.

"You're very welcome. Thanks for perking up my day. And I'll see you this evening," he said, glancing again at his watch then shaking his head. "I'm already late, which is out of character for me."

"Then you'd better hurry," she said, keeping her seat. She intended to have another cup of tea and absorb the flavor of a spring day in Paris.

"Bye," he called over his shoulder as he quickly paid and hurried onto the sidewalk. He walked in the opposite direction, so she could stare after him, sizing him up. He might be only a couple of inches taller than she, but his build suited him well. He was not too muscled, not too thin or heavy, and he walked straight and purposefully, as though he knew where he was going and exactly how he was getting there.

She gave the waiter a big smile as he poured more tea for her. She was having the time of her life.

Chapter 2

At precisely eight that evening, Melanie stepped off the elevator into the lobby and saw Dave seated on a sofa, dressed in a nice suit with a more conservative tie. As she walked toward him, she thought the blue eyes lit up as he came quickly to his feet.

"Hi. I hope you haven't been waiting long." She wondered if she had misjudged her timing.

"Just got here," he said with a smile. "You look great."

"Thanks."

His gaze swept down her new dress. The dress was a jade-green linen with a mandarin collar that hugged her neck. As the salesgirl pointed out, this shade of green accented her gray eyes and pink skin and picked up the highlights in her hair. It was a long dress featuring the popular slit on the side of the skirt. She had worn delicate gold sandals with flat heels so she wouldn't be taller than Dave.

She glanced through the hotel window. "I didn't bring a jacket," she said absently. She had picked a fine time to worry about that, but she hadn't the right jacket for the dress, anyway.

"You'll be fine. It's a wonderful evening, warm with balmy breezes. Not as warm as Atlanta, but that's a blessing."

"It's already warm in Atlanta in May?"

"It's warm in Atlanta as early as March, but March is usually windy and undependable. April brings the showers and flowers and all that. The summers are hot and humid." His hand cupped her elbow as they crossed the lobby to the revolving front doors.

"It's still cool and windy in Milton," she said as they stepped onto the sidewalk, and he hailed a taxi and gave the driver an address that meant nothing to her.

"You really know your French," she said with a smile.

"There are certain phrases that I do well because I use them often. But as far as carrying on a lengthy conversation with the locals, I'd be at a loss."

She felt he was deliberately being modest because he had already witnessed how little she knew.

He put his arm up on the leather seat above her head, and they both gazed out at the beauty before them as they sped past the Place de la Concorde.

"How beautiful," she said, looking out at the fountains and the Eiffel Tower in the distance.

"Yes, it is. How did you spend the day?" he asked.

She told him about the souvenirs she had purchased, and the cards, and admitted it was a relief to get that behind her.

"You too? I really hate that sort of thing. Mom and my sister Alison love it."

"So do my mom and Taylor; that's my sister."

"Older or younger?" he asked interestedly.

"A year older."

"Alison is two years younger than me. There are only the two of us. No other siblings. And your family?"

"Just Taylor and me," and they both laughed.

She enjoyed the full, rich sound of his laughter as she tossed her head back and looked at him a bit closer.

He reached over to brush a tendril from her cheek, and for a moment he stared at the strand of the rich brown hair, a color chosen by an expert hairdresser to relieve the mousy brown of before. "You have nice hair," he said, smoothing it back. "My sister would be envious. She's always fussing about her hair. Too thin, too curly, or too straight. Every day is a bad hair day for Alison."

She could relate to that but she didn't say so. She merely smiled. "How old is she?" It was a sly way of learning his age after he had told her Alison was two years his junior.

"Twenty-three. She's a registered nurse engaged to be married just before Christmas."

"Oh really? Do you like the guy?"

He chuckled. "He was my roommate at the University of Georgia. Yeah, I like him. Actually, I used to bring him home on weekends. We were sophomores and Alison was a big-eyed, high school senior. For her, it was love at first sight. Trey is more cautious, but I could see that he liked her right away. So could Mom and Dad. They got engaged the next Christmas when Alison was a freshman at Georgia. My parents insisted on her finishing college before getting married; that's the reason they waited."

She liked everything he had told her. He seemed to come from a good family, and she wondered about his faith but was unsure how to ask.

They had reached their destination, for the driver had pulled to the curb and Dave was paying the fare. Then they were out of the taxi, entering a restaurant that she recognized from a picture in the guidebook. She was impressed that he had taken her to such an exclusive place for dinner.

"I've been going on about my family. What about yours?" he asked, as they entered the candlelit dining room, which reeked of elegance and gourmet food.

"Taylor is married and has two children. She married her high school sweetheart, and she was *not* one to get her college degree. She went a couple of years and that was it. Said she always knew what she wanted to be: a wife and mother."

Dave nodded agreeably, as he held the chair for her while men in white uniforms rushed forward to attend to their every need. Never in her life had she eaten in such an elegant restaurant, even though Springfield and Cleveland had some fine ones. This one was different; and she remembered under the picture she had seen in the guidebook that this one was highlighted as a four-star with excellent French cuisine. There had even been something about the chefs, but she had forgotten.

Huge menus were spread before them. Water was delicately poured into fine crystal goblets; wine was offered, but Dave refused. "Unless you would like some?" he asked quickly.

"No, thank you. If you've dined here before, I'm going to depend on you to choose for me."

Somehow it didn't embarrass her to say that to him, for he seemed so accepting of her and she had really begun to feel comfortable with him.

He ordered a French dish that she interpreted as some kind of chicken. He handed the waiter the menu, smiled, then turned back to her.

"Tell me more about your family." He looked genuinely interested and so she tried to capsule their varied natures. "My mother teaches in high school, as you already know, and my father is an accountant. Both are very sensible, down-to-earth people. I guess Taylor is more sensible than I want to admit," she added slowly, speaking honestly to him.

"She's been a great mom to her girls, not spoiling them too much or giving in to their every whim. And yet she is kind and patient with them. I admire that," she added, hoping to assure him that she wasn't jealous of Taylor. But of course she was. In fact, she had always been jealous of Taylor, for whom life seemed to come so easy during their teens.

"Your parents are still together," he said, proving he had been listening. "So are mine. Most of my friends have stepparents and an assortment of family—you know, his, hers, ours. My parents will celebrate their thirtieth anniversary in July, and Alison wants to give them a party."

She had to laugh. "Mom and Dad celebrated their thirtieth last February, and Taylor did give them a party. Well, I did too. This is amazing."

"What?"

"I wouldn't have thought that first night. . ." Her voice trailed, as she dropped her eyes to the gleaming silverware.

"I know what you mean. I wouldn't have thought that first night we had so much in common. That *is* what you were going to say, right?"

She looked back at him, relieved to see that he wasn't making fun. He was admitting he had been just as turned off by her as she was by him. She smiled. "I was tired and grumpy."

"I was tired and rude," he said, taking the brunt of their unpleasant first meeting.

"No, you weren't," she laughed. "You were tired, I was tired."

They were both laughing as the waiter rolled up the salad cart and skillfully tossed their salad from a huge crystal bowl then expertly wielded his silver tongs, serving each of them a mixture of greens on a small crystal plate.

"Hey, it's interesting that we picked up the same flight in New York," he said, as his eyes roamed over her hair and settled on her gray eyes.

"Funny I didn't see you," she said, looking across at him.

"That's because I was buried down into the seat, half asleep when most of the passengers boarded. Our paths might not have crossed if—"

"If I hadn't jabbed you in the stomach with my bulky shoulder bag," she finished for him.

"And I wasn't planning to go out of the hotel for coffee

this morning, but it was such a pretty day, I decided to take a quick stroll before the afternoon meeting."

"Quite a coincidence," she said, and then an important question moved to the forefront of her mind. Whether it was coincidence or romance, she already knew quite a bit about him, yet she didn't know the most important thing.

"What do you do on weekends?" she asked, after she swallowed a bite of the tasty salad, enjoying the sweet delicate flavor of the dressing.

"If I told you I work most Saturdays, you'd probably think I was a workaholic."

"Are you?" she asked honestly.

"In a way. But it's been a tough year, and I try to do the best I can at whatever I undertake. I really like this company and want to stay with them."

She nodded. That still didn't answer her question.

"I manage to get in a little golf on Sunday, or go to the lake fishing with Dad."

She dipped into her salad again, feeling her spirits sink. "So that's how you spend Sundays?"

"Sunday afternoon, or I fish with Dad on Saturdays. We usually go to church on Sunday, then I go to my parents' house and pig out on Mom's Sunday dinners."

She leaned back in her chair and breathed a deep sigh of relief.

"What?" He apparently sensed there was something meaningful in what he had told her, but he had not yet figured it out.

"I go to church too. We're. . .a Christian family."

"So are we," he said, as though it were as natural as eating or breathing. "Oh, I get it." His eyes lit up again. "You were wondering if I was a party guy?"

"I was wondering if you were a Christian," she said seriously. "That's very important to me. My. . .former boyfriend wasn't, and we. . .well, it presented problems that we couldn't resolve. You see, he didn't believe in God. Neither did his family. It made a drastic difference in our values. I mean, he was a decent person, but—"

"I know what you're saying. Of course, I live in what is sometimes referred to as the Bible Belt, and yet we have nonbelievers there, just like everywhere else. I dated a girl in college who flaunted her atheism on our third date. Our last date," he added, shaking his head. "She was one of the prettiest girls in school, and I couldn't see past the huge green eyes and outgoing personality. Then I learned the true meaning of that old phrase Mom had worn out when I was growing up."

"Beauty is only skin deep?"

He laughed. "You're amazing. You know what I'm going to say before I say it, Melanie."

"My grandmother said the same thing to me, about beauty being only skin deep."

"But you are beautiful," he said quietly, his blue eyes sincere as he studied her face.

For a moment, the agony of sitting in the bleachers during the high school football games with Tracy, her best friend and mirror image, flashed into her mind. They would stare grudgingly at the long-legged majorette and bouncy cheerleaders and wish with all their hearts that they could trade places.

She hesitated for a moment then decided to tell him her true feelings. He was such a good listener that he seemed to pull the truth from her. "The truth is, when I was growing up, I was overweight, wore braces, and was quite plain compared to Taylor."

"See, that's the problem."

"Excuse me?"

" 'Compared to Taylor,' you said. No doubt you heard too many people make that comparison and drew the wrong conclusion."

"I was compared to Taylor openly and often," she admitted. "I always wondered why people didn't realize how much it hurt when guys looked at me and said, 'You are Taylor's sister?' in the tone of voice you would use if you were trying to figure out why someone had two heads. Or even worse, when Mom kept suggesting that I run track or play soccer or even basketball, which she knew I hated. What she wanted to ask me was why I didn't try for size six clothes like Taylor and compete in beauty contests."

"That must have been terrible," he said, the blue eyes sad, his face serious as he focused on her completely.

Her eyes met his. "It was. And you know what I never told Mom and Dad? I didn't *want* to be like Taylor. I preferred to work in Bible school with the little kids or take up a craft I could teach to the handicapped, something useful that made sense to me."

He looked at her in amazement. "You were remarkably mature for a teenager."

She shrugged. "Aside from that, I preferred to read

stacks of books or see a play or a movie that really touched my heart. I didn't care about being popular or going to all the parties. I guess it should have been more important to me," she said, breathing a heavy sigh. "But I did what made me happy. And that didn't always make my parents happy. Oh, they were happy about my grades, which were always better than my sister's. But I was a loner and didn't really mind it. They just never understood."

"You were being Melanie Roberts," he said, looking at her with admiration. She loved the sound of her name on his lips; she even liked the southern drawl, which was beginning to do strange things to her senses. She could almost smell the magnolias, and for a moment her romantic nature created a mental image of standing in a flower garden beneath a full moon with him.

And then he added the final words that truly stole her heart. "I admire your honesty and your courage."

"Well, I can thank my grandmother for that. She and I were very much alike. In fact, I was named for her," she continued, since he was so attentive. "She was Melinda Virginia. Kids started calling me Mel and I hated that, so Tracy, my best friend, and I had one of those very serious conversations over colas and chips."

"One of those late-night girl chats?" he teased.

"Right. I decided I liked the name Melanie after I had read *Gone With the Wind* for the fourth time."

"Melanie," he nodded slowly. "It suits you."

Then their attention was diverted by a flurry of silver-domed platters and a display of beautifully prepared chicken drizzled with an almond and mushroom sauce, complimented by a wonderful brown rice and lean spears of fresh asparagus and a skillfully designed fruit medley.

"You mentioned feeling that you were always being compared to your sister and that you always felt your mother wanted to change you," Dave said. "It took courage to grow up in those circumstances. Some people get bitter and ugly about it; but you seem like such a sweet, nice person."

"Thank you," she responded. Her eyes lingered on him for a moment, still amazed by the way Dave really listened to what she had to say. He was not one of those guys who had to constantly talk about himself.

He had turned his attention to the meal, and she did the same, appreciating the opportunity of dining on such an elegant meal.

"How did your meeting go today?" she asked, wanting to be equally interested in subjects he enjoyed.

"It was long and boring, giving me an idea of what the week holds. Lengthy debates between one of the leading executives from our company and one from another company here, who has unlimited questions about our programs."

Their server appeared refilling their water goblets as they worked their way through the meal.

"However," he added slowly, "I'm afraid I'll be forced to cancel a meeting or two."

She looked startled. "Why?" She had no idea.

"Because I have met a wonderful woman that I want to get to know better, and I'll be attending a hundred other meetings. But I won't get to see Melanie Roberts and I won't be in Paris with her."

There was a touch of romance to his voice, and she was pleased and relieved that she would be seeing him again. She had not allowed her mind to stray beyond tonight, for she didn't want to feel the ache of disappointment that she would surely feel when the time came to say good-bye to Dave Browning.

"And you don't want to miss hearing all about my dysfunctional childhood!" she teased, arching an eyebrow and deliberately making light of the situation.

"I don't want to miss hearing you talk about your life—whatever, however—and I don't want to miss walking along the Seine in the moonlight. Which is exactly what I suggest we do now."

She smiled. "Sounds like a good plan."

They had waved aside the dessert menu and coffee, and the server had appeared with a thick leather case containing their bill, which she didn't want to see. She knew their meal was very expensive, but Dave was generous and kind, and she didn't know how to express her appreciation other than to say, "Thank you for dinner. I enjoyed every bite and I have thoroughly enjoyed your company."

Her gaze took in the well-dressed people talking in quiet tones over the crisp linen tablecloths. Even the servers managed to deliver and retrieve silver in a way that muted the sound. One heard only the pleasant strands of classical music from somewhere in the background.

Chapter 3

Melanie and Dave had taken a taxi to a favorite spot for tourists to stroll over the Seine. Dave had removed the coat to his suit and placed it around her shoulders, as they walked hand in hand, staring at the glow of streetlights reflected in the Seine.

"It is so beautiful here," she said dreamily, studying the way the lights sparkled on the water. "I see why it's called the City of Lights."

"I'm still amazed that we met," Dave said, looking at her, rather than at the scene before them.

Melanie rolled her head lazily and looked at him. He was standing close to her, his arm around her shoulder. "So am I," she replied gently.

He was looking into her eyes, as though trying to see to the depths of her soul. He wouldn't have to. Melanie felt that her emotions were flashing in neon all over her face.

"Why did you choose this spring break to come to Paris?" he asked curiously.

"Because of my grandmother," she answered. "I'm seeing the Seine by moonlight for her." She took a deep breath and looked back at Dave, who hadn't questioned her. It was as though he understood.

She began to talk about her grandmother, how special she had been in her life, and that led to the wish money, and the reason she was here.

"I hope you have the most wonderful vacation ever," he said, squeezing her shoulder and smiling into her eyes. "I hope you will allow me to help make that possible. If I can," he added gently.

Gripping the front of his coat with both hands, to keep it snug and warm around her, she thought about their meeting and how romantic and wonderful everything had been. "You can make it possible," she said, admiring his modesty and a dozen other characteristics about him. "You know, you are a very thoughtful person, Dave. Are all southern gentlemen as kind and polite as you? I keep waiting for you to say 'ma'am' to me."

He laughed. "No, they're not all gentleman. They can be as disagreeable as men everywhere."

"Then you have been raised well," she said. Suddenly, she was beginning to feel like a teacher again, speaking to one of her students. "I noticed right off that you didn't just come plop down at my table today. You waited for permission."

"Well, that isn't being a southern gentleman," he said, tweaking her nose. "Most guys with half a brain would have waited in case you hated the sight of me."

She laughed, daring not to comment for fear of how much she would reveal. "It goes back to being a southern gentlemen," she insisted.

"Then I'll take that as encouragement to ask you to go sightseeing with me tomorrow."

Her heart jumped. It was as though she were spinning her own perfect dream. "What about your meetings?" she finally managed to ask though her tone was weak. Why was she reminding him? Now she was afraid he would start thinking more seriously and she didn't want that.

"I know the topic that's being covered. In fact, we've already been over it half a dozen times at the conference table in Atlanta. The competition is going to present their side, and we already know where they stand. I'll just say I have a more important appointment."

"Great. I'll have my own tour guide since you've been here before." She couldn't resist the smile that spread over her face. She fought the impulse to reach up and plant a kiss on his cheek, which would be quite a departure from the old Melanie Roberts. But she really wanted to touch his cheek, trace the outline of his broad jaw with her finger.

He glanced at his watch and took her arm. "Did you know it's ten o'clock in the evening in Atlanta?"

"What time does that make it here?"

He grinned. "Three o'clock in the morning."

"You're kidding!"

She couldn't believe they had spent so much time together and that, for the first time in her life, she was out at this hour of the night—no, morning, she corrected herself. There were still couples out strolling together, and one was actually clenched in a tight embrace, kissing as though they were the only couple in the world. This truly was a city of romance. Snuggling into Dave's coat and against his side, as he gently wrapped his arm around her, she thought how wonderful and *natural* this felt.

Their footsteps echoed over the sidewalk as they walked underneath a streetlight, enveloping them in a soft golden halo. She simply could not believe this was happening to her. Then she remembered the Bible verses Granny had taught her about patience and the importance of understanding that God works things out by His calendar, not hers.

She wished the evening could go on and on, even though they were already getting into a taxi and all too soon they were back at her hotel. He paid the fare, and automatically their steps slowed as they approached the door of the hotel. It was as though he regretted leaving her as much as she did him. But she was beginning to feel the weariness of a very long day. "You must be exhausted," she looked up at him.

"On the contrary," he said, nodding at the doorman as they entered the brightly lit lobby. "I'm wide awake."

He stopped in the lobby, and she realized that again he was being a gentleman. "Do you want me to walk you up to your room?"

She shook her head. "No, you need to get back to your hotel and get some rest." Reluctantly, she removed the coat from her shoulders and handed it to him. "I'll remember to bring a sweater the next time."

"Tomorrow will be a pleasant spring day," he said with only a trace of weariness in his voice. "Dress for comfort. And be sure to wear comfortable shoes."

She nodded. Her comfortable thick-soled leather loafers were already laid out.

They hesitated for a moment longer, as though unable to tear their gazes from each other. Then she did what she had wanted to do earlier. She reached up and kissed him on the cheek, not caring what the concierge thought. They had probably seen much more passionate embraces at this hour in the hotel lobby.

Her quick gesture pleased him, she could tell, for his blue eyes were glowing as he squeezed her hand. "Will ten o'clock be too early to get started? I only require about seven hours' sleep, but you may want to sleep in later than that."

She shook her head. "I have all summer to sleep in. I don't want to miss a thing while I'm here."

"See you then," he said, but he made no move to leave.

Melanie decided to take the initiative. She squeezed his hand back. "I had a wonderful time," she said, taking a step back from him.

"So did I." His eyes followed her as she took another step back, then she forced herself to turn around and walk to the elevator. But in her heart she had taken flight and was drifting through thin air like an angel. Or at least tonight she had become Cinderella, the enchanted heroine of the fable she often read to her little girls in school while the boys wiggled in their seats and pretended to be bored.

Chapter 4

When she looked out of the hotel window, she saw to her great pleasure that it was a gorgeous spring day. The chestnut trees were in full bloom and there was a slow, lazy beauty to everything. She took a deep long breath, feeling totally relaxed after a good night's rest.

Pink. This was definitely the day for the pink linen dress with the square neck, cap sleeves, and long skirt with its deep side slit. Too bad her skin wasn't yet tanned enough to do the dress justice. But she had her own opinion about tanning beds. She preferred the natural vitamin D. She hurried to the shower, deciding to shampoo her hair for the second day in a row, just to be sure it really gleamed in the sunlight. *Have I ever shampooed my hair two days in a row?* she asked herself absently as she gathered up her toiletries.

She was making progress toward being the desirable woman she had always dreamed of becoming. Humming an old song Granny used to sing about April in Paris, she smiled to herself when she got to the part about not feeling a lover's warm embrace until April in Paris. As she turned the shower on, she wondered if Dave had ever heard the song.

It was exactly ten when she stepped into the lobby, but Dave was already there, wearing khaki chinos, a white knit polo shirt, and a pair of loafers that looked as though they were made for comfortable walks around Paris. Clean and nice, but the leather was obviously a bit worn. Stretched to fit his feet, her father would say when he wanted to pay a compliment to his favorite shoes.

A smile quickly appeared when Dave spotted her and walked over to meet her. His eyes swept down her dress then returned to her face. He was looking at the short curly tendrils she had spent some time styling about her face before braiding the length of her hair in a French braid. It felt right, and she thought he must like it though he didn't say so. He merely smiled, as though she was exactly what he had expected.

"So do you have our itinerary?" she asked, initiating a conversation.

He whipped a pocket-size notebook from his pocket and flipped open the pages. "I studied the map last night and decided we should begin with the farthest point first, if that suits you."

"It suits me fine." She looked down at the notepad and saw the neat handwriting. Each line was numbered as though he had carefully outlined the plan. "You did all that after three this morning?" she asked, staring at the pad, completely amazed.

"Actually, I wake up every morning at six. Doesn't seem to matter if I went to bed at ten in Atlanta or at three in Paris," he said, placing the notebook back in his pocket. "I'm afraid I'm a slave to routine," he said. "When you get to know me better, you may not see that as an asset."

She had to smile at that. It had always been something she strove to accomplish. "Everyone needs a plan," she said, having told herself that each morning as she woke up and faced a stack of haphazardly folded papers that she had not graded. "Since I'm trying to set a better routine for my work habits, you'll be a good example for me."

They had crossed the lobby, taking turns through the revolving door, and were out on the sidewalk, where everyone around them seemed to be smiling and happy. Not one dour face like she often glimpsed in the adjoining cars at the corner red light on her way to school every morning.

He waved over a taxi and she looked at him questioning. "Thought we were walking."

"That's how we'll end up," he said, opening the door for her. "If it's okay with you," he added quickly. "I hope you're ready for brunch."

She hadn't even thought of food, which surprised her, when once she lived for meals. "I will be. I had a cup of tea in my room and that was all I wanted."

"And I had my usual pot of coffee," he said, laughing, as they settled into the backseat.

"I would have the shakes by now if I had drunk a pot of coffee," she said, glancing at him. She found it so easy to smile at him whenever they talked. She was not in the habit of smiling so much, except of course with her students, and they made it easy.

"And I would have a throbbing headache if I hadn't, addicted as I am to caffeine."

She shrugged and laughed softly. "Oh well, we all have our favorite things, I guess."

"Thank you."

"For what?"

"For not lecturing me like one anorexic friend who thinks caffeine is only half a step away from an illegal drug. Sorry that was an unkind thing to say about my last girlfriend."

She tilted her head and looked at him honestly. "It's your choice and your life. My parents don't even speak to anyone until they've had at least two cups of coffee, and we learned early to respect that."

He chuckled. "My brain doesn't truly function until it has been stroked by the presence of coffee." He had given the driver their destination and now the taxi was flying past all the landmarks she wanted to photograph. But then it occurred to her that she had forgotten her camera. What had happened to her common sense?

Dave had reached for her hand, and it seemed a natural gesture as they both took note of the passing scenery.

It would be a day she would treasure for the rest of her life. Dave solved her problem by picking up a disposable camera at a quaint little tourist shop.

"The pictures probably won't be the quality of the ones your camera would have taken."

"It doesn't matter. I can always buy postcards if I blur

the pictures or get them off center, which usually happens."

He laughed as they entered the Louvre and strolled leisurely to admire the statues. Out in the courtyard, she took a few pictures, and then they moved on to the Eiffel Tower, the statue of Napoleon, a museum that she found interesting, and finally ended up back at the hotel, their feet dragging. Dave was unable to suppress another yawn.

"What you need is a nap," she teased him.

"And miss dinner with you?"

She paused before the revolving door, since he had kept the taxi waiting. "Why can't you do both?" she suggested helpfully. It was something that she had already plotted sometime during the afternoon when she realized she enjoyed being with him so much that she dreaded saying good-bye. That would come on Friday; why not make the most of the few days together?

"Hey, great idea. So, a later dinner suits you?"

"Perfectly." She winked at him, pleased that he smiled at the gesture. It was amazing the way another person seemed to have emerged from the presence of Melanie Roberts, as though the fairy godmother had touched her with a wand and turned her into the woman she had always longed to be. She had never winked at a guy; it seemed so silly. But since meeting Dave, everything she said and did were honest reactions to his charm.

"Let's see. . ." He studied his wristwatch, which she noted was a frequent habit. He had admitted to routine, and she saw now how he stayed on schedule. He kept up with time, which always seemed to elude her. "It is now six o'clock. We could rest a couple of hours and meet up again at nine," he glanced at her, "or even ten."

She recalled he had admitted he only needed seven hours of sleep. She was an eight-hour sleeper, and a vague weariness clung to her body and dimmed her eyes. Yet in her heart, she was so exuberant that she wondered if she could even nap. But she must, her healthy nature reminded her. And she must have a cup of herb tea for energy when she awoke. She had come prepared with tea bags and vitamins.

"Nine is okay with me if you want to be here by then. If you don't make it until nine thirty, or even ten, just look for me on one of the sofas." She nodded in the direction of the comfortable areas within the lobby.

"See you tonight," she said softly, and this time it was he who reached down and touched his lips to hers in a sweet, brief kiss. He leaned back and stared down into her eyes and for a moment, neither said anything. Then she was conscious of the elevator opening behind her, at the same time she realized they were still holding hands. "See you later," he said, watching her as she got on the elevator and the door closed between them, closing off her view of him. She breathed a long, deep sigh of pure bliss. Was she dreaming? If so, she never wanted to wake up.

Chapter 5

He had selected another perfect restaurant for them. The one he had chosen last night had been exclusive and rather formal, and yet she was happy to have eaten there. It was one of those "must go" restaurants according to her guidebook—and even Nan Harper, who had gone once in her fifty-five years. After learning Melanie was going to Paris, Nan had tossed out names and places as though she hung out in Paris every summer. Melanie knew Nan's strategy: She had been studying the same tour book from their library. As usual, Nan always had to be one up on everyone else.

"We had authentic French last night; I thought you might like to sample a true Italian restaurant."

"How did you know it's my favorite food?"

He held the chair for her and she settled in, casting a glance over the wonderful ambiance of Old Italy recreated. "That's easy; because I always try to get one meal here whenever I come. Maybe I should just fly on over to Rome one of these days. I think there has to be Italian blood in my genes, the way I go after pasta."

Her eyes widened as he went around the table and took a seat while an eager waitress rushed to their side. "Which do you like best—lasagna or spaghetti?" Melanie asked, wondering if he really was that much like her.

"Pizza," he grinned, opening the menu. "But tonight I want something a little fancier. Do you like veal?" he asked.

She shook her head. "Not really. Just pasta of any flavor, any variation, as long as the chef uses pure olive oil and only a mild dash of garlic."

"Absolutely," he agreed, studying the selections.

She forced herself to do the same. The prices were less staggering than last night's famous French restaurant. Still, the food was expensive. She knew it would be, having done her research. But, thank God, he was buying. She had felt wealthy when she boarded the airplane, but already those funds were vanishing like magic, and she couldn't even remember what she had purchased. Souvenirs, naturally, and postcards, still unwritten, and the clothes, of course. *All a wise investment,* she told herself, as Dave ordered a veal dish and a spinach salad.

Melanie asked for the dish that seemed to offer the most tomato paste and pasta, which to her were twin components. It was authentic spaghetti, and when it was placed before her and she dipped a fork into it, a tiny mouthful thrilled her taste buds and she savored its delicate flavor.

They had both ordered coffee, an unusual departure for her, but she wanted to stay awake. Even though the French made their coffee strong, the rich cream made it pleasant. She discovered that it was possible for her to like coffee.

"Thought you didn't drink that stuff," he said, glancing at her half-empty cup, looking slightly amused.

"I don't. Often, I mean. But after watching you enjoy yours so much, I was tempted to give it a fair try. And I'm glad I did," she lifted the demitasse to her lips, taking another little sip.

"I've had a great time, Melanie," he said as they finished their meal and again refused dessert.

"So have I," she admitted, looking squarely into the blue eyes that she had come to adore. And as for the southern accent, it now lulled her senses; in fact, she was going to miss it. Somehow his drawl softened the harsh realities of the world and drew her into a special world that included only the two of them.

"I have to put in an appearance at tomorrow's meeting," he said, almost in apology.

"Oh, I understand. After all, you're here on business, not holiday, like me."

He looked across at her, and she saw genuine regret in his eyes. "I wish I were on holiday. There are so many things to do, so many places. . . ." His voice trailed, and she could see that he hated missing out.

She decided to make him feel better. "Actually, I need to write those postcards, so I don't beat them home, and I want to return to that little bookstore on the corner and browse. So I won't be doing anything significant for you to miss."

"It isn't that," he said, then hesitated.

"It isn't what?" she echoed, watching him carefully, wondering if it were possible that he had the same feelings for her that she had for him.

"I'd just like to spend the day with you," he added simply.

She smiled deeply. He was so honest and open and sincere about everything that she was deeply touched.

"Maybe it's my turn to do something nice," she said, wondering if she should offer to buy dinner.

"Like getting together a picnic lunch for us tomorrow?"

"What a wonderful idea," she beamed. "And go to a beautiful park someplace?"

He nodded. "Tomorrow I can sneak out about eleven and take a very long lunch hour. There's a beautiful park right across the street from my hotel." He repeated the address, although she had already memorized it. "Since it's so near my hotel, would you mind just meeting me in the park?"

"Not at all. In fact, I had hoped to stroll through one of the parks here before I left." Why did she feel she had to make excuses to justify every action?

He looked disappointed. "I don't have to be present for you to enjoy the park."

"Yes, you do," she said, tossing the old inhibited Melanie into the night. She believed in honesty and used it as a basic tool for her students. Why be different with adults? For the first time, the things she said and did seemed to make sense. She wondered why she had to come all the way to Paris, France, to resurrect the person who had been hiding underneath the layers of self-consciousness. She was shedding her defensive attitude much faster than she had shed the surplus twenty pounds. This pleased her.

Was it because of Dave Browning? Was it true that the right person complemented your strengths and softened your weaknesses? Yes, she decided, Granny was right. That was true! Or at least that was what was happening to her.

What else was happening? Melanie wondered as their gaze locked and neither spoke. It was one of those special moments when words are unnecessary, when eye contact is more important, when thoughtful silence allows one to slowly process what is taking place inside. It was something she had never been able to explain to Taylor, who talked incessantly. But Dave understood this; she could tell that he did.

He blinked and shook his head slightly, like one just coming out of a dream, and for a moment she felt it would be a necessary gesture for her too, but she refrained.

"Tell me more about your grandmother. She seems to have had a major impact on your life."

"She did." Melanie hesitated for a moment, studying his expression. He wasn't just being a polite southern gentleman. He was interested in her grandmother because he was interested in *her*. And when she realized that, she felt the same satisfaction that came to her from watching a beautiful sunrise or sunset, or hearing the church choir singing Christmas hymns.

Where did she begin in describing the woman who had been so important in her life? "She came to live with us after having a mild stroke that left her right side paralyzed so that she could longer be the independent woman she once was. She said her mind wasn't as sharp, but I never agreed. She had a remarkable mind, and she could captivate me with stories, which she often did. She even did a funny little shuffle of feet when she came into my room once and my radio was playing hits from the fifties," she laughed softly as she lifted her gaze over Dave's face and stared into space.

She raised a napkin to her mouth, aware she could no longer hold another bite. "My grandfather, Solomon Brown, was a salt-of-the-earth kind of guy, which Granny said was exactly the type she needed to keep her on balance. But she didn't like the name Solomon so she simply called him Brown. From their first meeting, I suppose."

Dave laughed. "I'm sorry I never met her. She sounds like so much fun."

Melanie felt the threat of tears. "Yes, she was many things. In fact, she's the reason I'm with you tonight."

Dave was suddenly serious. "How? What do you mean?"

She told him about the "wish" money she had inherited upon her grandmother's death in January and her grandmother's little note to see Paris for her. She had been determined to follow Granny's instructions, although her parents both argued she should pay off her car, or her college loan, or something typically sensible and responsible.

She was still talking about Granny when the waiter appeared rather discreetly at their table, inquiring again about more coffee.

Dave finally got the hint and looked at his watch. "It must be near closing time."

The waiter merely smiled, too polite to admit that it

was. When Melanie looked around the cozy restaurant, however, she realized they were the only couple left.

"I'm sorry. . . ," Dave began as his eyes followed hers. "I didn't realize it was so late."

He got up tucking an impressive wad of bills within the folder that held their ticket.

"Merci beaucoup," the waiter acknowledged.

They hurried out, both feeling a bit embarrassed as Dave hailed a taxi. "I can't believe the time went by so fast," he was saying as they hopped into a taxi and the driver roared off as though he was trying to set a record on speed. All too quickly, they were back at the Ritz and out on the sidewalk. Dave pushed the revolving door for her, and she stepped into the glass enclosure, glancing over her shoulder at him, directly behind.

Should she invite him up to her room? No, that wasn't quite right. It wasn't as though she were back at the apartment where she could invite him to take a seat on the sofa while she grabbed the fruit bowl from the eating bar and joined him with a handful of grapes.

She was vaguely aware that he was walking her to the elevator, pushing the button, and she felt nervous and awkward about what to do. But just as quickly, he settled the matter.

"Thanks for another wonderful evening," he said, lowering his lips to lightly brush hers just as the door of the elevator slid open. "See you tomorrow at eleven in the park," he called to her as she stepped inside the elevator. The door closed on his smiling face, and she stood very still, staring at the closed door as the elevator lifted upward.

It was absurd but she already missed him. She could spend hours with him and never tire of hearing him talk about his work, and he was equally interested in the funny little antics of her students. She had even told him about nosy Nan at some time during their hours together.

When the elevator doors parted, she stepped into the carpeted hall and sauntered down to her pink satin nest. Leaving Paris, and Dave, was going to be very difficult. But she refused to allow that thought to linger in her mind.

She inserted her card into the lock and held tight to the memory of his warm smile and the way his blue eyes took on a special light when he was amused. And she liked the aftershave and whatever he used on his hair that kept it soft and gleaming. The lock clicked, she opened the door, and floated off to her bedroom.

Chapter 6

Another beautiful day awaited them as she stopped at a market nearby, carefully choosing bread, fresh fruit, and cheese, and adding bottled water. That looked French and healthy, but she wondered if she should order an espresso for Dave and impulsively decided to do so, adding extra cream the way she had noticed him doing.

As usual he was right on time and found her easily under a large tree, their food tucked away in the picnic basket she had splurged on at the market.

"Hey, this is a real picnic," he said, looking around the grass.

She hadn't considered that he would be in his business suit and quickly suggested they move to a nearby table. When she laid all the treats out on the table he smiled with approval. Then, deliberately, she placed the espresso before him. "Hope it's okay."

"Thanks, Melanie. You really are a thoughtful person."

They began to eat heartily for it was a warm spring day in Paris and the pleasant breeze seemed to encourage their appetites. . .and romance. She was conscious of his gaze on her almost constantly, and once or twice she darted a glance in his direction. Once, she caught his blue eyes looking sad and regretful.

"What's wrong?" she asked, sensing something was spoiling the picnic lunch.

He sighed heavily. "I can't get out of the meeting today, and my boss has issued an ultimatum that we all get together in his suite until we iron out some complications that have come up in the meetings."

"You look worried," she said gently.

"We'll work out the kinks. It's just going to take a lot more work than I had thought. Which means," he had been staring into his cup but now his gaze rose to hers, "I may not get to see you again. Our plane flies out at seven in the morning."

Melanie's heart sank, but then she tried to gather her courage and be grateful for the time they had spent together. "Well, you have to do what you have to do," she said. She couldn't believe tomorrow was already Friday. Where had the week gone?

"I wish I could change my plans and stay over another day, but I can't," he said on a sigh. "My boss is great except for a few quirks. And one quirk is that no one gets special treatment in veering from the routine he sets."

She nodded. "Then I guess you've been pushing your luck, sneaking out of the meetings to sightsee with me."

He hesitated and shrugged, giving her time to wonder if maybe he had been scolded already.

"Melanie, I don't know how you feel, but I don't want

this to be the end of our. . .friendship."

She looked into his eyes, suddenly feeling all the emotion in her heart well up in her throat. "I don't either," she replied softly.

"Do you have E-mail?" he asked, glancing at his watch.

She sighed, hating to admit she didn't. "Actually, I'm getting it when I return," she said, instantly making up her mind.

"Great. We can E-mail back and forth and then. . . maybe make some plans to see each other again," he said, getting up from the picnic table, glancing back toward the hotel.

Her heart was beating faster and she again wondered if this had all been a dream. But as he reached out and squeezed her hand, she realized this was real, it had actually happened. Finally. To her.

She squeezed his hand back, and then he took a step closer and gently touched her shoulders, then lowered his head and gave her a deep, warm kiss that literally took her breath away.

"I do hate to go," he said.

She abruptly opened her eyes, realizing she was still locked in the sweet moment they had shared. She nodded, unable to say anything.

He reached into the pocket of his coat and withdrew a business card. "There's my address and telephone number, office and home, and on the back I've written my E-mail address at home."

She turned the card over and read the address. "I'll E-mail you as soon as I get hooked up," she promised.

He looked at his watch again, and she wished with all of her heart that she could make time stand still. But she couldn't. He kissed her again, more briefly this time, but the gentle brush of his lips still thrilled her.

"Good-bye," he whispered softly and quickly walked away.

She felt as though he was taking her heart with him. Her gaze sadly followed him. He purposefully crossed the street to the front of the hotel. Then he turned and looked at her again.

"Dave, I had a great time," she called to him.

He smiled. "Me too." Then he walked into the hotel and disappeared from her vision. She stood staring at the door for the next five minutes, aware that tears were gathering in her eyes. She wandered over and slumped down on the picnic bench, staring at their plastic plates and the leftovers that she would take back to her room. She reached over for his empty coffee cup and, remembering his kiss, put the rim of the cup to her lips.

"Dave Browning," she whispered, "you made my dreams come true."

Chapter 7

Melanie slept late the next morning and awoke feeling tired and something more. She rolled her head and glanced at the parted drapes. Outside, it was a gray day, and for the first time since she had been in Paris it was raining. She glanced at the ornate bedside clock. Nine-thirty.

She took a deep breath and hugged her pillow, as a deep sadness grew stronger. She frowned. *What?* And then she came fully awake and reality loomed to the front of her mind. Dave was already on a jet heading back to Atlanta. Just that knowledge brought a terrible emptiness to her heart. She tried to think of something fun to do today, but nothing appealed to her. She decided to order room service of croissants and a pot of tea and lounge around for a while.

The rain thickened beyond her window, and she forced herself to go down to explore some of the unique little boutiques inside the Ritz, but soon she was back in her room, slumped in the satin chair. Maybe she should call home. She calculated the time back in Milton. It was

Friday morning, and with Mom off from school, Dad had taken a week from his office as well. They had planned several projects for the home and flower garden, all of which sounded so boring compared to the week she had spent, a week she would never, ever forget.

Methodically, she checked her flight schedule and noted that she was scheduled to fly out early, as well. She really should force herself to go out and do something on her last day in Paris, and she wandered to the window trying to think of something that would appeal to her. But the truth was, without Dave, Paris had lost its charm. And her time would be better spent getting her clothes together, resting up for the long flight back, and mentally preparing herself to return to work on Monday. And first on her list, when she returned, was getting E-mail installed on her computer. The most sophisticated thing she had done on her computer was type up simple little tests or words on colored paper. She hadn't even bothered with the Internet. But now the computer held endless possibilities. Communicating with Dave was foremost.

Chapter 8

Melanie continued to marvel that it had only been two days since her return to Milton. To her parents, she had blamed her melancholy on jet lag and even skipped church on Sunday. She couldn't seem to get out of her bed for any reason other than to call Taylor with the pretense of a sisterly chat, but what she really wanted to know more about was E-mail.

And so, on Monday morning, as she greeted her second graders and proceeded with the difficult job of trying to establish a routine for them, and for herself, she hailed down the school's computer whiz over lunch. He agreed to come to her apartment that afternoon to show her the basics of E-mail and get her hooked up.

That idea lifted her spirits and she was actually humming "Somewhere over the Rainbow" by the end of the day, despite a barrage of questions over lunch from all the teachers; they wanted to hear every detail of her trip to Paris. She had always been a private person, and true to form, she did not mention Dave. The closest she came was to admit she'd met some interesting people.

But when nosy Nan Harper began to prod, she excused herself to get back to her room to work on a project.

That evening, the excitement of being "on-line" thrilled her as she shyly typed in Dave's E-mail address and sent her first message: a friendly hello to him and a thank-you for the wonderful time in Paris. Carefully she read and re-read her message and checked half a dozen times to be sure her E-mail address was correct. Then she placed a check mark in the box to indicate she wanted to be notified when her E-mail was picked up.

She managed to get through the morning, and with the excuse that she forgot her lunch, she dashed home to check her E-mail. Nothing. She rushed back to school, puzzled.

That night, she sent Dave another E-mail to inquire if he got her first one. She showered and dressed for bed, although in the next hour, she could not approach the computer without checking her message box, but there was nothing except a two-pager from Taylor with news of the kids and, predictably, only a few general questions about Melanie's trip to Paris. Taylor was basically selfish, and Melanie knew it. She dashed back a quick E-mail, then checked her message box again and saw with pleasure that her E-mail to Dave had been picked up. Tomorrow she would hear from him, and with that hope, she hopped into bed and turned out the light.

Did I give Dave my phone number?

The thought struck her seconds before the bolt of thunder that crashed outside her window, preceding the heavy rain that drummed on her roof. She loved the sound and usually it lulled her into a deep sleep. Not tonight.

She kept racking her brain to see if she had mentioned a telephone or address in Milton. He hadn't asked, a voice reminded her. She didn't want to hear that voice, so she turned the light back on and read the entire book of Psalms, got up at midnight, and checked her E-mail again. Nothing.

Sighing, she got back in bed and reminded herself that tomorrow was a school day. She forced herself to close her eyes and say her prayers.

The next afternoon, Melanie went to the video shop and picked up *You've Got Mail*, one of her favorite romantic comedies. She watched it as soon as she got home and then again after a light meal of soup and fruit. Every fifteen minutes she checked her computer, only to find to her dismay, and growing disappointment, that there were no messages. And that her E-mails had been picked up.

Her hopes grew dimmer as the week progressed, during which time she resorted to checking her message box several times a day. She even went into the principal's office and informed the secretary that she might be getting a call from a friend in Atlanta, and if so, to please come to her room and get her.

"You want me to take the number?" Mrs. Winters looked at her curiously, for she had been instructed not to pull teachers out of class for a phone call unless it was an emergency.

"Yes. It's very important," she added matter-of-factly and hurried out, vaguely aware that Brent Warren, the principal, had been watching her curiously the past two days. Her best plan was to simply avoid him, just as she had tried to avoid her parents; but there was no getting past the Wednesday night supper at the church before prayer meeting. She had decided she must attend; after all, she had missed church on Sunday, and she knew it would be easier to have a conversation with her parents with a group of church members eating beside them. This way her mother couldn't get too personal, although she doubted that her mother would ever envision her daughter having a romantic interlude in Paris.

Her father, on the other hand, was enough like Granny to glance at her occasionally and winked at her once when she was obviously out of the zone of conversation, her mind locked on Dave.

She simply smiled at her father, wondering if she could talk with him sometime, appealing to his softer nature, which occasionally surfaced when he was not immersed in tax figures or engaged in one of Mom's yard projects.

At prayer meeting, when prayer requests were taken, her throat suddenly felt tight and she wished with all of her heart that she could lift her hand and say, "Please pray that Dave Browning responds to my E-mail." Or more honestly, "Please pray that I don't get my heart broken."

The thought had crossed her mind more than once in the five days since she had been home. For as she gravitated toward Cinderella and all the romantic little fairy tales which appealed only to the girls, she realized that it had happened to her, despite everything.

She had fallen in love for the first time. She actually

understood now the "burning heartache" and the "incessant longing" she had read about could now be applied to her. All she thought about from the time she awoke until she crawled back in bed was the Dave she had met in Paris. But now that they were each back in their old environment, it was as if they'd never met. She missed him so much it was like a physical ache that could only be compared to the flu. Only the heartache seared into her soul in a way nothing ever had.

Each night when she checked her message box, her heart sank when there was no reply. . .except for the acknowledgment that her E-mail had been picked up.

She was renting romantic videos every night now, huddled on the sofa, picking at a light dinner on a TV tray. She had gone through the old classic *April in Paris*, and on this Thursday night, as she watched Cary Grant and Deborah Kerr in *An Affair to Remember*, she sobbed deeply and unashamedly. With only her cup of tea and the rapidly disappearing tissue in her box, she made a decision when at last the movie ended and she was weak from crying. As she pushed the rewind button on the VCR, she squared her shoulders and marched resolutely to her computer. This was her last attempt to contact him. But maybe, for some strange reason, her E-mails were not getting through. She took a deep breath and began the words that choked her as she typed them. For this could be good-bye.

> Dave,
> This is my last attempt to contact you. I've gone

past being offended to being concerned. Are you all right? I checked, there were no plane crashes, and in case you're interested, I arrived back in Milton on Saturday. I hope you will at least let me know that you arrived home safely.

Melanie.

After she finished the carefully worded E-mail, she checked her E-mail address again to be sure it was correct, then she glanced again at the check mark indicating that she wanted to be notified when the message was picked up. By 10:30, the message still had not been picked up.

As she crawled into bed and turned out the light she felt more than hurt, she felt confused and disillusioned. She just couldn't believe that Dave was the kind of person to be insincere in a relationship. He had cared about her; surely she hadn't just imagined it. Each day when she didn't hear from him, she reminded herself of how busy he was, the meetings, his rigid boss. . . But this was now Thursday and she had sent her first E-mail on Monday. And she knew how painfully quick it was to zip one off. No matter how busy he was, he could have found a few seconds to at least say, "Hi, Paris was fun, wasn't it?" Never mind, "I've missed you" or "I think about you" or any of the dozens of things that flooded her mind when she thought of him. Just a simple "Hi" would at least keep her hopes up, even though the idea of a continuing romance with him was fading fast.

The next morning, as soon as she awoke, she flew to her computer and waited impatiently for the message box to appear. No messages. . .except for the fact that her E-mail had been picked up. Again.

Tears filled her eyes as she slowly closed down the program and turned off her computer. *Maybe Paris and Dave were a dream after all,* she thought, feeling utterly miserable as she headed for the shower. Or if it were not a dream, it was painfully apparent that a week had gone by and now the dream was only a memory.

Chapter 9

She awoke on Saturday morning, wishing she hadn't committed herself to go along with the second and third graders to the museum. How would she dredge up the energy for such a trip? Not to mention the pretense she now kept of being happy, wearing a stiff smile, and trying not to remember Paris or Dave.

She forced herself to get up and shower, dress, and get ready to meet the bus at the school at twelve. Passing her computer as she gathered up her purse and lunch, she stared at the blank screen. Still no E-mail. She promised herself she was going to quit looking in that direction. The telephone rang, and she glanced at her watch, debating on whether to answer it. She hadn't the energy for another grilling from Mom. She walked past the phone, but then the possibility of the trip being canceled stopped her. On the fourth ring, she walked over and murmured a very unenthusiastic hello.

There was nothing but an odd croaking on the other side. She frowned, wondering if this was a crank call. But then through the muttered garble she recognized a name that struck magic and made her grip the phone tighter.

Dave? Had he said "Dave"?

"Who is this?" she asked pointedly.

There was a pause on the other end, and she could hear a shuffle. What was going on? Then a distinctly southern accent came on the line and her eyes widened.

"Melanie, this is Tom Barker. You don't know me but I'm Dave Browning's roommate. He's been in the hospital with pneumonia and bronchitis the past week, and though he's totally incoherent, he insisted on trying to call you. I've been delivering your E-mails to him, by the way."

"In the hospital?" she repeated, trying to take in everything he had told her, but it was quite a shock.

"Yep. He got sick the day he came home. Apparently, he picked up a flu bug in Paris and by the time he got to the doctor, he was so feverish and dehydrated that he was admitted to the hospital. He's been pretty much out of it until yesterday, but I've heard your name mumbled so many times, I think I can speak for him."

She smiled, sinking into the nearest chair, winding the phone cord around her slim fingers and feeling as though she had just been turned into Cinderella again. "I'm sorry he's so ill. Could I speak with him? I'll do the talking."

"Great!"

Another shuffle followed, and then a choked sound, and Melanie began to tell him how concerned she had been, that she was sorry he was sick, but that she hoped he would be out of the hospital soon. And she was glad to hear from him.

A garble followed but she made out the words "will call again."

"Okay, hope you feel better," she said, wishing she could be there at the hospital with him now.

It was the glance at her watch that forced her into action. She had exactly three minutes to get to school. But she felt she could fly, if necessary. Dave had not forgotten her! He had called her name often, or so his roommate said. She believed Tom. She believed Dave. And she believed that life was clouds and rainbows once again, just like the pictures she painted for her second graders.

Melanie approached her school day in an entirely different manner. Will's constant excuses to go to the bathroom did not ruffle her feathers, nor did Harry's antics on the back row, which usually required a stern voice. All the little girls were beautiful to her, and in a burst of appreciation for the spring day, she got permission from Mr. Warren, who was still watching her curiously, to take the children outside to examine the new rock garden the fifth graders had designed.

As they sat out in the warm sunshine with the kids playing happily, Mary Beth sidled up to her. It was hard not to favor blond little Mary Beth who was always bringing her gifts. They were in the midst of a discussion about Mary Beth's spring break to visit her grandmother in Springfield, when she noticed that Harry and Will were engaged in competition over who could throw one of the smaller rocks the farthest.

She jumped up from her comfortable spot on the lawn

and rushed to their side, scolding them more gently than usual and telling them they must pick up the rocks they had thrown, and now everyone was going back inside.

She hadn't even minded her mother's routine phone call every afternoon. This time she decided to favor her with a tiny bit of her news. She told her about meeting Dave from Atlanta, and one thing led to another, until Melanie stopped just short of saying she had fallen in love. Instead, she ended the conversation with a mellow admission: "He is the nicest guy I've ever met."

"But why haven't you told us about him? Why. . . ," and on and on.

"Er, Mom," she interrupted, "something is boiling over on the kitchen stove." Actually, her teakettle was. She had already had two cups of tea, but she couldn't seem to control herself; a wonderful sense of abandon had overtaken her. She loved the world, even Nan and her mother.

That night she rushed home and found her computer filled with messages—all from Dave. He had gone home from the hospital today, armed with antibiotics and fruit baskets. There were four E-mails written within an hour of each other. All began with an apology for not having contacted her sooner, then he was quickly into their trip to Paris, reminding her of places they had seen and things they had done.

"It's all I thought about when I lay in the hospital bed being poked with shots and fighting the frustration of losing my voice."

Each E-mail got more personal, and after she had read each one twice, she changed into her jeans and T-shirt, made herself tea, and bypassed food since her stomach had knotted up again. But it was a wonderful feeling. She had put on a CD and Harry Connick, Jr. was now crooning one of her favorite Cole Porter songs, and she felt her heart soar toward the heavens.

In the midst of her reverie she rushed to her bedroom, knelt by her bed, and said, "God, thank You. Thank You so much. Please don't let me lose Dave. I haven't asked for much in a long time, but I am asking You to bless my life with this wonderful Christian man. And I will be grateful forever," she added.

She had just returned to the computer when the telephone rang. During the conversation that followed, she could hardly believe that God seemed to be answering her prayer so quickly.

It was Tom again, Dave's roommate, and he was calling from his office.

"Melanie, Dave has had such a rough time the past week. Had to spend his birthday plugged into IVs and feeling miserable. His friends want to do something special for him. We're planning a surprise birthday party soon and. . ." He seemed to have difficulty going on with his plan.

"And?" she prompted. "What? I think it's great that you're doing that for him."

"Well, I realize you don't know me, but I've known Dave for years, and I can honestly tell you he is the greatest guy I've ever known."

A smile slipped over her lips, and she closed her eyes dreamily, recalling Dave's face when they sat talking that first day at the sidewalk café. But she was drifting again, so she yanked her mind back to the subject.

"So. . .I gather I can help in some way or you would not be calling?"

"I know it's asking a lot, and believe me, I will understand if you say no. In fact, he'd kill me—well, not really —just strangle me with one of his wild ties. . ."

She smiled recalling the one on the plane.

"But I'm going to be frank and invite you to fly down. We'll plan the party around whenever you can make it. We had a weekend in mind."

"Which weekend?"

He took an eternity before answering and then in a weak voice ventured the date. "This weekend. It's a surprise, and what I had in mind was paying for your plane ticket—our little present to him—and Julie, that's my girlfriend, can pick you up at the airport and you are more than welcome to stay with her. Her condo is only two blocks from ours." His rapid flow of words came to a thoughtful silence. "You probably think I'm being too forward. We Southerners tend to seem too friendly to a lot of people."

"Not to me," she said tenderly. "I think that is a wonderful gesture of friendship on your part, Tom. And I know Dave will be pleased. But. . ." She frowned.

The weekend! What would she wear? Could she possibly be packed and into Cleveland to catch a plane in three days? And could she even get a flight at this late date?

"I would really like to come, Tom. But it's such short notice. . . ."

"I understand completely. To make your decision easier, I took the liberty of making two plane reservations for you Friday night out of Cleveland. Whichever time is most convenient. There's a flight at seven and another at nine and—you must think I'm insane," he finished lamely. "But for as long as I've known Dave, I've never seen him so in love."

In love! The words jolted Melanie back in her chair, and she bit her lip as tears rushed to her eyes. Her heart felt as though it would leap from her chest and fly away like the little doves she loved so much. She swallowed hard. This was a big decision, and yet it wasn't. She had never met anyone like Dave; it might never happen again. And the sweetest miracle of all was that he was in love with her.

Tossing all of her mother's careful caution to the wind and conjuring up an image of Granny smiling down at her, she cleared her throat. "I'll come," she announced, and as she said the words, she knew she was making the right decision. In fact, she couldn't wait to see Dave again.

A huge sigh of relief filled the air. "You're just as great as he said you were. Most women wouldn't be as understanding or as nice. Which flight would be better for you?"

Melanie made a quick calculation, and since she had pondered plane schedules and fares for a month before scheduling her trip to Paris, she already knew the answer. "Seven."

"I hope you don't think I'm being too presumptuous but I'm a salesman and I tend to get aggressive. About the flights, I mean. Sorry."

She laughed. "Don't apologize. Someone has to think

fast in this situation." She debated the amount of time it would take her and immediately realized she would have to leave school early, but she would not be deterred. She rarely asked for time off, and Mr. Warren would just have to understand.

"What time does it arrive in Atlanta?"

"Well," he hesitated, "you're going to lose some time because that particular flight makes a stop. But we won't expect more from you than a good night's sleep at Julie's and then we'll plan the party for Saturday. Actually, we'll start early, and that will surprise Dave even more."

She was laughing like one of her second graders. She loved the idea, and with Tom and Julie so accommodating, how could she refuse? In the split second she was having those thoughts, Tom rushed in with one more appealing plea to cinch the decision. "Dave hasn't had a real birthday party in years. Says he prefers his birthdays low-key. He's so good to everybody else it will be our pleasure to do something special for him."

"And mine too," she added, feeling the warm fuzzies inside.

"How will I recognize Julie at the airport?"

"She'll be the little blond with the big smile, probably wearing jeans and a University of Georgia sweatshirt. Dave has described you enough for her to easily spot you."

Melanie lifted an eyebrow. "Really?"

"Just teasing. You won't have any trouble finding each other. Meanwhile, I'll have Dave occupied with something so he won't suspect anything. Actually, I'll probably have to go drag him away from his desk at the office. He's practically holed up there day and night, until he drags in and puts Harry Connick, Jr. on to play with the same CD over and over until I have to put in earplugs. He's kind of eccentric at times." He stopped talking, which seemed abrupt. She had already learned that Tom was the kind who liked to talk, and she wondered how well he and Dave got along because she had an idea that Dave might need more silence.

"I hope you don't play hard to get," he said, sounding more southern now as his words slowed down.

"Why?" she asked curiously, staring across at her CD as it lulled out a soothing Harry Connick, Jr. tune.

"Because I've really ruined it for him if you do. I mean some women think the chase is half the fun."

"Not me." Melanie smiled again, thinking how blessed she was. "No, actually Dave and I are very much alike. That's why we got along so well in Paris." *And that's why we both like the same music,* she could have added. But Tom already knew enough to be dangerous; he didn't need any more ammunition. Dave would probably want to strangle Tom at all the private things he had revealed to her, but she was glad that he had. During her week of torment the old insecurities had toyed with her mind. Staring into the mirror, she felt fat and ugly again, though she knew she was not. And she felt scattered and dumb and overemotional. But now one phone call had restored her self-confidence. And her simple, humble prayer had been answered.

"Okay, Tom. I'll come. And let's keep it a surprise. I think that's a great idea."

"Fabulous. Your ticket will be waiting at the airport."

He gave her the airline's gate and flight numbers and she wrote them down, astonished at all he had accomplished. "Sorry if I've assumed too much, but I just wanted to make it as easy as possible for you. And I really did not want you to say no. Thanks, Melanie. I understand why he said you were such a terrific person."

"Thanks, Tom. Oh, by the way, what should I bring? I've never been to Atlanta."

"It's already hot and humid. Dress for comfort because we're very casual. Well, we will probably go out for dinner Saturday night, but just something a bit dressy will be fine. Not too dressy. I mean, the kind of outfit you'd wear for dinner there."

"Okay." Dinner at the best restaurant in Milton wouldn't be dressy enough for Atlanta, she decided. But her new Paris wardrobe presented her a wide array of choices, and as soon as she hung up she flew to her closet and started mulling over her options.

Chapter 10

There was definitely an air of "what's going on?" among the teachers' buzz during their coffee break and lunch. After she had answered the anticipated questions of why she was going to Atlanta so soon after her return, she gave a simple, honest answer. She had looked everyone directly in the eye and said, "I've met someone, and he's being given a surprise birthday party. I'd like to be there."

Everyone simply stared, totally at a loss for more questions. It was unlike Melanie to share her private life; it was even more unlike Melanie to "meet someone" and then go dashing off to. . .Atlanta, Georgia!

Her mother, on the contrary, had insisted on knowing every detail, but for once Taylor, thank God, had come to her rescue. "Mom, for heaven's sake, let her have a life," Taylor had scolded more than once. "We want to see her happy, and I've never heard her voice so soft and dreamy."

Even her dad seemed to understand, and she noticed he had been staring more at his mother's portrait, deep in thought.

She left school early and arrived at the airport in plenty of time to board. True to his word, Tom had seen to it that a round-trip ticket was paid for and waiting for her at check-in. She boarded the plane in comfortable slacks, a knit top, a lightweight jacket, and loafers and did her best to nap on the flight to Atlanta.

As the plane approached Atlanta she stared out the window in awe at the millions of lights spread out underneath the canvas of black sky. Melanie found herself wondering precisely which part of this huge city Dave lived and worked in and whether Julie would have to drive far to get to the airport. When the plane touched down, she could feel the humidity seeping into the jet at about the time the pilot informed the passengers it was a pleasant seventy-eight degrees.

She was struck by a pang of nerves as she deplaned and walked up the concourse. As Tom had predicted, Julie was easy to spot. She was the first person in the reception line. A wide smile flew over her face when she spotted Melanie. It was obvious that Julie was a bundle of nervous energy, fidgeting as she waited, shuffling from one foot to the other, and tossing her short blond hair back from her face.

"Melanie," she called out in a thick southern drawl.

"Julie?" she asked, smiling, although there was little doubt.

As soon as she reached Julie, who was no more than five-foot-two, Melanie felt herself being enveloped in an affectionate hug. "I'm *so* glad you came," she said, her blue eyes twinkling.

"Thank you. Me too," Melanie added, returning her

smile as Julie quickly ushered her down the escalator to the baggage area. "How was your trip? Long and boring of course. I just hate plane rides, don't you?"

Melanie opened her mouth to respond but quickly realized a reply was unnecessary because Julie plunged right on. "Last December Tom and I flew up to New York to see a Broadway show and do some Christmas shopping. . . ."

"How fun," Melanie interjected, not wanting to seem void of personality, but Julie wasn't worried about that.

"Have you ever been to New York at Christmas time? Well, don't bother. It's a mad scramble, although I guess it's worth it. The shopping was the best part, but we were disappointed in the play that had been so highly recommended to us."

Melanie merely smiled down at Julie, aware that it was unnecessary to try to answer every question. Julie usually answered them herself. In an amazingly short time they had retrieved her canvas bag, but then Julie turned to her with a frown of concern. "Just one?"

"I decided to keep it simple."

Julie nodded, apparently seeing the logic to that. "And you had very little time to get ready, right? Well, you've really been a good sport about this," she said, motioning for a skycap to pluck the bag from Melanie's hand, although she could have managed. However, she had decided it was easier to let Julie take the lead, since she seemed to take her job seriously. Clearly, she was in charge of getting Melanie safely to. . .wherever they were going.

"I'm parked right out front," Julie said, slipping a bill

to the porter then offering a blazing smile to the security guard patrolling the parked cars. Melanie watched with fascination as Julie charmed her way past all obstacles, and soon they were settled safely into her little convertible.

"I put the top up," Julie glanced at Melanie with a smile, as she turned the key in the ignition and they plunged into the traffic. Another blazing smile toward the man she had cut in front of, and they were off. "I know we can all be fussy about our hair. That's why I keep mine short and simple."

"It looks nice," Melanie said, observing the very short, casual cut that allowed her hair to be easily maintained.

"You have a Southern name," Julie said, whipping onto the interstate, even though traffic was heavy. "I love it, though."

"Actually, I was named after my grandmother," Melanie said, leaning back against the thick leather seat and relaxing a bit. "She was Melinda, and Dad was insistent about my being her namesake."

"It fits." Julie shot her a quick glance before careening into another lane, barely missing an SUV roaring up just behind them and responding with an ugly screech of brakes. "Guess you've read *Gone with the Wind?*"

"Half a dozen times," Melanie laughed. She found it so easy to talk with Julie whose chatter and laughter was infectious.

"I always think of myself as Scarlet," she whipped her head toward Melanie, sending her short waves toppling about her face. Above the faint glow of the dashboard, Melanie could see the twinkle in the wide blue eyes and could only imagine how crazy Tom was about her. She decided to get to the point, since Julie was an easy conversationalist.

"So tell me about Dave's friends. I already like you and Tom and—"

"You do?" She giggled. "Tom said I would talk your ear off but he knows I'll just be me and can't help it. Tom and I are probably the most liberal of Dave's friends. As you must know, he's a bit conservative, works too hard, never plays, all that. Tom and I barely get through the week until Friday and then its nonstop playing until the weekend's over. He's usually at my place or I'm at his, but it seems to be no problem for Dave because he works all the time. Too much," she said, frowning for the first time since Melanie had met her. "We've been relieved to see a more relaxed, happy Dave since he returned from Paris. Actually, since he got out of the hospital. In fact," she stopped at the light and took the opportunity to give Melanie an appraising eye, "we all think you've been very good for him. That's why it was so important for us to get you down here for his birthday party. We wanted it to be perfect."

Melanie liked the sound of that. "What do you have planned?"

"I'm going to get you settled in, and then let you shower and get comfortable, then I'm dashing back out to meet Tom at the Party Place. We're buying some stuff for tomorrow. As usual, Dave is working tonight and probably plans to go into the office in the morning. Because he was out sick for a week, he feels he'll be letting his co-workers down if he doesn't catch up on his part of the project by yesterday." She paused and shook her head as if she found him hopeless. "But that's Dave. Dedicated and conscientious. I used to complain to Tom that Dave was boring, but I've seen a different side of him lately. I hope we can be good friends," she said, tossing a glance at Melanie as Julie steered her little car into the driveway of a huge apartment complex.

"I'm sure we will be," Melanie said, turning to survey the nice surroundings. "I'll grab a luggage cart from the garage closet and we'll dash on up to my place."

Melanie had already figured out that Julie did nothing in slow motion, so she hurriedly got out of the car, hooked her shoulder bag on her arm, and ran a hand over her hair.

"You look great," Julie said, not missing a single gesture as she managed to find the cart, roll it to the trunk of her car, and pop the lid. "Love your hair. The length is right, and those highlights compliment your facial features and those fabulous gray eyes." She stopped suddenly in the midst of her fast-forward movements and peered closer at Melanie. "Do you wear contacts?"

Melanie laughed. "Yes, I do."

Julie nodded, turning back to her task of pulling out Melanie's bag, though Melanie tried to assist her. "That's why your eyes look so clear and gray. Thank God, I've never had to bother with glasses. I'm too scatter brained to keep up with them."

They were practically racing toward the elevator, and Melanie grabbed a breath, aware that the humidity was causing her to move slower. Her clothes suddenly felt slightly damp, as did her skin.

"What's your part of Ohio like?" Julie asked, as they stepped onto the elevator and she pushed a button as she rearranged her ring of keys.

Melanie was fascinated at how Julie always managed two things at once. "It's a small town, but we're not too far from Cleveland."

"I've never been to Cleveland," Julie glanced again at her.

"Then I'd love for you to come visit."

Julie smiled at her. "I like you, Melanie."

Her honesty almost startled Melanie, but then she remembered Dave explaining that some of the people he knew were outspoken and frank, but everyone was friendly and to some people almost seemed insincere because of their responses. Melanie realized Julie was being honest, and she smiled and accepted the compliment.

"Thank you. I like you too. Bet you wondered what kind of person Dave had met?"

Her thin blond-brown brows shot up and down. "I wondered that any woman could steal his heart so fast. I've fixed him up so many times that I finally gave up. He was too hard to please." The elevator door slid open and they stepped out onto the soft, plush beige carpet. "But I see why now. The right person is worth waiting for, don't you think?"

Melanie looked at her carefully, wondering if she should commit herself to that. "When you're sure it's the right person."

Julie was unlocking the door but just before she pushed it open, she shot a questioning glance at Melanie.

"Haven't made up your mind yet, huh?"

"Well, we've only known each other a week," Melanie tried to be rational, though Julie obviously believed in love at first sight.

She hurried on ahead, switching on lights, and Melanie looked around, impressed with the nice furnishings and the good taste of the decor. "This is your room," she said over her shoulder, leading the way into a comfortable room done in soft blue with an adjoining bath. "If there's anything you can't find, just prowl through my room across the hall." She waved a little hand in that direction. "The fridge is stocked, so help yourself." She paused to draw a breath.

"Thanks, Julie. You've been most gracious. I'll be fine. You go on and meet Tom and do whatever you need to do about tomorrow. I'd like a hot bath—about half an hour in that tub." She glanced toward the bath.

"We knew you'd be tired after working all day, driving into Cleveland, and then the long flight. It's after eleven," Julie glanced at her watch, "so I have to hurry. The party supply store closes at midnight, and I have to call Tom on my cell phone to say I'm on the way."

"Go ahead. I'll be fine."

"See you in the morning," Julie called over her shoulder, grabbing her purse from the hall table and rushing out the door. The latch clicked loudly, assuring Melanie that she was safely secured.

She found the kitchen and grabbed a bottle of milk and located the cereal, dishes, and flatware. She had a bowl of cereal with a banana from Julie's fruit bowl, feeling the weariness of the strenuous week and the long trip settling into every bone of her body. And yet her mind was wide awake and spinning with everything Julie had told her and the awesome realization that she was in Atlanta, near Dave, and that she would see him tomorrow. After a relaxing bath and a couple of aspirin, she crawled between the smooth, crisp sheets, turned off the light, and dissolved into the softness of the bed.

The distant bounce of music reached her slowly. She noticed her door had been closed sometime during the night, a thoughtful gesture on Julie's part. As she lay there luxuriating in the soft bed and wondering what the day held, she recognized the music as a popular group whose songs were not particularly to her taste, but she realized that Julie's quick personality would respond to that type of beat. The bath had eased her sore muscles, and now her eyes moved toward the closet and the clothes she had brought—those she had worn in Paris. She remembered exactly the ones Dave had complimented.

She had already planned to wear the skirt and blouse she had worn when they met. And if they went out for dinner, she would wear the dressy jade number. She hadn't brought heels, because Dave was only a couple of inches taller and she wisely chose dressy flats and gold sandals.

Tossing the covers back, she rushed to the bathroom to wash up, pulling on her new terry cloth robe as she went. After quickly freshening up, she wandered out into the living room where she spotted Julie perched at the eating bar, the wall phone cord stretched to accommodate her as her hand sped over the notepad.

The smell of fresh coffee filled the air. Since meeting Dave, Melanie had developed a taste for coffee, so she quietly crossed to the kitchen with a brief wave at Julie, not wanting to interrupt her conversation.

"She's up now," Julie said, looking fresh and bright-eyed in a short white sleep shirt that showed off her deep tan. "So we can get right on with it. This is Tom," she explained to Melanie. "Yep, we can be there in an hour."

An hour? Melanie hastened her movements around the kitchen, wondering what time it was. She spotted a kitchen clock and noted that it was only eight, which meant this was the earliest Saturday morning she had seen in awhile. But she'd had plenty of sleep, and she didn't want to waste another second of her short weekend.

"Okay. Love you," Julie said sweetly and hung up. "Glad you found what you needed," she said, as Melanie poured cereal into a bowl. "I never eat breakfast. Well, maybe a banana on the run."

"That's how you keep your nice figure." Melanie glanced at her, amazed at her perfect size.

"Now, here's the plan. Dave just left for the office, so we'll get dressed and Ginny and Chad, that's our two other mutual friends, will meet us at the apartment, and we'll string up the decorations we got last night. Tom is blowing up balloons already."

Melanie smiled at her. "Dave is going to be so pleased."

"And so surprised, I hope. The pleased part will take place when he sees you. I'm so glad you came," she said on a slow romantic sigh. "Well, I'm going to shower and dress. Is forty-five minutes too soon?" she asked suddenly, as though aware she might have acted hastily.

"No, that's fine. I'm accustomed to hurrying to get to school."

"That's right!" Julie suddenly looked amazed. "Second graders, right?"

Melanie nodded, amazed that Julie and Tom knew so much about her.

"I work over in Buckhead. Assistant manager of a little boutique in the mall. It's fun." With that explanation, she hopped off the barstool, and her bare feet with their bright red toenails padded quickly toward her room.

"I'll be ready," Melanie called after her. It seemed the appropriate thing to say. They had all gone to so much trouble for Dave's party. She only hoped he would be surprised and pleased at their efforts. *What will Dave really think about my coming?* she wondered as she finished her breakfast and put away the cereal and milk. Would he think she was being too presumptuous? Julie and Tom didn't seem to think so, but knowing them, he would understand that maybe they had pressed her to come. The truth was, it had taken very little persuasion.

After washing her bowl and drying her hands, she hurried back to her room to make her bed and begin dressing.

Chapter 11

Between Julie and Tom and Ginny and Chad, whom she also liked, they seemed to have thought of everything. Melanie relaxed and began to enjoy stringing up the Happy Birthday signs, then joined Ginny in putting out a lunch buffet they had picked up at a local delicatessen.

Ginny was easier to be with than Julie was, because, like Melanie, she ran at a slower speed. She was a physical therapist at one of the hospitals where Chad worked as a medical technologist. Their tie to Dave was first high school and then Georgia where they had all gone to school.

"We've been friends for years," Ginny said, arranging the finger sandwiches on a platter and then glancing up at Melanie, who was about the same height and size. "Dave is a great guy. We just want him to meet a girl deserving of him."

Melanie didn't know how to respond to that, because she didn't know if she was that girl, so she merely smiled at Ginny and spread dip on crackers.

"And you seem deserving," Ginny added thoughtfully.

"Thank you. But we really haven't known each other very long."

"I know. But it doesn't take long to know, does it?"

Their eyes met and Melanie knew exactly what she meant. She decided to be honest with her. "No, it doesn't."

"Hurry up, you guys!" Tom called from his perch on the ladder where he was adding one last cartoon sign to the chandelier. Melanie had thought him the perfect match for Julie; he was tall and lanky, calm when she was in high gear, yet aggressive when she couldn't make a decision. They looked at each other with adoring eyes, and that fascinated Melanie. To have been blessed with a good relationship for so many years seemed strange to her. When she considered her short time with Dave, the first twinge of doubt crept in.

Were they rushing into this? They didn't really know one another, she hadn't met his family, nor had he met hers.

And then Julie was motioning wildly toward the kitchen. "Everyone in there quick. He just drove up."

Tom cast one last satisfied glance around the room, and Melanie had to admit it was perfectly decorated and was sure to surprise and please Dave. It was twelve o'clock, and Dave had told Tom he would be in to relax for a quick lunch before going golfing with Chad. But Chad was hiding in the kitchen with the rest of the conspirators, and they had something quite different planned. Melanie found herself extremely nervous. Her hands were cold and her throat dry, as they grouped together in a quiet little circle in the kitchen, awaiting the key in the lock.

All was silent, the music had been turned off, along

with all the lights, and the cassette Tom had made of deep snoring was propped just behind the door so that would be the first sound that greeted Dave. When the door opened and Melanie glimpsed his crisp white business shirt and perfectly groomed hair, her heart jumped to her throat and her hands turned to ice. He had already heard the snoring and was quietly closing the door and gently opening the closet door to hang up his jacket.

At that moment all the lights went on, and everyone yelled "SURPRISE!"

He whirled, turning pale as his eyes widened on all the decorations and the sudden blare of a CD playing an old-fashioned "Happy Birthday." One by one they moved into the living room, though Julie motioned for Melanie to stay in the kitchen.

Melanie waited, holding her breath, as he hugged Ginny and Julie and shook hands with Tom and Chad, thanking them for the party. "We're on a budget and couldn't afford a nice gift," Chad began to explain.

Dave put up his hand, and now she caught a side profile of him, for he still had not turned toward the kitchen. She felt a surge of tenderness well up within her just at the sight of him.

"So we decided to try to get you something you really needed," Tom said matter-of-factly, and Julie gave her the eye signal to come forward.

Slowly, Melanie came out of the kitchen, and Dave, following everyone's gaze, turned around. For a moment, he could only stare as though unable to believe his eyes. Then he covered the distance between them in a few short steps and pulled her quickly to him, smiling into her face.

"Melanie. You came down for my birthday."

She could only nod as she looked up at him and realized that nothing had changed. He was still just as she imagined him, except a bit thinner from his illness and a bit peaked. But the blue eyes that blazed into hers told her everything she needed to know. And then his lips were brushing hers, and she couldn't keep her arms from sliding up his arms to his shoulders. The kiss deepened until someone cleared his or her throat and Melanie jerked back, startled.

What was happening to the self-conscious girl who never made a move without thinking it over at least half a dozen times?

"Okay, time to eat," Tom broke the moment.

Dave's eyes still held hers, as though there were only the two of them in the room and the mood of Paris was still very much with them. The crowd was putting out the food, gathering around the counter, while Dave kept holding Melanie's hand and thanking her for coming.

"You've lost weight," she said, hoping to bring them both back to the moment.

"Yeah, but I'm fine now."

"Come on, you two," Chad nudged him. "Fill your plates. You're too thin, Dave. See, Melanie has already noticed."

"Oh, I didn't mean. . . ," she began then stopped. Those days of apologizing for everything were behind her now, and standing next to Dave she felt herself being led toward a bright new and very different future. She took a deep breath and forced her eyes away from Dave toward the crowded buffet.

"We should at least be sociable," she said gently. "They've really worked hard."

Dave blinked and turned around, surveying the food, the decorations, everything as though for the first time. "You are the greatest friends a guy could ever have," he said, and to everyone's surprise it looked like businessman Dave was about to cry.

She slid her hand into his. "Come on, I'm hungry."

They joined in then, filling their plates and joining in the conversation as Chad related news of the new golf course that was being built, knowing this would capture Dave's attention. The meal went pleasantly and then they moved to the sofa, talking easily, the way friends who had known each other for a very long time often did. Strangely, Melanie felt as though she fit right in, because she could relate to some of the things they were saying. She was delighted to learn that Ginny enjoyed reading, knew where the best bookshops were located, and that they shared a fondness for the same authors.

A knock on the door startled all of them for a moment, then Tom leapt to his feet and rushed to the door. A cart of sweets was pushed into the room by a pleased-looking caterer. A giant chocolate cake was the centerpiece, flanked by an assortment of other little goodies. And there were special decorative candles, already on the cake.

"Hey, this is too much."

The caterer was generously tipped in the background by Chad and disappeared back through the door.

"No. . .actually, we had planned to have Melanie jump out of the cake," Tom said, with mock seriousness, "but we couldn't find the right size cake."

Everyone laughed uproariously while Julie reminded Dave that he *had* to make a wish and blow out the candles. All of them. Tom was dutifully lighting each candle, as though there were hundreds, instead of twenty-six.

"Okay, you've made your point," Dave laughed. "But this is the happiest birthday of my life," he said and looked at Melanie.

"Make your wish," she reminded him.

"That's easy," he said, his eyes lingering on her before he turned and with a great whoosh of breath blew out each candle. Ginny and Julie then set about serving the rich cake with a colorful mint and a fortune cookie tucked on each side of the delicate china plate.

Everyone had fun reading their fortunes and debating whether there was anything to them or not. Julie staunchly believed in fortune cookies. Chad did not. Meanwhile, Ginny was busy in the kitchen.

"Hey, knock it off," she called. "I'm making Dave his special espresso."

With that Julie joined her in the kitchen and they began to load the dishwasher. "We've made reservations at The Globe for dinner at nine. But that gives you two a few hours together before dinner," Tom began.

"In privacy," Julie called from the kitchen.

Melanie glanced toward the kitchen and then said to Dave, "I really would like to help them clean up."

"Okay."

A couple of gifts had appeared out of nowhere for him; golf balls with engraved hand towels and a new desk set. Melanie decided to wait on hers.

When the party began to wind down and the others had gathered up all the debris, thrown it away, and pushed the caterer's cart into the kitchen, they made their excuses.

"See you at The Globe," Ginny smiled first at Melanie then Dave.

"And don't be *too* late," Chad teased.

At that precise moment, the bedroom door opened and the sound of accordion music, mostly out of sync, reverberated across the room, drawing everyone's attention to Tom who was wearing a French beret and had an accordion strapped to his chest. He was doing his best to give an imitation of a French song, but everyone erupted in laughter, quickly offending him.

"Thank you, Tom," Melanie called out. "That was very thoughtful of you."

He shrugged as Julie tugged at his sleeve while he removed the beret and placed the accordion on a chair. He started to go then turned back and looked at Melanie and Dave.

"You were right," he said to Dave. And they both understood the meaning, and strangely, Melanie did too.

After the door had closed and the voices had died away down the hall, Melanie realized that someone had put on a romantic sound track from a favorite movie, which seemed perfect for the occasion.

"You know what?" Dave said, lifting her hand to his lips and kissing each finger.

"What?" she asked softly, staring up into his eyes and feeling as though they were drifting on a cloud again.

"We're not in Paris," he said slowly, "and I'm more in love with you than before."

Tears glowed in her eyes for a moment as the romantic words about two people falling in love forever echoed to her. "Me too."

They reached for one another and at last Melanie knew the meaning of being a complete woman, of knowing the wonder of romance.

And she knew Granny was probably smiling down from her own special cloud.

PEGGY DARTY

Peggy has been spinning wonderful tales of romance for several years—and winning awards along the way. She had her first inspirational romance published by Zondervan in 1985. She started writing articles of inspiration about family life, but fiction was her real joy. After an editor suggested she try inspirational fiction, she found it to be a way to share messages of hope and encouragement that she feels are desperately needed in these difficult times. She loves to hear from her readers and says, "When I get a letter from a reader who tells me one of my books touched her heart, lightened her load, or helped in some way, I feel my goal has been accomplished." At home in Alabama, Peggy has been married to her college sweetheart for more than thirty years, and she is the mother of three and grandmother of two little boys.

Wall of Stone

by Nancy J. Farrier

Dedication

To Audrey, Dell, and Jeri,
who keep my writing on course;
my husband, John, who says, with good cause,
that writers starve because they forget to stop and cook;
my son, Adrian, and my daughters,
Anne, Abigail, Ardra, and Alyssa,
whose enthusiastic encouragement keeps me going.

"O afflicted city, lashed by storms and not comforted,
I will build you with stones of turquoise,
your foundations with sapphires.
I will make your battlements of rubies,
your gates of sparkling jewels,
and all your walls of precious stones"
(ISA 54:12 NIV).

Chapter 1

Chandra Kirby stared a moment longer at shimmering hazel eyes flecked with bits of green and yellow then slipped her mirror back in her purse as the plane taxied to a stop. She blinked back tears, dabbing at her eyes with a tissue. *Get hold of yourself,* she admonished. *Some vacation this will be if you cry the whole time.*

"You're running away." Her sister Clarissa's statement still hurt. *I am not running away.* Chandra's tears dried as her stomach churned. "You ran away from love, you ran from facing death, and now, a year later, you're running away from the fact that our parents are still dead."

Clarissa's voice from their last phone conversation echoed through her head. Clarissa wanted Chandra to come back to Indiana for a week. *I already had plans. I am not running away,* Chandra defended herself fiercely as she edged her way into the center aisle of the plane.

Standing in the slow moving line of people waiting to exit the plane, Chandra thought about the reason for her trip. All her life she'd dreamed of taking a bike tour through the English countryside. Then, after her parents' murder a year ago, she'd immersed herself in her work, trying to escape the anger and total abandonment she felt. As the anniversary of their deaths approached, Chandra knew she needed to get away in order to deal with it. A long dreamed of trip looked like a good answer to the problem.

Chandra followed the crowd through customs in Heathrow Airport and headed for the baggage claim area. Her body felt heavy from fatigue and stress. She walked slower than most of the people swarming past her. Without warning, she stumbled to the side, nearly landing on the floor as a man's body hurtled into hers.

"Excuse me," he said, his hand wrapping around her arm, steadying her. "I have to catch up to my party, and I'm sorry. Chandra? Chandra, is that you?"

Chandra tried to calm the thud of her heart, knowing who touched her from the sound of his voice. She looked up into the astonished face of Pierce Stillwell, childhood friend and, although unknown to him, the love of her life. "Hello, Pierce."

She almost sighed in relief at the even tone of her voice. It betrayed none of the inner turmoil.

"I can't believe we would run into each other in London of all places. What are you doing here?" Pierce's dark blue eyes sparkled, and his smile warmed the space around them. He glanced toward the exit doors. "Oh, sorry, Chandra. I've got to run. I'd love to stay and talk, but they're waiting for me, and I don't want to be too late. I'll call you sometime."

He leaned over, kissed her lightly on the cheek, and

dashed away. The crowd eagerly swallowed him, and Chandra stood silently staring after him, her hand covering the place where his kiss burned into her skin. The longing to run after him, almost overpowering in its intensity, nearly caused her to forget he was the reason she'd left home in the first place. A lone tear slipped from her eye, wending its way slowly down her face. Chandra pulled her long French braid over her shoulder and twisted the ends through her fingers as she began to once more move with the crowd.

Approaching the luggage bay, Chandra noticed a young woman holding a placard with her name printed on it. She smoothed the skirt of her midnight blue suit, trying in vain to wipe away the travel wrinkles. Weaving through the crowd, she slowly approached her. "Hello, I'm Chandra Kirby." She shifted the overnight case and held out her hand.

The petite brunette smiled, wrinkling her pert, freckled nose, and grasped Chandra's hand. "Glad to have you here, Chandra. I'm Leah, from Bikeway Tours. Let's collect your bags. Then we'll join the others in the van and motor to the inn."

"Here we are," Leah said cheerfully as she set Chandra's bag next to a gray twelve-passenger van. "Go ahead and find a seat while we load your bags."

Chandra smiled at the young couple on the first bench seat behind the driver. She could hear other people talking in the back of the van, however the middle seat beckoned her with empty arms. She edged past the first seat, maneuvering through the narrow space and into her seat. Before fastening her seat belt, she glanced back at the couple seated behind her.

"Pierce!" Chandra's involuntary gasp reverberated in the quiet of the van.

"Chandra! I can't believe this." Pierce's husky voice brought back a rush of forgotten emotions. "I didn't know you were going on this bike tour. Do you remember Morgan Wilson?" Pierce indicated the gorgeous blond seated next to him.

How could I forget my worst nightmare? Chandra wanted to say as she watched Morgan snuggle closer to Pierce. "Of course, I remember Morgan. Who could forget our senior prom queen?" Chandra struggled to keep her tone light.

Pierce turned to Morgan. "Morgan, do you remember Chandra?"

Morgan's smile didn't reach her eyes. "Of course. She was the little shadow who followed you everywhere. I'm sure this will be fun, Chandra."

The look in Morgan's eyes chilled Chandra. She barely listened as Pierce introduced her to Kurt and Gina Holman, the young couple in front of her. She turned around as Leah and the driver of the van climbed in. Pulling a paperback novel out of her purse, she fastened her seat belt and pretended to read words she couldn't even focus on. *Oh, God, I can't take this. I've always loved Pierce, and he's always loved Morgan.*

Chandra tried to ignore the soft murmuring from the seat behind her as the English countryside flashed by. Not wanting to picture Morgan with Pierce's arm around her, Chandra tried to concentrate on the emerald green hills dotted with sheep, thinking how beautiful they were compared with the dry brown hills around L.A. In the spring, L.A.'s hills were green but not like this. These rolling slopes blossoming with thatch-roofed cottages looked like something out of a fairy tale.

Leaning her head back against the seat, Chandra's thoughts filled with a warm smile and midnight blue eyes. Pierce. Her childhood friend and confidant. When the other girls her age were giggling about boys, trying out makeup and perfume, and longing to meet the latest movie heartthrob, Chandra preferred bike rides and hiking with Pierce. They dreamed for hours on end of taking bike tours all over Europe when they grew up, planning each trip and the order in which they would take them.

Although to Pierce they were only friends, Chandra had always longed for a deeper relationship. She loved him for his easy smile, his wonderful sense of humor, and the fact that he put up with her constantly organizing his unorganized life. Only Pierce understood the hurt she felt from being continually rejected by the girls her age because she didn't share the same likes and dislikes.

Chandra turned to look out the window, blinking back tears as she recalled the last time she had been home. At her parents' funeral, only Pierce had understood her grief. She still remembered the comfort of his arms around her. The safe, protected feeling Pierce gave her turned out to be her only solace during that miserable time. They hadn't seen or spoken to each other since.

Anger bubbled up inside as Chandra thought about her parents and their needless deaths. They were such good people. Always ready to help anyone in need, Chandler and Darlene Kirby were well loved in Newbury. Serious crime rarely happened in rural Indiana, and the whole community suffered a shock over the cold-blooded murder of her parents.

It didn't take long for the authorities to track down the young men responsible, but that didn't bring back her parents. Drugs and alcohol were the contributing factors. It turned out her parents had helped these young men because they were needy. Then, high on drugs and alcohol, the two men decided to see if they could get some more money. Her parents refused, probably recognizing the disoriented state the young men were in. Thinking to ransack the house, the boys tied up her parents, and when they couldn't any find money, they shot them. Chandra clenched her fists, her stomach knotting.

Chandra hoped this trip would help her forget the anger and the pain. *God, I don't know why You allowed this to happen,* she thought bitterly as she did every day. *They loved You. You should have been there for them.*

"Well, we're almost to Winchester," Leah's cheery voice cut through the silence, startling Chandra. "The inn is only a couple of miles away."

In the distance, Chandra watched a windmill slowly circle its arms through the gray haze as if beckoning her to come closer. She grimaced, thinking of Don Quixote trying to conquer windmills. Sometimes she thought her anger toward those young murderers was her windmill—

a useless effort. Yet she couldn't seem to give it up, no matter how hard she prayed. *They deserve my anger,* she thought, clenching her teeth.

The van pulled to a stop close to the door of the quaint, country style Green Meadow Inn. Chandra climbed stiffly from the van, watching the daffodils in the flowerbeds lining the walkway as they nodded their yellow heads at her. A light mist washed her face.

She tilted her head back and gazed up at the old lime-stone building, ivy snaking up the gray walls. The windows on the second floor opened out, and Chandra could visualize a young maiden leaning over the ledge, looking down the road, waiting for her favorite knight to ride by on his fiery steed.

After listening to instructions for meeting at the evening meal, Chandra followed the directions to her room. She opened a door to a small but neatly furnished bedroom complete with two twin beds. Chandra crossed to the window and, ignoring the weather, leaned out, wondering if her knight in shining armor would ride by.

Chandra sighed and sank down on the bed nearest the window. She couldn't remember being so tired. Before leaving on this trip, she'd spent a full day at the office tying up loose ends and preparing her staff for her absence. She didn't even have time to change clothes before catching her plane.

Groaning, she slid off the bed and opened her neatly packed suitcase to get some fresh clothes. They were to meet downstairs for dinner in an hour, and she wanted a shower first. Maybe then she would be able to stay awake during the meal.

After a long hot shower, Chandra undid her French braid and slowly brushed out her long hair. Her thick tresses hung in waves below her waist.

The door to the room suddenly burst open. Morgan stalked in and plunked her suitcase down in the middle of the floor. "It looks like we'll have plenty of time to reminisce, since we'll be sharing a room most of the trip." Her ice-covered words trickled bumps up and down Chandra's arms.

Chapter 2

W hy did you choose cross bikes for your tours?"
Pierce asked, looking up from the bicycle he
knelt beside. Dale, the tour guide, glanced
over from the Bikeway Tours bike he was examining.
"Most of the trip is along back roads. A lot of them are
fine for road bikes, but some are a little rough for those
thin tires. Then we throw in a few paths for fun and a little off-the-road scenery. You don't necessarily need a
mountain bike, but you need something sturdier than a
road bike. These seemed to meet our needs, and we've
never had a complaint about them."

"The components are good," Pierce admitted. "I like
the Ultimate ones. I sell a lot of them in my bike shop."

Dale nodded and continued to check the bicycle's
brakes, shifters, and gears, getting ready for the first day's
ride. The sun, peeping over the rolling hills, bathed them
in its warm glow.

"Good morning." Chandra stepped around the side
of the inn. Pierce smiled at her, noting her black and purple paneled biking shorts and matching jersey top. Her

purple and gray fingerless biking gloves and helmet dangled casually from one hand.

"Good morning to you." Pierce's husky voice broke the silence. Bikes forgotten, he found he couldn't take his eyes off of Chandra. The morning light made the auburn highlights in her hair stand out like a halo. The green of her hazel eyes glinted warmly. Her smile, fresh and open, beckoned him invitingly.

"Are you ready for the ride today?"

Pierce forced his gaze down and ran his hand once more over the bike frame before answering. "I'm ready. How about you? Have you kept up on your riding?"

"You bet." She stepped forward and ran her hand lovingly over the nearest bicycle seat. "I try to ride a little bit every day, and I do longer rides on the weekends. And you?"

"I started a bike club eight months ago." Pierce smiled at her and found himself trapped in her gaze again. "I guess I got tired of riding by myself. We do mostly road trips that are fairly short, but one weekend a month, part of the club gets together to do some off-road mountain biking."

"Are the others on the tour in your club or just from your church?"

Pierce nodded. "Morgan doesn't usually participate, but Kurt and Gina started the club with me. At first Gina ran the support team and wouldn't ride with us. Then after a couple of months she got tired of that and talked Kurt into buying her a bike." Pierce grinned. "She didn't have to talk much. Kurt and I were already discussing this tour, but he didn't want to do it if Gina wouldn't come with us. Now Gina rides every day and loves it."

"Oh, there you are." Morgan's sultry tone drew Pierce's attention like a magnet. Even in her unitard, a one-piece bike suit, and helmet she looked breathtaking. Her blue eyes captured his, drawing him away from Chandra. "You disappeared after breakfast, and we wondered what happened to you."

Pierce noticed Kurt and Gina standing behind Morgan. "I wanted to check out the bikes we'll be using," he stated lamely. "You know I always have to give them a once over."

A half hour later, Chandra swung her leg over her bike, flipped her long braid over her shoulder, and pushed off. The morning air, cool and moist, brushed against her skin like a damp washcloth. The village houses lined the road like a row of limestone checkers. A stream meandered alongside the trail, small footpaths crossing it at intervals.

Breathing deeply, Chandra relaxed, feeling her muscles tighten then gradually begin to loosen and adjust to the rhythm of her peddling. Once out of town, she would work up to the proper cadence, but just now she wanted to enjoy this quaint little village at a slower pace.

Chandra maneuvered to the front of the line at the town limits and picked up her pace a little. The clean country air almost made her lungs ache, as if they weren't used to such luxury. A click of bike gears alerted her that someone was catching up. Chandra glanced over her shoulder to see Pierce coming alongside.

"I see you're out front as usual." He grinned and

slowed his peddling slightly to match hers. "I always did have to work to keep up with you."

Chandra laughed. "I seem to remember it the other way around. I think that's why I'm so competitive."

Pierce's deep blue eyes sparkled with laughter. "We sure had good times together. I think you were the best thing for me. You wouldn't believe how disorganized my life is without you around."

Groaning, Chandra rolled her eyes. "I can't bear the thought. I had to constantly keep after you. It's been ten years, so it might be impossible to get you organized after all that time," she teased. His warm smile lit up the morning, and Chandra felt her pulse quicken. Pierce always had this effect on her, yet she knew it was a one-sided attraction.

"Pierce!"

Pierce glanced back over his shoulder. "I'd better go," he said. "Morgan refused to take our advice on preparing for the trip. To her the thirty miles we're covering today will seem like a million. I'd better go see if I can encourage her." He gazed for a moment at Chandra. "Sometime this trip we'll have to find the time to catch up. I've missed having you around."

Chandra bit her lip as he slowed his pace and drifted back toward the others. He missed her? What did that mean? Did he possibly feel something for her just as she felt something for him? Or was it simply her friendship he wanted, not a deeper relationship? Obviously, he reserved that for Morgan.

Chandra slowed her pace while keeping an even

cadence. Even though she'd prepared for this trip, she knew the first few days were designed to ease the group into the rhythm of steady biking without wearing them out. That's why the first days were the shortest distances. Despite the best training, any bike rider could be susceptible to fatigue, aching muscles, or sores where the bicycle seat rubbed the skin raw.

"Hi, Chandra." Kurt's cheerful voice cut through her reverie.

Chandra glanced over and once again felt warmed by Kurt's friendly brown eyes and welcoming smile. "Hi, Kurt."

"Isn't this the most beautiful country?" Kurt nodded his head toward a cottage near the road where two apple-cheeked girls waved excitedly, their brown braids bobbing with the motion. "I think this must be the best way to visit a new place. If we were in a car, we'd never see it in such a personal way."

Chandra nodded. "I hope we have time to look around. I wanted to examine the little village where we spent the night. I'd like to get to know some of the people, too. I love to travel and meet people."

"You work for a travel agency, don't you?"

"Yes. I enjoy working at Fantasy Travel and arranging people's dream vacations. It gives me the chance to visit places most people don't get to see." She paused a moment. "Tell me, how long have you known Pierce?"

"We moved to Newbury a year ago. I'm the assistant pastor at Pierce's church. We hit it off right away—you know how some people click? Well, Pierce and I were like that. Later we started the bike club and that really cemented our friendship. How long have you known Pierce?"

Chandra frowned in thought. "I barely remember a time when I didn't know Pierce. Our parents were close friends, and we grew up together." She smiled as a fond memory surfaced. "As the tomboy of the neighborhood, I didn't get along with the other girls. Pierce always stepped in, and we spent hours together riding our bikes and talking. He was the slightly older brother I wanted but never had." *At least, that's what everyone thought.*

"Then you must be Chandler and Darlene Kirby's daughter." Kurt's casual comment struck deep. "I'm sorry about what happened to them."

"Did you know my parents?" Chandra tried to still the tremble in her voice.

"I met your dad and mom when I interviewed for the assistant pastor's position. They took Gina and me to dinner and made us feel so welcome. We were only in Newbury three weeks when they were murdered. I still can't believe it happened."

A tear trickled slowly down Chandra's cheek, and she angrily brushed it off. "I still miss them so much," she whispered. "I can't understand why God did this."

"But Chandra, God didn't do it." Kurt leaned forward to look at her. "We don't understand why God may have allowed it to happen, and I know this may sound trite, but He works out everything for good."

"Well, I can't imagine a loving God bringing some good out of this. Two wonderful people were murdered while the scum that killed them are allowed to live. Not only are they allowed to live, but they were barely punished because they were young and didn't know what they were doing." Chandra couldn't keep the sarcasm from her voice. "Now, please excuse me," she said as she pushed harder on her pedals and raced ahead of Kurt. Tears traced down her cheeks as she fought to control the anger and hatred that knotted her stomach.

Pierce watched as Kurt dropped back beside Gina, and Chandra pushed ahead once more. Chandra's shoulders were hunched over her handlebars and her head bent low as if a great weight were on her. Pierce glanced over at Morgan, her face reddened with exertion, any attempt to be alluring momentarily forgotten.

What's wrong with me? Pierce thought. *Ever since high school I wanted to date Morgan. She's the most beautiful woman I've ever seen. I planned to ask her to marry me on this trip, yet now all I can think of is Chandra and how much I want to be with her.*

"Pierce, I think I need to stop for a while," Morgan panted as she slowed her bicycle. "I can't believe how hard this is."

"It's too bad you didn't make some of our longer trips."

"I rode my bike every day," Morgan snapped impatiently. "Some days I even rode through the trails in the park, so I'd be ready for the off-road part of the tour."

"Morgan." Pierce took on the tone he used when instructing a group of children. "You didn't ride that far. And the trails at the park are only three miles long, so the most you ever rode is five or six miles at a time. That's a lot different than the thirty to fifty we're doing each day on this tour."

"Maybe you didn't explain how far we'd be riding." Morgan's voice began to emulate the whine of an airplane engine preparing for take off. "Not only are my legs dying but I'm sure I'm getting sores from this bike seat."

"We'll stop for lunch before long. We can borrow a tool from Dale and check the slant of your seat. What kind of unitard did you get?"

"How should I know? I just picked one out of a magazine and bought it."

"I warned you to be careful to get clothing designed for women." Frustration crept into Pierce's voice. "The padding is different for us, Morgan. That might be why you're getting sore. We'll see what we can do at noon."

Pierce looked down the road to where Chandra and the others steadily pulled away from them.

"Oh, I see." He turned to see Morgan watching him. "You'd rather be riding with her—your old girlfriend. I suppose she trained properly for this tour."

"Chandra isn't my old girlfriend. We grew up together and have been friends for years. She's like a sister to me, and yes, I know she trained for this tour." Pierce stopped, wondering why he felt like he betrayed Chandra when he told Morgan she was like a sister. Hadn't they always been like brother and sister?

Morgan's cold tone jerked him back to the present. "Just remember, you invited me on this trip. I expect you to stay with me, not with your long-lost sister."

Chapter 3

Chandra hopped out of bed and stretched. Sharing a room with Morgan last night had been better than the first night. Morgan, too tired and sore to do or say much of anything, had climbed into bed early and fallen asleep instantly.

Crossing to the small window, Chandra peered out to see what the day would be like. The sun, playing peek-a-boo with gray clouds, promised possible showers and cool riding. Today they would see the famed Salisbury Cathedral and take a side trip, if they wanted, to Stonehenge.

A low moan from the bed adjoining hers alerted Chandra that Morgan had awakened. Chandra did her best to ignore Morgan's discomfort as she slowly pulled herself up in the bed. She and Morgan hadn't exactly hit it off, and Chandra didn't want to risk Morgan's anger this morning.

"Good morning," Chandra called over her shoulder, trying to sound cheerful. "Do you want to shower before breakfast?"

"I don't care," Morgan snapped. "You go ahead and

I'll take mine later."

Chandra quickly grabbed a towel and washcloth and headed for the bathroom. *Why in the world did Morgan come on this bike tour?* she wondered as the warm water poured down on her, loosening her slightly stiffened muscles. *Surely, it can't be for the sole purpose of being near Pierce. God, please help me see Morgan as You see her. I know You love her, so help me to at least tolerate her presence.*

"How are your saddle sores this morning, Morgan?" Chandra asked after her shower.

"I don't know that it's any of your business," she snapped. "They hurt like crazy, if you must know. I don't have any idea how I'll ride that stupid bicycle today."

"Did you bring some salve?" Chandra held up a small tube of her favorite salve. "If not, you can borrow some of mine."

Morgan stared at her, looking surprised, then nodded and reached for the tube. Slowly, she pushed herself off the bed and hobbled toward the shower. Chandra pulled the hairbrush through her wet hair, staring at the closed door thoughtfully, wondering how Morgan would manage.

Chandra stared in awe at the towering Salisbury Cathedral. The cathedral, bearing the tallest spire in England, definitely displayed the mastery of medieval architecture.

"Marvelous, isn't it?" Chandra jumped as Pierce's husky voice sounded close to her ear. Her pulse quickened, and she felt a blush warm her cheeks as she looked into his deep blue eyes. "No wonder so many people thought God lived in these buildings. They hold a presence that reminds one of God," Pierce said softly.

For a moment they stood in companionable silence, gazing at the rows of arched windows and alcoves lining the sides of the buildings. Suddenly, Pierce began to chuckle, and Chandra glanced at him.

"Care to let me in on the joke?"

Pierce grinned at her. "Do you remember Pastor Robinson? He led our youth group for a while."

"I remember him," Chandra said, a smile tugging the corners of her mouth. "We were so mean back then. We used to refer to him as our favorite horse, because he had such a long face."

"That's him. I don't think I'll ever forget his face and the way he talked so slow." Pierce laughed. "I used to watch old Jimmy Stewart movies and wonder if Pastor Robinson did the voice parts for him."

Chandra giggled. "So what reminded you of him?"

Pierce gestured toward the cathedral wall. "See that alcove, the second one from the end? The figure in there could easily pass for Pastor Robinson, don't you think?"

Chandra strained to pick out the stone figure Pierce pointed out.

"You're looking at the wrong row," he said, leaning closer and lifting her chin with his hand. Chandra bit her lip as his light touch set her pulse pounding. She could feel the warmth of his nearness and fought a longing to lean against him.

"You're right," she gasped, pulling away from his disturbing touch. "Do you suppose his great-great-great-grandfather posed for that statue?" Chandra looked up at

Pierce as his husky laugh drifted toward the imposing structure containing the statue in question. As she turned, she glimpsed Morgan watching from the edge of the grounds, her blue eyes blazing daggers even at that distance.

Quickly, Chandra moved away from Pierce. "I think I'll go inside and look around for a while. If the outside is this magnificent, I can't wait to see the inside. I'll see you later, Pierce." Chandra walked away, denying the look of hurt she'd seen in Pierce's eyes at her abrupt departure.

Pierce watched in shock as Chandra crossed the lawn and disappeared into the depths of the church. *What did I say?* he wondered. *Why did she leave like that?* The memory of those almond-shaped hazel eyes flecked with gold and green stayed with him. *She's always been special to me, Lord, but she just thinks of me as a brother. Help me get rid of these strange feelings. I plan to ask Morgan to marry me.*

Slowly, Pierce wandered over to the walled-in garden area of the church and slipped in through a doorway. For the next hour he wandered through the building and the grounds, admiring the medieval stonework and architecture.

Pierce paused to admire a particularly intricate piece of stonework, and the silence of the huge building closed in around him. It felt as if he were the only person in the whole world. The sound of quick footsteps and voices echoed down the hallway.

"Chandra." Morgan's sharp command echoed through the hall. "I want to talk to you."

Pierce glanced down the hall, wondering what he should do. He wasn't an eavesdropper, but this hall dead-ended, and the only other way out would be to pass them. As he stepped quietly down the hall, the conversation got louder, and he paused, not wanting to intrude.

"Hi, Morgan, isn't this a magnificent place?"

"You can quit with the concerned goody-two-shoes routine, Chandra. I saw you outside with Pierce, and I want it to stop."

"You want what to stop?"

"I know what you're doing. You're doing your best to take him away from me. Well, it won't work. I won't give him up."

"I don't know what you're talking about. Pierce walked up to me outside, not the other way around."

"She's right, Morgan." Pierce said.

Morgan's mouth dropped open then closed. For a moment she stared at him then turned to walk away.

"I want to talk about this later, Morgan," Pierce called after her.

Pierce reached over and pulled Chandra close for a moment. "I'm sorry, Chandra. Morgan is usually so sweet," he murmured.

How could she have changed so suddenly? Have I just been blind? Pierce wondered. *Oh, God, help me know the right thing to do,* he prayed.

"Everybody ready to set off?" Dale asked as Chandra stuffed the last bite of her sandwich in her mouth. "For those who want to, you can take a side trip to visit Stonehenge this afternoon. It's on the way to your lodgings tonight." He glanced at the overcast sky. "In case of rain, you have rain slickers in your pack."

Nearing the turn to Stonehenge, Chandra slowed, noticing the sluggishness of her bicycle. She looked down and groaned. "I hate changing flats."

"You hate what?" Pierce's voice so close startled her, and she nearly swerved off the road.

"Pierce, how do you manage that?" Chandra gave him an exasperated look. "You are always sneaking up beside me. I think you like to scare me like you did when we were kids."

Pierce laughed. "I didn't try to scare you. You just didn't hear me coming. Now, tell me what you hate."

Chandra gestured to the back tire on her bicycle. "Changing flats, especially on a back tire. Oh well," she sighed. "I guess it can't be helped."

After removing the tools and spare tube, Chandra flipped the bicycle upside down, balancing it carefully on its seat and handlebars. Pierce laid his bike down in the grass at the side of the road and stepped over to help her remove the tire.

"Pierce." The sugary sweetness in Morgan's tone turned Chandra's stomach. *What does he see in this woman?* she wondered.

"Pierce, I need you to ride with me." Morgan moaned slightly as she stopped and rubbed at her sore legs. "I don't think I can make it without your encouragement."

Chandra watched as Morgan widened her blue eyes and pursed her pink lips in a deliberate pout. Chandra remembered that same expression from high school days.

Pierce stirred beside her then slowly stood up. "Here comes Dale, Chandra. He can help you with this flat."

"That's fine, Pierce. Thanks anyway." Chandra bit her lip as Morgan flashed her a triumphant look. Pierce and Morgan pedaled slowly down the road as Dale stopped beside Chandra and hopped off his bike.

"Looks like you could use a bit of help here," Dale stated. He deftly turned the wheel around, searching for a nail or thorn that might have punctured the tire. He frowned up at Chandra. "You know, we use these tires because they're so hard to ruin. They rarely ever go flat, and when they do it's usually something obvious. Do you remember running over anything?"

"Nothing big enough to hurt one of these thick tires." Chandra leaned over to join in the search for the offending object.

"Well, I don't see a thing," Dale admitted finally.

Dale slipped the tire tool between the tire and the rim and expertly slipped the tire off. Unscrewing the cap, he pulled the tube out and slowly checked it over. Chandra peered at the flattened tube, unable to see anything wrong with it.

"Maybe a rock got in the tire." Dale pulled the tire apart and ran his fingers around the inside of the rubber. "No, I can't feel a thing." He sat back and stared at the tire, a puzzled look on his face. Dale shrugged and picked up the new tube Chandra had already laid out.

As Dale began to install the new tube, Chandra carefully inspected the flat, running it slowly through her hands. She couldn't find a single puncture or even a worn place. Slowly she examined the valve stem, knowing this could be a problem area. As she turned it around, something caught her eye, and she peered down into the stem.

"Look at this." Chandra held out the valve stem. "I think I found the culprit."

Dale reached for the flattened tube and looked down in the valve stem. "You're right," he said. "How do you suppose that got in there?" He pulled a pocketknife from his pouch and carefully dug the tiny pebble from the stem. "Did you take the valve cover off when we stopped for lunch?"

"I haven't taken it off at all. There hasn't been a need to."

"I can't imagine this rock getting in there all by itself." Dale held up the offending piece of rubble. "It's possible this was placed there on purpose." Dale looked at Chandra grimly. "I'll have to keep a better watch over the bikes. Now, let's get this tire pumped up, and we'll be back on the road."

Gritting her teeth, Chandra thought of how much she hated people who resorted to treachery. A picture of the young men who'd murdered her parents flashed through her mind. *Is this the way they started?* she wondered. *Did they begin with seemingly innocent pranks?*

The trip to Stonehenge passed without incident. When she arrived, Kurt, Gina, and Pierce were already strolling around the towering rocks. Visitors were not allowed to actually walk up to the rocks, but they could get a good view of them nonetheless. A rain-laden breeze brushed across Chandra's cheeks, sending a shiver down her spine. She didn't see Morgan or her bicycle.

"I see you got your flat fixed," Kurt called. "Come, look at these rocks. I'm trying to convince Pierce he should sneak in and pick one of them up."

Chandra laughed and warmed herself in Pierce's intense gaze. "I'd like a ringside seat for that. When we were growing up I used to think Pierce could do anything, but this might be stretching his abilities some."

They all laughed, and Kurt and Gina wandered off together. Chandra wished she could touch one of the rough pebbly rocks. "I wonder how they did move these rocks," she mused.

"I haven't any idea," Pierce answered, moving to stand beside her.

His nearness unsettled her, and Chandra thought about putting some distance between them. "Where's Morgan? I didn't see her bicycle with the rest."

"She didn't want to do the extra ride, so I sent her on to the inn."

Chandra leaned back and looked at Pierce. His closeness took her breath away. As he leaned toward her, Chandra's heart began to pound. For the first time she wished she had never moved away from Newbury or from Pierce.

Chapter 4

A huge drop of rain splattered on the tip of Chandra's nose, dribbling down the side. Pierce could not help laughing at the shocked look on her face.

"Pierce, Chandra!" Kurt's voice echoed off the rocks. "I think we're about to get an impromptu shower. We're heading on to the inn. You coming?"

"Right behind you," Pierce called back. He gave Chandra a crooked grin. "Looks like we'll be needing those rain slickers after all."

Once they reached the inn, Pierce hurried through the front door. He hoped to get to his room with a minimum of dripping on the carpet.

"I'm sure you had a wonderful time without me."

Morgan's acid tone chilled Pierce's already cold body. The ride to the inn had been chilly, as the rain turned from a light smattering of cold drops to a deluge. The foursome had stayed together, riding slowly at the edge of the road. Pierce felt at times as if he needed a windshield wiper, even though he didn't have a windshield. Now, before he even had time to dry off, Morgan wanted a confrontation.

"You're right, I did have a wonderful time," he retorted. "I even enjoyed riding in the rain. For once on this trip, no one complained about anything, even though they had plenty of reason to complain." Pierce brushed past Morgan. She stood with her mouth hanging open, her beautiful face flushed, her eyes flashing angry darts his direction.

Pierce climbed the stairs to his room, each step getting harder and heavier. He stopped and turned to look at Morgan, still watching him. What was happening here? All he'd ever wanted was to have Morgan's love. He had insisted she accompany him, yet now he resented her being here.

Despite the shivering in his limbs and the primal urge for a warm shower, Pierce retraced his steps until he stood face to face with Morgan. "I'm sorry," he said. "I'm half frozen and tired. I shouldn't have snapped at you like that."

Morgan's smile warmed the room. She raised her hand to touch his cheek then, as if thinking better of it, gestured toward the stairs. "Why don't you go get a shower and warm clothes? Then we'll snuggle up down here and make up."

A few minutes later, Pierce sighed as the warm water beat away the chill. *God, I'm so confused. I thought I knew exactly what was right for me when I invited Morgan on this trip. Now, I find I'm irritated with her most of the time. Is this Your way of showing me that Morgan isn't the wife You have for me? Please, help me see clearly. And why am I so attracted to Chandra? I can't get her out of my mind.*

The dark blue, baggy sweatshirt momentarily shut out the

already dim light as Chandra pulled the shirt down over her head. She shook out the folds, letting it drop easily over her slim hips, ending half way to her knees. She traced the picture of two cats on the front of the shirt, right above the saying, "You're purrrrfectly wonderful." The shirt reminded her of her favorite things—Fluffy and Tinker, her cats, and Pierce's midnight blue eyes.

She ran a brush through her still damp hair, slipped on some shoes, grabbed her book, and headed downstairs. On the way up, she had noticed a crackling fire in the common room. Sitting in front of that warm fireplace looked like the perfect way to get completely warm and cozy.

The common room was larger than a living room in most houses but furnished much the same. Variegated blue carpet rippled across the floor, the colors emulating the swell of ocean waves. Blue and brown easy chairs held out inviting arms, beckoning all visitors to sit and relax. A high-backed, overstuffed couch and love seat rested in the middle of the floor near the fireplace. Everything in the room whispered comfort and peace.

Chandra headed for the smaller love seat. She sank into its softness and curled her feet underneath her before she realized she wasn't alone in the room. Pierce stared at her from the couch while Morgan, seeing she had Chandra's attention, snuggled close to him, a look of triumph in her eyes.

"Excuse me." Chandra jumped up. "I didn't mean to interrupt."

"No, please stay." Pierce struggled to sit up straighter, obviously trying to move Morgan farther away. She wasn't cooperating. "We certainly don't have dibs on the room. Besides, I'm sure you'll enjoy the warmth of the fire. I know I do."

Morgan sat up slightly then ran her hand up and down Pierce's arm, her eyes never leaving Chandra's. "Please do stay, Chandra. Perhaps we can reminisce a little."

Chandra hesitated. She knew who would come out looking good if they talked about old times. It would be the ever-popular Morgan, not Chandra, the little nobody. The sound of the rain drumming on the roof echoed in the tense silence. For a moment Chandra pictured Morgan tossed out in the wet night while she snuggled on the couch with Pierce. A thrill of satisfaction raced through her.

God, forgive me. I know You want me to see Morgan as You do. She sank back down on the couch and tried to smile. "Of course, I'd love to talk about old times. Or perhaps we could just sit here and enjoy the fire." She held up her book. "I brought my own entertainment, so you needn't worry about me."

"How quaint." Morgan's mocking voice cut through the air. "You still have a thing about sticking your nose in a book."

Chandra bit back a sharp retort. What did Pierce see in this woman?

"I, for one, am glad you're still reading." Pierce grinned at her, warming her clear through. "I've even started reading more than I used to. It's a good way to relax."

Chandra smiled back, ignoring the daggers shooting from Morgan's eyes. Before a fight commenced, she opened her book and began to read, effectively ending the conversation. She didn't know how long she could keep up the pretense, but she didn't want to appear cowardly, running every time Morgan said something hateful. She had to stand her ground—without stooping to Morgan's level.

The next morning dawned bright and beautiful. Everything had a fresh-washed look to it. The grass sparkled with dew. Flowers eagerly reached toward the warm sun. Even the air smelled crisp and clean, a wholesome earthy scent permeating everything.

Pierce stepped out of the inn and stretched. He could not wait to start the day's ride. They would be taking a side path part of the way, weaving through countryside rarely seen from a car. *Someday I'd like to have a bike tour business in Indiana,* he thought. *Maybe Chandra could give me some tips on arranging tours.*

He smiled thinking of Chandra and her interest in his business. Morgan rarely asked him about anything. She always talked about her little boutique that carried pricey, name-brand clothing and accessories. He frowned. Come to think of it, Morgan knew nothing about his likes and dislikes, even though they'd been dating for months. Chandra, whom he hadn't spent much time with for years, knew more about him than Morgan.

"Hey, Pierce, ready to go?" Kurt's words and hearty slap on the back startled Pierce back to reality.

"Yeah, I'm ready." Pierce tried to force a smile.

Kurt, ever the pastor, halted in mid-step. "Looks to me like you lost your best friend. Something I can help you with?"

Pierce shrugged, not wanting to talk just yet. "Maybe later. Right now I need to sort some things out."

Kurt squeezed his shoulder. "Whenever you're ready, we'll talk. Okay?"

That evening, after a long day of listening to Morgan's complaints about the bike trip, the food, the company, and a myriad of other woes, Pierce needed to get out. He slipped through a side door of the inn, wandering down a well-worn path to a little stream. It would be a couple of hours before dinner. He hoped a little prayer would help.

He'd barely settled on a smooth rock when he heard cracking sounds coming from the brush. *Oh, Lord, please don't let it be Morgan. I can't take any more of her complaints right now.*

"Pierce?"

Kurt's deep voice sent a feeling of relief sweeping through Pierce. "Over here, Kurt."

Kurt sank down next to the rock, sitting cross-legged on the grass. The stream gurgled a soothing melody. For a few minutes they contemplated it in quiet.

"I need to talk, Kurt, but I don't know exactly how to begin."

Kurt picked a blade of grass and ran it through his fingers. "Why don't you just start. If it doesn't come out right, we'll work on sorting through it together."

Pierce sighed. "When I came on this trip I knew exactly what I wanted. I had it all planned out, and I thought it was right. Now, I'm not so sure."

"You said you knew what you wanted. What about

what God wanted?"

An arrow of pain arced through Pierce. "I guess that's the problem. I always thought I knew what God wanted so I forgot to ask Him about it." He bent to pick up a stick, rubbing the bark from it. "Ever since I can remember, Chandra has been my best friend and Morgan has been the one I wanted to marry. I've always seen Morgan as beautiful and sweet. I know they say love is blind, but I'm beginning to wonder how I could have been so blind. She hasn't been so sweet on this trip."

"What about Chandra? Is she still your best friend?"

"That's the thing. Suddenly, I find I don't want Chandra just as a best friend. I want more from her or, maybe, I should say, with her. But when I think like that, I feel as if I'm betraying Morgan. I planned to ask her to be my wife."

Kurt looked up at Pierce, his brown eyes probing. "A wise mother once told her son that finding a virtuous woman isn't easy, but when you do she's worth more than rubies."

Pierce grinned. "That sounds like some sort of Scripture, Pastor."

Kurt laughed. "You're right. I can't seem to get away from it. You might try reading what Lemuel's mother tells him about a wife in Proverbs thirty-one. Maybe you can use that to discern what woman God has for you. Meanwhile, I'll be praying about your decision. It's easy to fall into the rut of assuming we know what God wants and forgetting to consult Him on the matter."

"I've heard you tell the teenagers over and over how God will stir things up if we're not listening. Well, I do believe there's some stirring going on here and it sure is uncomfortable for me."

Kurt stood and stretched. "That's all right. We all need stirring up now and then. If everything was easy and went our way all the time, we would have a tendency to forget our need for God."

"Thanks, Kurt. I appreciate the talk."

Patting Pierce's shoulder, Kurt replied, "Anytime, you need me, I'm there."

Pierce watched Kurt walk back up the path to the inn then bowed his head. *God, please show me Your will here. I'm not so sure about Morgan anymore. In fact, I'm beginning to wonder why I ever liked her in the first place. Help me make the right choice.*

Pierce walked slowly, his footsteps silent on the hard dirt track. Twilight deepened and stars were peeking through the leaves overhead. He rounded the corner of the inn and stopped. Someone was by the bicycles. The slight figure wasn't Dale. In the dim light he leaned forward, straining to see what was going on. The inky shadow bent over, and a slight clink carried on the still night air.

Before Pierce could call out, the ethereal shape straightened and darted off into the darkness.

Chapter 5

The next morning, Pierce stepped outside early. Plants still dripped tears of water from the night's rain.

"Dale, I looked all over for you last night." Pierce's voice sounded loud in the quiet of the dawn.

"Don't tell me you wanted a moonlit ride." Dale grinned. "This is the one stop where I don't stay with the team. I have family living here, and I spend the night with them. What did you need?"

"I took a walk last night, and when I came back, I saw someone messing with the bikes." Pierce gestured toward the row of bicycles at the side of the inn.

Dale frowned. "Who was it? What did they do?"

Pierce followed him across the drive. "It was too dark, and I couldn't see much. I did hear a metallic sort of clink, but I couldn't figure out what would cause it." He hesitated. "I have an idea that it might pay to check Chandra's bike."

Dale stopped and gave him a sharp questioning look. "Why is that?"

"I. . .uh," Pierce stammered, "I don't know if I can explain it."

Leaning over Chandra's bike, Dale squeezed the tires and ran his hands over the gearshifts. "Any idea what part of the bike they touched?"

"I remember the person leaning over the front of it and then straightening."

Picking up the bicycle, Dale moved it away from the others then flipped it upside down to rest on the seat and handlebars. Pierce moved up beside him, and they both studied the gears and chain.

"I don't see anything wrong here." Dale set the bike back on its tires.

"Let me see if I can remember exactly where and how the person was leaning on the bicycle." Pierce moved to the bike as if he were going to mount it and bent forward. Looking down, he frowned as something caught his eye. "Look at this. There's a scratch mark on this bolt. Was this here before?"

Dale ran his finger over the gouge in the metal. "No. I go over these machines every day." He pulled a wrench from a pouch at his waist. "Someone loosened the handlebars just enough to cause an accident."

Pierce gritted his teeth in anger. "The bike would have worked fine until a downhill or rough stretch of road, then the wheels would go one way and the steering another. Chandra would have had no control."

"That's right," Dale agreed. "If you know who did this, I want you to tell me. I don't like anyone sabotaging my equipment."

"Like I said, I didn't get a good look. They ran off before I could even get close."

After breakfast Dale stood and faced the tour group, his face grim. He held up the wrench, twirling it between his fingers. "I want you to know that someone tried to impair one of the bicycles last night. I don't know who did it, but I wanted to tell you that I check those bikes daily. If I find out who did this and it was one of you, that person will be asked to leave this tour immediately. Understand?"

Pierce watched Morgan's face as Dale made his announcement. Her eyes narrowed and a faint flush crept into her cheeks. Had she been the one? Did she hate Chandra so much that she would try to hurt her by wrecking her bike?

Chandra stopped at the side of the road and straddled her bike, looking at the idyllic scene before her, glad that she always rode ahead of the others for the quiet. A hill rose gently, terraced by stone walls and dotted with sheep contentedly munching on the emerald grass. A small stream wended its way along the bottom of the hill, and she could hear the soothing melody of the water tripping over the rocks.

"That's a beautiful sight."

Pierce's voice startled her out of her reverie. She looked into his laughing blue eyes and wondered briefly if he were referring to her or the vista before them.

"I didn't hear you," she blurted out. Looking back at the lambs frolicking through the grass, she took a deep breath, trying to calm her nerves. Every time Pierce came near, she felt like a silly schoolgirl with a crush.

"I can't believe we're finally here." Pierce spoke in a hushed voice. "I remember how often we used to talk about and plan the trips we would take. I didn't dream we would really be able to do it."

Chandra chuckled. "Do you recall some of the stupid things we decided on?"

Pierce managed to look wounded despite the grin on his face. "Now, what would we have done that was stupid?"

"I seem to remember wanting a basket on the front of my bike so I could carry my cats in it. And you wanted to bring your parakeet and have it ride on your shoulder."

"Well, pirates always walk around with parrots on their shoulders. I don't know why cyclists can't have parakeets."

"Did you ever try it?" Chandra asked.

Pierce lifted his foot onto his pedal. "I think it's time to get going."

"Not so fast, buster." Chandra grabbed his handlebars. "I think you're avoiding my question. Come on, fess up. Did you try to ride a bike with your parakeet?"

"Do you know how fast a parakeet can fly when it's outside?" Pierce's laugh echoed off the hills. "I never did see the poor thing again. And I thought we were best of friends sharing an experience."

Chandra doubled over with laughter. "I can't believe you really tried it."

"Okay, Miss Smartie, how about you? Did you ever take your cat for a ride?"

"I think you're right. We should be going." Chandra

pushed on her pedal, but Pierce was faster. He grabbed her bike before she could even get started.

"Oh, no you don't. This is true confession time. Let's hear it."

Chandra felt the heat rising to her cheeks. She grabbed her braid that had fallen over her shoulder and twisted the end. "I suppose I could tell you that my cats don't appreciate moving faster than their four legs will carry them. Now, they walk a wide circle around my bikes."

Pierce leaned closer, his fingers running softly down her cheek. "Why did you leave, Chandra?" he asked softly. "I've missed you so much."

She opened her mouth, searching for the words to say, but his nearness stole her breath. She closed her eyes, trying to think of one reason why she had moved away. Nothing came to mind.

"I wish you would move back, Chandra. I have some plans I'd like to tell you about and see what you think. Maybe you could help me." Before Pierce could say any more, the staccato click of a bicycle changing gears alerted them that the others had caught up.

"You took so long to catch up, I was beginning to think we'd have to send a search party for you." Pierce grinned as Kurt and Gina rode up beside them.

Morgan, red-faced, forced her bike the rest of the way up the hill and stopped at the rise next to Pierce. Chandra bit her lip. Did Pierce really want her to move back because he liked her? Wouldn't he always be attracted to Morgan? Even with a flaming face, sweat dripping down her cheeks, and a helmet squashing her bouncy hair, she looked devastatingly beautiful.

"What a gorgeous view," Kurt exclaimed. "No wonder the two of you stopped here."

For a few minutes Chandra saw the vista afresh. The brilliant blue sky, white clouds scudding past, the sun bathing the hills with warmth, and the sheep, now resting in the grass in a contented group, tugged at her heart.

"This reminds me of your parents' farm, Chandra," Morgan spoke up. "Every time we drove by there were sheep in the fields. I wonder what ever happened to all those sheep."

Although the scene hadn't changed, Chandra felt as if the sun had dropped from the sky, leaving her chilled inside and out. Pain flared fresh inside, and she wanted to cry out. One glance at Morgan's face told her that the hurt was intentional. Her gloating look was unmistakable. A heavy silence descended over the group.

"My sister and her family live at the farm now." Chandra's throat closed painfully as she choked out the words. "I think they sold the sheep."

Anger welled up inside at the unfairness of it all. Her parents should still be alive and would be if God had taken care of them. Why hadn't He protected them and watched over them? Weren't they His sheep and He the Shepherd? A shepherd should watch over his sheep and keep them from being harmed by wild animals, and that was just what those two kids were—wild animals.

"Chandra?" Pierce's soft voice captured her attention. "Are you all right?"

She nodded, fighting back tears of anger and frustration. She looked at him, begging him silently to leave her alone.

Pierce knew her so well. He turned to the others and motioned down the hill. "I, for one, would like to cool my feet in the little brook down there. Anyone care to join me?"

"You're on," Kurt agreed.

Chandra closed her eyes and listened to the click and whir of the bikes racing down the path. She needed a moment alone to pull herself together.

"I know what you're trying to do," Morgan hissed close to her ear making Chandra jump. "You're trying to get Pierce not to like me anymore. Well, it won't work, and I'm telling you right now to stay away from him. Do you understand?"

Anger and revulsion fought a battle within. Chandra tried to hold her temper, but it didn't work. "I'm not the one turning Pierce away from you, Morgan. It's you and your whiny, attention demanding ways. Why don't you start thinking of someone else for a change?"

"I think of Pierce all the time," Morgan spat out.

"You only think of how you can trap him. He's a conquest to you just like all the other boys were at school. Having one worship at your feet wasn't enough. You had to get them all to bask in adoration of you."

"You're just jealous because I'm prettier and more popular than you." Morgan's eyes flashed fire.

Chandra shook her head, realizing how foolish it was to argue about this. "Morgan, don't you think I've seen the little notes you've left in our room? Mrs. Pierce Stillwell. Morgan Stillwell. They're all over. That's something girls did back in high school. I don't care about being popular. I'm content with who I am and with the job I do. Maybe you should try to be the same."

Pushing against the ground, Chandra shoved off, heading down the hill. She heard a low growl from Morgan and glanced back. Morgan, her whitened fingers gripping the handlebars and her teeth clenched like a growling dog, bore down on Chandra's bike.

Swinging back around, she could see the others at the bottom of the hill, removing their shoes and dipping their toes in the stream. Pierce and Kurt were laughing. Even Dale seemed more relaxed than he had been all day. She tried to ignore Morgan's furious pedaling beside her.

"You think I'm a baby. I'll have you know I could have any man I wanted, including most of the so-called happily married ones. I won't have you taking the man I've decided to marry." Morgan's voice carried more than a hint of a threat.

A sharp jolt caught Chandra off guard. Before she could react, her bicycle jerked to the side. She slipped off the path and on to the rocky hillside. Her bike bounded crazily across the grass. Chandra fought to bring it under control. She squeezed the brakes tight, trying to stop. A huge rock, hidden in a patch of long grass, loomed before her. The front tire hit it, and Chandra flew into the air, bike and all.

She thudded to the ground and rolled toward the brook at the bottom. For an instant she caught the look of horror on his face as Pierce ran toward her. A sharp pain radiated through her body as she came to a stop near the edge of the stream. Something sharp jabbed at her cheek. She turned her head to see a sharp rock. Broken pieces of her helmet littered the ground around it.

"Chandra, are you hurt?"

Chandra looked up. Morgan knelt over her in pretended concern. Only Chandra could see the victorious smile spreading across her face.

Chapter 6

"Chandra." Pierce knelt on the other side of her, holding her hand in his. "Don't try to move until we check you over. Thank God, your helmet protected your head."

Morgan backed away as Dale knelt on the other side of her. "I want you to move a little at a time as we tell you to," Dale spoke softly.

Chandra tried to smile. Her leg ached. Her whole body felt bruised. "I think I'll be fine. Let me sit up."

Dale started to object, but Pierce held up a hand. "It's okay. She's been biking for years, and I know she's had some nasty spills. She'll tell us if it's serious."

The warmth from Pierce's hand holding hers gave Chandra incentive to move. With a moan she sat up. Her left leg stung, and she leaned forward to get a closer look. A rock had gouged a cut down the side. Bright red blood stained the green grass. "What happened?" she asked softly. "Did I hit a rock?"

"You hit your head on one." Pierce bent over her leg, his fingers probing gently. "Do you have a first aid kit, Dale?"

Dale nodded and ran to the bikes.

"Pierce, I think he can handle this," Morgan called in a soft voice. "Why don't we go on? I don't want to get in too late."

Pierce gazed at Morgan for a long moment. A hush fell over the group. "I'm staying here with Chandra, Morgan. Why don't you go on without me?"

Morgan's blue eyes welled with tears. She bit her lip as if trying to hold back a sob. "If that's the way you want to be, then it's okay. Stay with her. Maybe you should have invited Chandra to come with you rather than me."

No one spoke as they watched Morgan climb on her bike and head down the road. Finally, Kurt broke the silence. "Do you want me to ride ahead and have someone come with a car?"

"No, please," Chandra said. "I've been in plenty of accidents. I'll be fine. As long as the bike works, I'd rather ride and loosen up the sore muscles."

Dale smiled as he finished taping a bandage on her leg. "I'll check the bicycle for damage. The good news is that we'll be staying two days in this town. There are some great antique shops to browse through. Also, you'll have a room of your own tonight."

"That will be a treat," Chandra admitted.

When Kurt and Gina followed Dale to see about the bike, Chandra suddenly realized she was holding Pierce's hand again. Or was he holding hers? She couldn't really tell, but it felt wonderful. She looked up into his dark blue eyes and serious face.

"What did happen?" he asked. "How did you wreck

on such an easy hill?"

Chandra looked down and rubbed her finger lightly over the bandage on her leg, trying to decide what to say. "I'm not sure," she replied. "I felt a jolt, and the next thing I knew I was flying down the wrong side of the hill."

As he wrapped his arm around her and pulled her close, she could hear the deep breath he let out. "Just be careful," he cautioned. "I can't stand the thought of you really being hurt."

Chandra relaxed, listening to the steady thump of his heartbeat. Her aching muscles, the pain in her leg, and the world around faded away. It would be utter delight to stay here in Pierce's arms forever.

Before evening, Chandra already regretted her eagerness to have a room to herself. Even though sharing a small room with Morgan proved difficult, it was better than being left alone with her thoughts. For the whole trip she had managed to keep herself busy or around other people so that the upcoming anniversary of her parents' deaths wouldn't bother her so much. Now she found she couldn't erase the hurt and anger from her mind.

She closed her eyes, surrendering to the awful memory and accompanying sense of panic when her sister, Clarissa, called to tell her of her parents' murder. She recalled with absolute clarity exactly where she'd been at that moment. Snuggled in bed, the red clock numerals blinking 5:30 in the morning, Fluffy still curled in a warm ball at her feet, and Tinker rubbing against her arm, purring his reminder that it was nearly breakfast time. She could still feel the coldness of the phone pressed against her ear and the unreality of the message being relayed.

Shock. She knew it must be shock. She hadn't cried. There must be a mistake. Her parents were going to live long lives serving God. They loved Him. He protected them. It was that simple. There must be a mistake.

It wasn't until she looked at the empty shells of her mother and father lying cold and still in their caskets that the truth finally sank in. They were dead. God had failed. He had allowed a stupid crime to happen to those who loved Him most.

A sob wrenched its way from deep inside. Chandra turned her face to her pillow, drowning the sound. *Why, God? Why did You do this? I needed them. I need them now.*

Only as her sobs quieted did she hear the small voice whisper, *You need Me, My child. Only Me.* Oh, how she wanted to believe that. She longed to surrender all her hurt to God, but the thought of the two young men pushed to the front. All she could see was them being allowed to virtually go free because of their youth. Yes, they'd gotten a prison sentence, but it was such a short one it was like nothing at all. How could the jury have been so gullible?

The soft whisper of God's voice fell farther away as bitterness pushed its ugly face into view. Soon the voice was only a faint memory. Self-righteous anger once again filled her.

Pierce strolled through the countryside. He loved England. It seemed so quiet and peaceful compared to the hectic lifestyle in the States. He felt like he had journeyed back in time when he came here. The old houses with stone walls and thatch roofs reminded him of tales in story-books. The people were quaint, the children ran barefoot in their yards. Life was definitely slower here.

He lengthened his stride, enjoying the feel of stretching his muscles. From his second-story window at the bed and breakfast where they were staying for two days, he had noticed a stream that meandered through this pasture. Hoping the owner didn't mind, he crossed the stone wall surrounding the field and looked for a place to relax next to the water.

He sank onto the grassy bank, the cool of the ground seeping into his legs. Leaning back on his elbows, he watched the puffy clouds float across the sky. Smiling, he remembered when he and Chandra used to see who could find the best shapes in the clouds. It was never a contest. She always won. She had the best imagination and could pick out outlines he never would have thought of looking for. Now, as he gazed heavenward, he only saw a sweet smiling face with hazel eyes staring back at him.

Pierce shook his head and sat back up. He picked up the Bible he had brought with him and turned to the book of Proverbs. *Okay, God, I really need some help here. I need You to show me Your will. I don't want to just follow what I think You want. When I do that, I seem to just do my will, not Yours. Please, show me what You have in store for me in a wife.*

Bending over so his body would shade the words, Pierce began to read: "The words of king Lemuel, the prophecy that his mother taught him."

Pierce smiled. *I remember my mother teaching me wise*

things too. Of course, at the time I didn't think they were so wise. Now, though, I can recall her telling me what to look for in a wife. Why didn't I think of that?

He noticed a title heading at verse ten, "The Capable Wife." Skipping several verses, he began to read once more. "Who can find a virtuous woman? For her price is far above rubies. The heart of her husband doth safely trust in her, so that he shall have no need of spoil. She will do him good and not evil all the days of her life."

Pierce looked up again and chewed his lip. "She will do him good," he whispered to himself. "What good has Morgan ever done for me? She doesn't even know what I like or what interests me. All we ever talk about is what she likes and wants. All we ever do is what she suggests we do. This trip is the first time she's ever done something I wanted. I think the only reason she came is because she expects me to ask her to marry her.

"I don't think I could ever trust in her. When we're at home I find I'm constantly watching other men, jealous if they so much as look at her." Frowning, Pierce realized that was because Morgan usually took advantage of those looks. She enjoyed attention from other men. In fact, she thrived on it. He didn't know if he could ever be content with that type of threat to his marriage.

Reading on through the wise words of Lemuel's mother, he marveled at the work that this wife did. She cared about every aspect of her family's life. "She openeth her mouth with wisdom; and in her tongue is the law of kindness."

He shook his head. Morgan certainly didn't fit very

many of the verses here. Her words could be honeyed and sweet when she wanted them to be, but now that he thought about it, she didn't speak with a lot of wisdom or kindness.

"Favour is deceitful, and beauty is vain: but a woman that feareth the Lord, she shall be praised."

The words jumped off the page and grabbed him. Hadn't his mother said that more than once? She had told him over and over that beauty was only skin deep and you have to look farther than that.

God, is this what You're trying to show me? Is Morgan only something beautiful and vain? For long moments he thought about the years he chased after Morgan, hoping that someday she would be his. Now, he saw the truth. That had been a fruitless chase after a vain and empty woman.

Who can find a virtuous woman? God, forgive me for not seeking Your will earlier. Help me to set things right. I can see Chandra in these verses, Lord. I believe I've always loved her but was too blind to see it. Help her to return my love. Give me the right words to say to Morgan, too, Lord. I don't want to hurt her.

Evening shadows stretched across the field before Pierce was finished praying. He knew dinner would be ready soon and hurried as quickly as he could without stumbling in the growing darkness. Anticipation of seeing Chandra made his heart pound. He could still feel her snuggled up against him. It felt so right to hold her. He wanted to be there for her every time she needed him. Maybe tonight he would get the chance to talk about it with her.

The smell of roasting meat and potatoes wafted through the air when Pierce swung the front door open. He breathed deeply, his stomach rumbling a protest at being empty. He bounded up the stairs to put away his Bible and change for the meal. Chandra, because of her hurt leg, had a room on the ground floor. He couldn't wait to see how she was and walk with her to the dining room.

A few minutes later he stood outside her door. He ran a hand over his damp hair, smiling at the giddy feeling that made him so antsy. He had checked in the dining room, and Chandra hadn't been seated around the table with the others. He knocked, trying to calm his pounding heart.

"Yes?" The muffled reply barely sounded through the solid door.

"Chandra? I came to see if you're ready for dinner." He slid the door open slightly so he could be sure she heard him.

"Go away."

"Are you okay?" Pierce leaned farther into the room and could see her huddled in bed.

Chandra turned to him, and even in the dim light he could see the redness around her eyes. "Just go away and leave me alone. I'm not hungry and I don't want to see anyone."

Chapter 7

T aking the steps slowly, Pierce rubbed his sleep-laden eyes as he came downstairs the next morning. Rest had been an elusive companion after the brush-off Chandra had given him. He stayed awake most of the night wondering if it was something he had done that caused her to cry so much. He thought she'd enjoyed it when he held her after she was hurt. She seemed content to lean against him. Had he said something then or later that caused such a negative reaction?

Then, last night, as he turned away from Chandra's room, he saw Morgan with her inviting smile. For once, he hadn't wanted to spend any time with her. He wanted to tell her it was over between them, but he had been so upset because of Chandra that he couldn't even think straight. He spent much of dinner and the evening trying to act normal when his heart was breaking in two.

Only Kurt seemed to sense something was amiss. He and Gina stayed with Pierce and Morgan, talking and laughing as if trying to make up for Pierce's quiet. Pierce knew Kurt wanted to talk. It hadn't been easy to avoid him all evening. What happened was between him and

Chandra, though. Perhaps later he could talk to Kurt about it.

Sunlight streamed through the windows next to the front door, highlighting the gleam of the polished oak floor. Pierce paused to look out at the tree-lined avenue passing by the bed and breakfast. Situated on a hill at the edge of town, it would only be a short walk to the streets that were lined with antique shops. Dale had pointed them out yesterday.

Heavy hearted, Pierce stepped toward the dining room. He had looked forward to spending the day combing those shops with Chandra. Now, he didn't know if she even wanted to see him again. And he still hadn't been able to say anything to Morgan. She would be expecting him to go with her. Well, first things first. He would have breakfast and then talk to Morgan.

The spicy smell of sausages drew him toward the table. Chandra was seated across from Kurt and Gina, laughing at something Kurt must have said. Morgan wasn't anywhere around.

"Good morning." Pierce slipped into the chair next to Chandra's. He could see a slight puffiness around her eyes, but other than that there were no traces of last night's tears. "Did I miss something?"

Chandra grinned. "Kurt was just telling me about some of your mountain biking experiences."

Pierce groaned and pretended to glare. "I thought pastors could be trusted to keep things in confidence."

"I believe that's only when they are things told in confidence." Kurt chuckled and Gina laughed. "Besides, half the congregation was there—or at least the half that rides bikes with us."

"So what deep, dark secret did he tell you?" Pierce tried to put on a wounded martyr look. Chandra's entrancing smile nearly undid him.

"Oh, I just heard about the time you decided to try a new trail. When you went over the hill you landed in a big mud bog that was being prepared for a dirt bike race." She leaned closer, and he could see the green and yellow flecks in her hazel eyes. In a loud whisper she continued, "I have it in strictest confidence that even your very blue eyes turned brown."

Laughter rumbled up as Pierce remembered the very humbling incident. "I do believe God brought me down a peg or two that time. I know I needed it. I had mud everywhere—in my hair, my ears, up my nose. I was a mess."

"Pierce."

Morgan's hoarse call interrupted the fun. They all looked at where she leaned on the door of the dining room, her hand pressed to her forehead in a dramatic pose. Her legs wobbled, and Pierce and Kurt both jumped up to help her.

"What is it?" Pierce asked. He and Kurt helped her to a chair.

"I'm not feeling so well this morning. I think that maybe it's something they fed us yesterday. I should complain to the management."

"None of us is sick," Kurt said, "and we ate the same food. Do you need to see a doctor?"

"No, I think I'll just stay here today. Maybe by tonight

I'll feel better."

Pierce brushed her forehead with his hand. She didn't feel exceptionally warm. He didn't think she had a fever. "I hate to see you miss out on the shopping. I thought you might be able to find something to take back for a souvenir."

Morgan put her hand on his arm and gave a pleading, puppy-dog gaze. "Please stay with me today, Pierce. I don't want to be by myself in a strange place."

Pierce forced a smile. How could he possibly give Morgan the news that it was over between them when she was sick? "Let me help you back to your room."

"No." Morgan pushed him away. "I'll let Gina help me. You go ahead and have breakfast. After I rest a little longer I'll come down and we can spend time together here."

Watching Morgan lean on Gina as they left the room, Pierce felt some of the carefree joy leave as well. *God, nothing is working out. What do I do now?* As if the Lord spoke directly to his heart, Pierce knew he had made his decision last night and he would stand by it. He had seen enough of Morgan's manipulations to recognize her "illness" for what it was. He would send Gina back up to tell her he was going shopping, and then he and Chandra would have some time together. Maybe he could even find out what had been bothering Chandra last night.

Chandra watched Kurt and Gina stroll arm in arm down the narrow roadway toward a bakery. She could still hear Kurt's words. "With all this biking, I'm wasting away. I'm sure I need a sweet pastry to get me through the shopping."

Gina had laughed and asked what his excuse was all the other times he wanted something sweet in the morning. Chandra didn't know how he could even think of food after the huge breakfast they'd been served earlier.

"So, I'm ready to look in some of these shops. How about you?" Pierce's dark blue gaze captured and held hers. "You sure your leg is up to this?"

"Positive. But before we start, I have something to say." She took a deep breath. "I'm sorry about last night. I didn't mean to be churlish. I just miss my parents." She looked away, fighting against the lump in her throat.

"Hey." Pierce tilted her chin up with his fingers and planted a soft kiss on her forehead. "Enough said. It's forgotten."

She smiled, relieved to have the apology over. "Well, then, where shall we start?" She hoped her wobbly voice went unnoticed. She didn't want Pierce to know how his nearness set her heart racing.

Placing his hand under her elbow, Pierce propelled her forward. "I think the best way to do this is to start with the closest shop and work our way through the whole bunch."

Chandra gasped in mock astonishment. "You mean you brought that much money with you? How will you carry everything on one little bicycle?"

"It's easy, my dear." Pierce wiggled his eyebrows at her. "Did you ever see Mary Poppins? All I have to do is buy a bag like hers and stuff everything in it."

For the next three hours, Pierce and Chandra wandered through the shops, exclaiming over their various finds. Everything was charming in an Old World way. Chandra spent a long time looking at the assortment of beautiful dishes. Clarissa collected antique dishes, and she wanted to get something special for her. Finally, she settled on a white cream pitcher, exquisitely decorated with blue flowers and trimmed in gold. The graceful handle and tilt of the pitcher spout reminded her of a pitcher her mother had given to Clarissa for a wedding present.

Pierce spent much of his time browsing through old books and tools. Chandra stepped into another room, waiting for him to finish. The musty smell of old dust made her sneeze. The walls were covered with artwork of various sorts. A ship tossed on restless waves. The wind whipping through its sails caught her eye. She shuddered. Sailing had never appealed to her, and she didn't want to imagine how frightened she would be in a storm like that.

Moving on, she stopped to look at pictures of the English countryside. Leaning forward, she gasped. One of the smaller pictures looked exactly like the scene she had stopped to look at yesterday. There were the rock walls terracing the hillside, the grazing sheep, and the small brook. She could almost hear the bubbly melody it had played. Even the clouds looked the same.

"That looks familiar." Pierce's low voice next to her ear startled her.

"I can't believe it, but it looks like the same place." She glanced up at him and found herself unable to drag her gaze away.

"It looks the same to me."

He spoke so softly she had to lean closer to hear the

words. Pierce tucked a strand of hair behind her ear then trailed a finger across her cheek. A tingle of excitement coursed through her.

"Why don't you buy the picture?" he asked. "You could have a memento of the trip that will remind you of a place you actually saw."

"It could remind me of why I have the scar on my leg." She grinned. Tearing her gaze from his, she looked back at the idyllic scene. "I don't know why I like this picture so much. I love the walls and the sheep. It's something about them, but I don't understand what it is." She shrugged. "I think I'll look around some more."

They wandered out of the shop. Pierce slipped his hand around hers. "Look. There's Kurt and Gina. Shall we see if they're ready for some lunch? Shopping always makes me hungry."

Chandra smiled and nodded, not trusting her voice. She wondered if Pierce felt any of the electricity that raced up her arm from the contact with his hand. This day was so perfect. Nagging thoughts of her agony last night tried to intrude, but she pushed them away. She didn't want anything to spoil this closeness with Pierce.

By late afternoon they had visited nearly every little shop in town. Chandra's leg ached as they headed back to the inn. She tried to keep from limping, but Pierce must have noticed.

"Are you okay?" The concern in his eyes warmed her.

"I think my leg's had enough walking for one day," she admitted. "Maybe we could sit somewhere and rest before we climb the hill to the bed and breakfast."

"That's what I like about England." Pierce grinned and gestured to the side of the road. "There's always a wall to sit on when you need it. Imagine back home. You'd have to sit on a barbed-wire fence."

"Ouch!" Chandra grimaced. "I think I'd rather put up with an aching leg."

Pierce sat close to her, his arm brushing against hers. As if reading her thoughts and knowing how she longed to rest her head against his shoulder, he put his arm around her and pulled her close.

"Do you know how much I've missed having you around?"

She could only shake her head in answer. His hand cupped her chin and pulled her close. He ran his thumb gently over her lip, and she thrilled to his touch. Slowly he bent his head and lightly brushed her lips with his.

"I can see you're worried to death about me being sick."

At the sound of Morgan's voice they both jumped. Chandra started to pull away, but Pierce pulled her closer, his arm tightening protectively around her shoulders.

"I'm glad to see you're feeling better Morgan." Pierce didn't look too happy. He let his arm drop. "If you'll excuse us, Chandra, Morgan and I need to talk."

He stepped toward the beautiful blond, and Chandra shivered as his warmth left her. Morgan shot her a look of victory as Pierce took her arm and turned her toward town. Chandra watched them walk away, the lump in her throat nearly shutting off her air. How could he do this? One minute he was kissing her and the next he was walking off with Morgan.

Y ou're dumping me for that skinny little nobody?" Morgan's voice carried such a threat that Pierce actually stepped back a pace.

"I'm not dumping you for anyone," Pierce tried to explain. "I can see it won't work out for us. You aren't interested in the things that interest me. We don't have anything in common."

Morgan flipped her blond hair over her shoulder and pointed a purple-nailed finger at him. "What do you mean I'm not interested in things you're interested in? How many boring church services did I sit through for you? All the time I would smile and act like I loved it, yet I only did it for you."

Pierce felt as if someone had knocked the air from him. He floundered for an answer. "Do you mean you don't believe in Jesus?" he choked out.

Looking annoyed, Morgan answered tartly, "Of course, I believe in Jesus. Even when we weren't dating I went to church at Christmas. I always enjoy watching the manger scene reenacted."

"But, Morgan, it's more than just believing in a baby in a manger. What about Jesus dying on the cross? What about His resurrection? You have to repent of your sins and ask Jesus into your heart as Savior. Have you ever done that?"

"I don't need to be fanatical about religion like you," she retorted.

Morgan's words wrenched at his insides. Pierce watched helplessly as she stalked off toward the inn.

By midmorning the next day, Pierce thought he might freeze to death despite the warm sunshine blazing through a partially clouded sky. After last night, both Morgan, who rode behind him, and Chandra, who rode ahead of him, were giving him decidedly chilling glances.

I guess I shouldn't have gone off with Morgan like that without an explanation to Chandra, he thought for the millionth time. *I only wanted to set things right. I wanted Morgan to know our relationship is off. I can't continue with her after finally seeing that she is self-centered and not even interested in following God.*

Recalling the confrontation with Morgan, Pierce nearly groaned aloud. She hadn't taken rejection well. Morgan apparently was used to attracting any man she wanted and then casting him off when she finished with him, not the other way around. As if his eyes were opened suddenly after years of blindness, he could see how she had left a string of broken hearts and affected lives behind her.

Even now, he felt utterly incapable of reaching her. *God, I don't know what to do to help Morgan understand her need for You. Please work on her heart and give me the opportunity to talk to her. If not me, then send someone who can speak to her, Lord. I believe under all her sophisticated veneer, she's lonely and lost. She needs to know You.*

As for Chandra, Lord, I don't know what I've done to alienate her. She was so wonderful yesterday. I'm sure she feels something for me, too. I know I should have explained why I was leaving with Morgan, but all I could think of was getting it over with. Help Chandra to forgive me. I know I've offended her.

Yesterday evening, after his talk with Morgan, Pierce couldn't wait to see Chandra and talk to her about his feelings for her. When he returned to the inn, he found that she'd gone to her room and didn't want to be disturbed. She didn't come for the evening meal, and this morning she had already eaten before he got down to breakfast. She barely returned his greeting before hopping on her bicycle and heading off for the day's ride. Now he rode a few yards—what felt to be several miles—behind her, hoping she would give him a sign of some sort to let him know she wanted to talk.

Chandra steadied her bike with one hand and reached up to rub her eyes with the other. If someone had thrown a handful of sand in her eyes, they couldn't have felt worse. Dry and gritty, they burned from lack of sleep and too much crying. Last night, every time she closed her eyes, a picture of Morgan walking off with Pierce drifted across her eyelids. Of course, that was better than the few times she managed to get some sleep. Then the dreams of

Morgan in Pierce's arms, wearing a gorgeous wedding dress, made her wake in a cold sweat.

This morning she had been unable to face Pierce. Why had he kissed her and then walked off with Morgan? Did he think he could just toy with her affections? Had he meant it as a brotherly kiss? It sure hadn't felt like one. Even now, she could remember the feel of his fingers tracing a path down her cheek.

To make matters worse, this was the anniversary of her parents' murders. Oh, how she longed to have Pierce hold her and comfort her. Instead, she found herself pulling away, estranged by his feelings for Morgan and her own hesitancy to trust anyone.

By late afternoon when they stopped for the day, Chandra was ready to quit. Her leg ached a little, although the cut was healing nicely. Thanks to being in good shape, her bruises were fast disappearing. She hadn't spoken more than two words to anyone all day, and all she wanted was time alone. With that in mind, she headed down a narrow path that meandered through a small grove of trees.

Birds twittered overhead. The rich, moist smell of freshly watered woods filled the air. Chandra bent down to push her finger into a piece of moss at the base of a tree. She smiled as water welled up around her finger. She had loved doing that as a child, admiring the moss's ability to store water. It had been years since she had seen such succulent plants growing wild.

The path turned and ran alongside a low rock wall. Chandra climbed up and sat cross-legged on the top, gazing at the valley stretched out before her. She didn't think she would ever tire of the green hills.

A small scuffing noise on the path behind her set her heart thumping. She swivelled around and saw Pierce, his hands stuffed in his pockets. His blue eyes studied her with a pleading little-boy look. She couldn't help but smile.

"I hope I'm not disturbing you," he said.

She shrugged, not sure what to say. She didn't really want company, but she just couldn't turn him away.

"Are you sure you won't offend Morgan?" She hadn't meant to sound so catty.

"I need to talk to you, Chandra." He climbed up on the wall and settled down beside her. "I've tried to talk to you all day, but you wouldn't let me. I know this is the anniversary of your parents' death. Is that what's bothering you?"

Tears welled up in her eyes. She thought after the last few days she wouldn't have a single drop left to shed, but they still rose to the surface all too readily. "I'm sorry I haven't been good company. You could have talked to Morgan." *Oh, God, I sound like some bitter, old shrew. Please help me.*

"That's who I wanted to talk to you about."

"No, I can't talk about you and Morgan right now." Chandra looked away, so he wouldn't see the pain she knew was showing in her eyes.

"Would it help to talk about your dad and mom?" he offered. She could hear his desire to help.

"I don't know." Her voice caught. She bit her lip, trying to control her wayward emotions. One minute she didn't want to ever see him again, and now she couldn't bear to have him walk away.

Pierce scooted closer. He slipped his arm around her and pulled her against his side. For a minute she resisted, then she relaxed against him, feeling his strength as a comfort seeping through her.

"For as long as I can remember, I loved your dad and mom." Pierce spoke softly, almost as if he were afraid of saying the wrong thing. "I used to watch your dad as he worked on the farm. He always whistled a hymn or sang while he worked. He told me more than once that when you give your all to Jesus, He gives you more blessings than you know what to do with."

Pierce paused and Chandra wanted to ask him to continue, but she knew she couldn't say a word right now without crying.

"Your mom always treated me like a son. She fed me every time I came over. She even chewed me out when we would ride through the mud and get our clothes filthy. If you remember, I got yelled at right along with you." A low rumble of laughter echoed through Pierce's chest.

Chandra couldn't keep the chuckle inside. Pierce was right. Her parents never treated him as a friend; he was always family to them.

"Do you remember the time we decided to round up the sheep on our bicycles?" Chandra asked. She could feel the vibration of Pierce's laughter as he squeezed her tight against him. "We thought we were sheep dogs," she said, "and the sheep thought we were monsters. It's a wonder the poor things lived through it."

Pierce's laughter rang across the hills. "It's a wonder

we lived through it. I don't think I'd ever seen your dad quite that shade of red."

"That's true," Chandra agreed. "I don't think he whistled the rest of the day. That's what showed me how mad he was."

"But, you know," Pierce spoke thoughtfully, "the best thing about your dad was his ability to forgive. He certainly let us know we were in the wrong and we never were to do that again. But as soon as it was over, he'd forgotten it. Oh, maybe not forgotten, but he never brought it up again, and he treated us with the same love and respect he always did."

"You're right," she agreed. "My dad and mom were both that way. I remember Dad saying if Jesus forgave him, then who was he to hold anything against anyone else?"

For several long minutes, Chandra and Pierce sat quietly. She could feel the soft rise and fall of his chest and the slight pressure of his fingers on her arm. She tried to concentrate on him, but other thoughts pushed insistently to the surface.

What about you, child? Can you forgive as I have forgiven you?

Chandra shivered at the words spoken to her soul. "Cold?" Pierce asked. She shook her head no, and the quiet settled over them again.

God, maybe I should forgive, but I don't know how. I can't even feel You there most of the time. Why did You let this happen? My parents loved You. Why are they dead and those animals that killed them still alive?

Once again anger welled up inside. Chandra wished

she could face those two boys. How would they feel tied to a chair with someone threatening them with a gun? They wouldn't be so cocky then. How would they like it if someone they loved were brutally murdered? Forgive them? Not likely. They didn't deserve it.

Chandra pulled away from Pierce, ignoring the cold that settled over her when she did. She swung her legs over the side of the wall, kicking the rocks as if the aggressive act would allay some of her feelings of hatred.

"Are you okay?" Pierce's soft question irritated her.

"I just need to be alone for a while. If you want to talk, you have friends back at the inn." Chandra glanced at Pierce and hated the hurt look that crossed his face. Why did she always hurt people she loved? She wanted to reach out and stop him from leaving, but the bitterness welling up inside forced her to turn away. She pulled her knees up and buried her face in them, trying to ignore the sound of Pierce's receding footsteps.

Chapter 9

Scraping up a few pebbles from the top of the wall, Chandra plunked them one at a time into the green grass beyond. She was glad Pierce had left. Now she could just spend time thinking. Maybe if she thought the hurt through a few more times it would ease some, and the hatred she felt toward her parents' murderers would ease also.

"Chandra?"

She threw the pebbles in the air and let out a screech. Pitching forward she nearly fell off the wall.

"I'm sorry." Kurt appeared genuinely concerned. "I didn't mean to startle you like that. Pierce reminded me that this is a hard day for you. I thought you might like someone to pray with you."

Chandra felt like a fool staring at this pastor as if he were some sort of freak. She couldn't think what to say. "I. . .I think I just need to be alone." She felt her face warming with embarrassment. What would Kurt think of her hatred and anger?

As if reading her mind he asked, "Are you able to deal

with the anger that generally follows an act of violence like your parents' death?"

She stared, groping for words, hoping he would just leave.

"I didn't know your father very well, but I've heard a lot about him. I know he loved Jesus, and he is remembered in the church for his ability to forgive no matter what." Kurt paused and rubbed his hand over the back of his neck. "I don't know why, but I feel I need to tell you that when we are unwilling to forgive others, it becomes a root of bitterness. Pretty soon, that root grows into a wall that comes between us and God."

"I know," Chandra heard herself whisper. "I can't even feel God out there anymore. I've tried to tear down the wall, but I can't."

Kurt smiled, and she felt he truly understood. "Of course, you can't. Only God can do that."

Chandra closed her eyes and thought of the voice earlier that had asked her about forgiving. "I suppose in order for Him to tear down the wall, I have to forgive those boys who murdered my parents. Well, I don't think I can do it. I don't even want to try."

"Chandra, I remember being really hurt. I didn't want to forgive either. Sometimes, I've had to ask God to help me want to forgive someone."

She studied him for a moment then nodded. Kurt bent his head and prayed, "Father, You know how Chandra's hurting. It's hard to lose someone you love, especially to an act of violence. Please help her turn all her hurt and anger over to You. Heal her, Lord."

It was such a simple prayer that Chandra ached inside. *Oh, God, help me have that kind of relationship with You.*

After Kurt left, Chandra watched the light grow dim as the sun set behind her. The shadows lengthened, and still she sat, thinking about the wall that stood between her and the Lord. Had she built the wall? Was her bitterness keeping her from having the joy God intended?

She bowed her head, resting it on her upraised knee. *God, I don't want to live like this. I remember how my father forgave. I know You've forgiven me, but Lord, I don't know how I can forgive those young men.*

She sat for a moment lost in thought. *God, I guess I need to forgive You, too. I've felt all along that all You had to do was intervene and my parents would have been okay. I blamed You for their deaths. I forgot that Satan still causes evil to happen, and that You can redeem such horrible things by bringing good from them. Help me, Lord, to forgive.*

Cleansing tears flowed down her cheeks as, for the first time in a year, peace swept through her. Stars began to twinkle in the darkened sky. It still hurt to think of her parents' death, but for once, there was no bitterness and hatred accompanying that hurt.

Chandra made her way slowly back to the inn. As she let herself in through a side door, she saw Kurt, Gina, Morgan, and Pierce relaxing in the front room. They were laughing about some funny story Kurt must have told. Chandra smiled and quietly made her way up to her room. Tonight, she wanted to spend time in prayer, relishing the complete contentment she now had.

Early the next morning, Chandra brushed out her hair and braided it, trying not to disturb Morgan. Morgan had come up late last night, mumbling about Pierce and how she wouldn't let some little nobody like Chandra take him away from her. Chandra had pretended to be asleep, yet she couldn't help wondering why Morgan thought she was losing Pierce. Had something happened between them?

Now, as she prepared to leave the room, Chandra glanced over at Morgan. Eyes narrowed to slits, Morgan looked at her with such an expression of hatred that Chandra shuddered. She quickly slipped out of the room and downstairs. She might miss an evening meal, but never a breakfast. It was her favorite meal of the day.

"Pierce?"

Morgan's cloying whine made his hair stand on end. They'd only been on the road for about an hour, having done a little sightseeing before they set out. All Pierce wanted to think about was Chandra. He didn't know why she wanted to be rid of him last night. This morning she seemed fine. In fact, she appeared happier than he had seen her for the whole trip. Now Morgan was back in her demanding mode again. He thought he'd taken care of that when they'd talked the other night.

"Yes?" He tried not to be short with her.

"I know you're sorry for talking to me like that the other night." Morgan gave him her most dazzling smile—the one she usually reserved for getting her own way. "I want you to know I forgive you completely. You don't have to be so moody. I know you've been upset about our talk."

Pierce just stared at her, not believing what he was hearing. "Morgan, I was serious when I talked to you the other night. I haven't changed my mind."

The scrunch of bike tires and the whir of the wheels turning grew loud in the silence that followed. Morgan's face whitened, and then a red flush crept up her neck into her cheeks.

"I can't believe you would really choose Chandra over me. She'll never be able to help you like I will."

"And just how will you help me?" Pierce tried to keep the aggravation from his voice.

"I am a business woman. I can help with your image as a business owner. Together we can make a name for ourselves." She almost sounded as if she were pleading.

"Morgan, I don't want to make a name for myself. I never have. I enjoy my bike shop and would like to expand a little, but my main desire is to have a wife and family. I want a wife who believes in Jesus Christ as her Savior and Lord. You've made it clear that you don't have the same beliefs I do."

"Fine," Morgan hissed. "Have your little family and go to church every Sunday. If those are your ambitions, I'm sure Little Miss Nobody will do fine. As far as I'm concerned, our relationship is over."

She threw her weight onto the pedals and pulled ahead. Pierce stopped in the middle of the road, totally dumbfounded. "I do believe she just wanted to feel like she's the one who ended it," he said aloud, startling himself. "I cannot believe it. She just couldn't let me have the final word."

Pushing off, he started down the road after Morgan and Chandra, the only ones ahead of him. *God, please touch Morgan. I think she is really lonely, but she's afraid to admit it. And, Lord, help me get things right with Chandra.*

Chandra breathed deeply. The fresh air in the country here couldn't be compared with the smog-laden fumes in Los Angeles. Here, it rained so often everything always had a newly washed appearance. She smiled. No wonder the story of Camelot, the perfect kingdom, had been born here. Then again, maybe it was just her outlook that was different today. She hadn't noticed everything looking so bright and pretty any of the other days. She laughed at the antics of a pack of dogs cavorting over rock walls in the distance. Even the animals were excited.

Yesterday she'd felt like the weight of the world sat on her shoulders. The feelings from her parents' deaths and her confusion over her love for Pierce and his love for Morgan all weighed heavily. After her hours of prayer and healing, she felt like a new person. She wanted to sing and dance. She was more carefree than she could ever remember being. God was in charge of her life and it felt good.

Slowing her bike, Chandra noticed for the first time that she didn't have the insistent urge to always be in the lead. She wanted to take it easy. Maybe it would be fun to slow down and spend some time talking with the others. She was even looking forward to talking to Morgan. She wanted a chance to heal the rift that had always been between them.

A crunch of gravel alerted her to the bicycle pulling up beside her before she saw it in her mirror. Morgan, pushing hard on her pedals, gradually closed the distance between them. Chandra glanced over at her and flashed what she hoped was a friendly smile.

"Hi," Chandra called. "You've really improved your riding on this trip."

Morgan glared back. "I didn't ride up here to chit chat with you."

"Did you have something you wanted to talk about?"

"Yes." Morgan glanced over her shoulder. "Pierce."

"What about Pierce?" Chandra couldn't imagine what Morgan wanted this time.

"I just wanted to warn you about what happened the other night," she said, her voice gloating. "Pierce proposed to me. Of course, I had to turn him down. He begged me to marry him, saying if I didn't, he would be stuck asking you to be his wife."

The breath left Chandra and she forced her feet to push the pedals, hoping the familiar motion would calm her. *God, help me understand this,* she cried. In that instant she knew Morgan was lying. Pierce wouldn't say that about her. If he had proposed, Morgan would be flashing a diamond at her, not telling her how she'd turned him down.

Chandra glanced in her rearview mirror. Pierce was catching up to them. She could hear the barking dogs getting closer. Stopping the forward motion of her feet, she began to coast. She looked up and met Morgan's eyes, noting the challenge sparking from them.

"Maybe, I'll just wait and ask Pierce about that."

Chandra tried to steady her quivering voice.

"You wouldn't dare."

Was that fear Chandra detected in Morgan's voice? Tightening her hands around the brake levers, Chandra let her bike drop behind Morgan's. A hoarse yell sounded faint above the din of the dogs. Suddenly a mass of bodies flowed over the wall beside the road. Tails wagged and tongues hung from panting mouths. Chandra braked hard.

The pile of dogs hit Morgan's bicycle full force. Morgan screamed. Her bike wobbled as she shifted her weight, trying desperately to stay upright. Then one last dog raced over the wall, hitting her front wheel on its way through. Morgan flipped, smashing into the rocks at the side of the road. She lay there, her leg tangled in the bike frame at an awkward angle, her face white as chalk.

Chapter 10

Chandra gathered with the others around the stretcher Morgan was strapped to. She had broken her leg in the fall, and the ambulance attendants were waiting to take her to the hospital to have it set. Morgan's blue eyes, glazed slightly from the pain and medication, narrowed when she saw Chandra.

"Pierce has always loved you, even though he was too stupid to see it," she murmured as the pain medication began to take effect. "I tried to get rid of you. I loosened the handlebars on your bike, but they found it. Then I kicked your bicycle so you would wreck. I hoped you'd be hurt so badly you'd have to leave the tour. I said hurtful things whenever no one else could hear. But no matter what I said or how I treated you, you never took revenge." She shook her head as if to clear her thoughts. "Maybe there's something to your God after all." Her last words were barely audible as she drifted off into a drug-induced sleep.

The small group stood in stunned silence as Morgan was loaded into the ambulance. Dale pulled Pierce off to the side to talk with him. Chandra hurt for him, knowing how Morgan's admissions must have been a blow. She watched silently as the van carrying Morgan's bicycle headed down the road toward their next stop.

"Chandra, are you okay?" Kurt asked.

"I'm fine," she whispered in a voice that sounded hoarse. She knew that learning the depth of Morgan's hatred for her should hurt, but instead it seemed as if a protective shield were in front of her the whole time.

Thank You. Lord. I know this state of calm must be Your doing. It must be the peace that passes all understanding Mom used to talk about. Thank You.

She looked over to where Pierce stood talking with Dale. His eyes met hers. He smiled and a tingle raced down her spine. How she longed to have him hold her. How did he feel about Morgan now? Would he still want to marry her?

A subdued group climbed back on their bikes for the remainder of the day's trip. Chandra hoped a hot shower would wash away the cold that seeped into her bones, knowing all the while that it wouldn't really help.

Pierce stopped in the open doorway of the den, clutching the small package tightly in his hand. Chandra stood across the room talking to Kurt and Gina. Her light brown hair swung in loose, shimmering waves to below her waist. He longed to run his fingers through it. *Oh, God, how I love her. Morgan was right. I've always loved Chandra. I was only enamored with Morgan, and I couldn't see the difference. Thank You for showing me the right qualities to look for in a wife, Lord. And Father, please help Morgan to come to know You.*

Earlier, Pierce had learned that Morgan had asked Kurt and Gina to visit her in the hospital. Maybe at last she was willing to admit her need for God.

Kurt glanced up and beckoned Pierce to join them. Chandra turned and gave him a half-smile. He could see the uncertainty in her eyes. He crossed the room in three long strides. Taking Chandra's hand in his, he pulled her close to him.

"If you'll excuse us, I'd like to speak to Chandra outside." Pierce barely waited to see Kurt's answering grin before he headed for the door. He had to slow his eager steps so Chandra wouldn't have to run to keep up.

"Pierce, where are we going?" Chandra gazed up at him with her gorgeous hazel eyes. For a moment he almost forgot the reason he wanted to talk. All he wanted to do was stroke her honey-colored cheek and kiss her upturned lips.

Taking a deep breath, he tugged on her hand, leading her toward a copse of trees down the road where they could talk in privacy. "I need to talk, Chandra. There's too much that's gone unsaid between us lately. I also have some plans I've been trying to share with you for several days."

She smiled and his heart skipped a beat. He wanted to draw her into his arms and forget all about talking.

"Well, what's so important?" she asked as they entered the shelter of the trees. The hesitant look on her face told him how unsure she felt.

"I've been wanting to talk to you," Pierce repeated. He took a deep breath, praying for the right words. "It seems like every time I try to talk to you lately something interferes. A couple of times I've been sure you were mad at me."

"I'm sorry." Her sad expression reminded him of a forlorn puppy dog, admonished for some misbehavior.

She looked up at him and explained. "It's just that for the last year I've been struggling with the senselessness of my parents' deaths. Kurt showed me I needed to forgive before I could go on with my life, how bitterness was building a wall between me and God. Last night I finally turned all those feelings over to God. I can't believe how free and clean I feel today. I'm sorry I was so difficult."

Pierce wanted to leap for joy. Instead he gave her a quick hug then gestured at an open grassy knoll. When she sat down, he dropped down beside her, once more picking up her hand. He ran his thumb over the palm of her hand, trying to think where to start.

"First of all, I have something for you." He handed her the small package wrapped in brown paper.

"What is it?" Chandra looked like a child with a gift. Excitement sparkled in her eyes as she tore the wrapper off. She gasped. "It's the painting. I thought about this last night while I was praying. I know why it's so special." She slowly ran her fingers around the frame. "It reminds me of how I need to be the sheep in God's pasture and let Him put a wall of protection around me. For a long time I've been on the outside with a wall of bitterness separating me from Him."

A tear of joy traced a path down her cheek. Pierce gently wiped it away. Chandra gulped in air, fighting her swirling emotions as Pierce slowly touched her cheek and then smoothed her hair. How could he do this to her if he still cared about Morgan?

He looked into her eyes, and she nearly drowned in his midnight gaze. "Chandra, Morgan was right."

She hesitated. "Right about what?" she finally asked.

"I've always been enamored with Morgan, the beautiful prom queen, but until the last few days I didn't realize that's not what I should look for in a woman—particularly one I want for a wife."

She pulled her hand away. "Are you telling me you're planning to ask Morgan to be your wife?"

"No." He grabbed her hand again. "I'm trying to say that Morgan isn't right for me. I don't love her. I never have. I've always loved you. Since you left, part of me has been missing. I didn't know what was wrong until God hit me over the head. I love you, Chandra. I have ever since I can remember." He leaned forward and cupped her cheek with his hand.

Chandra sat very still, relishing the feel of his warm fingers on her cheek. Had she heard right? Did he say he loved her?

"But, Morgan said you proposed to her."

"I didn't." Pierce drew her even closer, slipping an arm around her shoulders. "I told her there was nothing between us because she doesn't share my interests or my beliefs. I hope these experiences will lead her to God, but even then, we are too different to ever be able to share a life together."

"But I live in L.A. and you live in Indiana. This will never work."

"I've been thinking about that, too." Pierce smiled and leaned so close she could feel his breath brush across her cheek. "I would like to start a tour business to go along with my bike shop. You could move back to Newbury and help me with arranging the tours."

Her heart pounded. She needed to gasp for air but couldn't. "And would we be partners in business?"

"I'm hoping we'll be more than that." Pierce's lips were only inches from hers. "Will you marry me, Chandra?"

She gazed up at him, not sure she could even answer. Slowly she reached up and traced her finger down his jaw, smiling at the rough, stubbly feel of him. Slipping her hand behind his head she pulled him to her. The kiss lasted for a long moment of ecstasy.

He lifted his head and looked at her. "I don't believe you answered me, Miss Kirby."

She giggled and threw her arms around his neck. "Yes," she almost shouted. "The answer is yes, Mr. Stillwell." Looking into his eyes, she could hardly wait for the adventure of life together to begin.

NANCY J. FARRIER

Nancy resides in Arizona with her husband, son, and four daughters. She is the author of numerous articles and short stories. She also is a monitor at the small Christian school her daughters attend and homeschools part time. Nancy feels called to share her faith with others through her writing.

River
Runners

by Marilou H. Flinkman

Chapter 1

Anthea busily worked with the rest of the river guides getting the boats ready for their new group. Two women from the office of the Colorado Rafting Company had met the passengers at the hotel the night before for an orientation meeting. "Are the boats all filled now?" Anthea asked Rick, the crew boss for this trip.

"One more to pump up. Ben is getting the supports into the ones we have air in. You and the others can start hauling stuff from the truck down to the beach." He straightened up from the pump he'd been using. "Watch out for Steve. He gets testy about loading the food."

"Hey, always treat the cook with respect," Anthea joked. As she walked back to the truck, she thought about the passenger list. She made a game of reading the names of people and where they came from and then trying to put names to faces when they got off the bus the first morning. This trip there would be a teacher from Ithaca, New York. Since she attended college at Cornell, she had a special interest in meeting someone from the same town as her school.

"I'll hand sleeping mats down to you," Karen called to Anthea from the back of the large freight truck.

Grabbing mats and then waterproof bags, Anthea hauled gear to the waiting rubber rafts. Her tall, slender body hid a physical strength she'd gained from years of trips like this one.

When all the gear had been carefully lashed to the rafts, the crew took a short break. Rick faced them as they sat on the sand. "We've all run the river before, so you know what to expect. Jeff is going with us as an apprentice this trip. Gus is our swamper. He'll help out wherever we need him. Anthea, Karen, Petula, and Ben will be paddle raft guides along with me. We'll take turns on the four rafts and spell Jeff and Steve on the oared boats."

He looked up as a bus pulled into the parking lot. "Here come our paddlers." He waved to the driver and approached the people getting off the bus.

Anthea stood back, assessing the people she would be running the river with for the next two weeks. When she saw a middle-aged man with white hair get off the bus, she thought, *Bet that's him. Sheet said schoolteacher, and that guy has got to be a teacher.* A young man, obviously his son, and a woman who was probably his daughter-in-law stood together as Rick welcomed the group and gave instructions.

Within a matter of minutes, the personal gear had been taken off the bus and strapped to the rafts. The rafters were fitted into life vests and headed for the rafts. Anthea watched as six people got aboard the raft she would guide. She smiled and greeted each one, showing them how to fasten their backpacks to the straps holding the gear in the center of the raft.

A young couple took the front seats as Anthea handed out paddles. A young muscular man took the middle seat on the left. *He'll be a strong paddler,* Anthea thought. As she guided the raft into the river current to follow the other boats, she gave instructions. She tried to give practice drills in right and left turns and how to back paddle. The couple in the front seemed to be in a world of their own.

"Bill," Anthea called to the husband who had the front right seat, "in that spot you are lead paddle. You'll have to keep a steady stroke and listen to me for instructions. You guys with the paddles are the power in this boat."

"No problem," Bill replied.

Anthea sat on the back edge of the raft with a long paddle she used as a rudder. She watched the currents and knew just how to guide the raft where she wanted to go. "Let go; all forward," she called, letting the raft drift into the current in the middle of the river.

Bill could not keep a steady rhythm. His wife Sue would stroke a couple times and put the paddle over her lap to watch the scenery. The young man behind Sue looked back at Anthea. She shrugged her shoulders, and he smiled in reply. Looking into his friendly blue eyes above the full brown beard, Anthea knew she had a cohort. "You rafted before?" she asked him.

"Not unless you count a canoe in the Adirondacks," he replied. "My dad and I have done a lot of canoeing on the lakes in the mountains there."

"You're from New York?"

He grinned. "Is that a problem?"

"Sorry, didn't mean it to sound that way. Are you the guy from Ithaca?"

"Yes, I teach high school English there."

She shook her head. "I guessed wrong again."

"Did I do something wrong?" he asked still keeping a steady paddle going while he looked back at Anthea.

She laughed. "It's a game I play. I see names on the list of people going on the trip and try to match them to faces. You didn't look like a schoolteacher."

He tipped the Australian hat he wore strapped on his head. "This isn't normal school day garb."

Anthea had been keeping an eye on the river while visiting with the young man. "Since I got the name and face mixed up, what is your name?"

"John. My students call me Mr. Briggs. And I didn't get your name in all the confusion."

"I'm Anthea Hoyt, and I also spend time in Ithaca. Have one more year before I take my degree as a veterinarian from Cornell."

"I'm impressed. Tough school to get into."

She laughed, "Took me two tries, and I really think the personal interview with the dean who wanted to raft the Colorado got me in."

"Left turn," she called out to the paddlers. Bill was fiddling with his backpack and didn't even put a paddle in the water. She watched as John dug his paddle in to compensate. "Thanks," she said quietly when he looked back at her.

They continued on the water for about three hours when Rick took the lead and headed for a sandy beach. "We'll stop here for lunch," Anthea explained to her crew.

John stayed by the raft to help her tie up. "Need anything carried?" he asked.

"Steve has the food stuff. He'll want a table set up and will have his lunch box where it is easy to get to." She pointed to the middle-aged man who kept his bald head covered with a floppy hat. "If he needs help, he'll let you know."

"I'll go offer my services."

After lunch was over and the gear had been lashed in Steve's boat, the people headed back to the rafts. Anthea watched Bill start for the front seat again. "Would you mind switching, Bill?" she called to him. "I'd like to have John in that position for the afternoon. We'll keep changing off each day," she explained.

John nodded to her with a smile and took the lead paddle position.

The afternoon went smoothly in spite of Sue and Bill not following directions. If she wasn't rummaging in her pack for food, he would be standing up taking pictures. Anthea politely tried to get them to be part of the team, but they remained in their own little world.

"We're going to camp in the rocks tonight," she told her paddlers." She quieted the groans. "These are big flat rocks that go up like steps. The farther up you go, the better the view."

The sun went behind the huge cliffs early so it seemed dusk when the rafts pulled in to make camp for the night.

John jumped out as soon as they hit the shore of the river and held the raft while the others got out.

"I'll tie up for the night," Anthea told him. "Thanks for all your help."

"At your service," Again he tipped his Aussie hat. He went off to help unload the rafts and assist people in sorting for their bags.

"Looks like I've got an extra swamper." Rick held out a hand to John. "Thanks for pitching in. Others will as the days go on, but the first day is a time for getting used to the routines."

"Where are the tents?" a women asked Rick, who turned to find the tent bag.

Anthea looked up to see John take his gear to a quiet spot. He didn't put up a tent. Instead he took out a notebook and started writing. Karen called to her, and she went to help cook supper.

After the meal had been eaten and cleared away, she went in search of John. *I need to thank him,* she told herself as an excuse for her action. She found him back in his quiet spot with a notebook in his lap.

"You keep a diary?" she asked.

"Sort of. I will want to put stories with the pictures I take for my parents."

"Is that why you're making the river run?"

"Dad and I talked about making this trip many times. Things finally came together, and here I am," he told her.

"And your dad?" Seeing the grimace on his face, she quickly added, "I shouldn't intrude."

He sighed. "It's okay. Dad and I had many good times

together, and we can still talk about them. Guess that is another reason to take notes. I don't want to forget any of the details when I tell him about the run."

"Your father's ill." It came out as a statement rather than a question.

"Dad got hit by a drunk driver. He's a paraplegic." He looked at her. "He kept teaching from a wheelchair for a few years, but the New York winters are terrible. Especially when you can't walk."

"I can walk, and I will be glad when next winter is over. I grew up in the desert. Cold and snow are not my idea of ideal living conditions," Anthea told him.

"That's what my parents have decided. Mom is a librarian and has found a job in Chandler, south of Phoenix. Dad had thirty years of teaching and retired this spring."

"Your parents moved to Arizona?"

He nodded. "Another reason for this trip. I drove the moving van out here for them and decided while I was here I would run the river."

"Going to be lonesome for you back in Ithaca."

He reached to touch her hand. "Maybe I've made a new friend."

Anthea felt her face grow hot. "I study all the time. Not much company."

He shrugged. "You can't blame me for trying. I didn't mean to offend you."

"It's okay," she said quickly with a smile. "I'm not offended. As a matter of fact, I owe you. Once in awhile we get people who don't fit into the scheme of rafting.

Looks like Sue and Bill are in that category. I appreciate your help."

"I'll be there for you tomorrow, too," he assured her with a smile that gave her shivers.

"Thanks. I've already asked Gus to ride with us. If you two take the front seats, we can keep up without wearing out the two paddlers in the back. We'll keep Sue and Bill in the middle."

"What happens in the rapids?"

She shrugged. "We'll try to train them. If they don't listen, they will be swimming. You know how to pull someone back into the boat?"

"Yes, you did a good job of explaining that task." He grinned. "It will be a temptation to push Bill under for a bit before pulling him in."

She laughed with him. "Not the Christian thing to do."

He shrugged without comment.

Puzzled by his reaction, Anthea rose. "I better get my bed roll set up. Morning comes early."

"How early?" He looked up at her, making her conscious of her bare legs in the shorts she always wore on the river.

"Crew is up by four to get water going for coffee and start breakfast. Someone will blow the conch shell at five to wake the rest of the camp."

John put his notebook down and got up. He stood just a few inches taller than her five-foot, eight-inch frame. She had pulled off her hat, and her long dark hair fell over her shoulders. She could tell by the warmth in his blue eyes that he liked what he saw.

"You going to put up a tent?" she asked to break the spell.

"No. It looks clear. I'll just roll out my mat and sleeping bag right here."

"Should be a good spot. I'll see you in the morning." She scrambled back down the rocks to where the camp kitchen had been set up. She looked up to see him watching her as she unrolled her sleeping bag.

The next day went better. With Gus and John in the front, Anthea found it easier to control the raft. Bill and Sue remained in the center. At the back she had an older woman on the right and a boy of about nineteen on the left. The woman had done a lot of rafting and maintained a good steady paddle. The boy followed her instructions and did well. The four of them worked as a unit in spite of the couple who didn't fit into the system.

"Have you done much rafting?" Anthea asked the boy in back.

"My mom, brother, dad, and I did this run about ten years ago. We went in one of the big motorized rafts. I always wanted to do the paddle trip, so the folks gave it to me for high school graduation."

"Great gift."

"Sure is, and wait 'til my brother finds out I rafted with John Briggs."

"John?" Anthea looked at the lead paddler.

"My brother has read all his books."

"I thought he taught school." Anthea wondered where

she's missed this bit of news.

"I think he does, but mostly he writes adventure stories for teens. I wish I had one of his books for him to autograph for Freddie."

"Maybe at the end of the trip you can get one."

"Hey, great idea. Thanks."

Anthea mulled this information over in her mind. *So that's why he takes notes. It's more than his father he plans to tell about this adventure.*

When the group stopped for lunch Steve spread out his usual array of vegetables, meats, and breads for sandwiches. The clients had been allowed to bring cases of soda pop. Steve kept them in the hold in his supply boat. Rick would keep some of them in a burlap bag and throw the sack over the back of his raft for an hour to chill the drinks in the cold river water before a meal.

As the afternoon wore on, Anthea kept up a running lecture on the geology of the riverbank. "The youngest rock we've seen is 245 million years old. God had a creation plan that doesn't deal with time the way we do," she explained. John turned to look at her, but she couldn't read his expression. *I don't think he's a Christian,* she thought.

The wind started to pick up. Anthea ceased her commentary on the river and urged her crew to paddle. "This head wind is going to be tough. We need to work together as a unit or we won't make it to camp 'til midnight." She checked the current, even though she knew it would not be strong in this section. "Bill, could you try to follow John and stroke in unison? It helps keep us steady."

As usual Bill had been standing in the raft taking

pictures. No sooner did he sit down after Anthea spoke than Sue put her paddle down to dig in her backpack. Sighing, Anthea sent a short prayer for patience winging its way to heaven.

Four of her crew plus herself were exhausted by the time they pulled in to make camp for the night. Anthea smiled to herself when she heard the older lady tell her husband she would make sure not to get in a raft with Sue and Bill again. *Wish I had that option*, Anthea told herself.

She saw John carrying buckets of water. They used river water, but it had to be pumped through a filtering system first. Rick had asked people to help out, and John had taken him seriously.

Anthea helped Karen make a bowl of tossed salad for supper. "Saw you got the couple Rick warned us about."

"Two days in a row. Gus and one of the clients took front paddles, and we did okay in spite of the head wind."

"I've been looking at that client. The guy is a real hunk. I never had a schoolteacher like that." Karen sighed.

"Back then anyone over twenty looked ancient. We wouldn't have given him a second look." Anthea tossed chopped peppers into the salad bowl.

"I've noticed you talking to him a lot. You getting chummy with a passenger?" Karen teased.

Anthea felt her face grow red. "He's been nice to help out. He took lead paddle for me when I got stuck with the couple who should have taken a motorized trip."

Karen raised her eyebrows. "Don't keep him all to yourself. He can paddle my boat anytime."

Anthea scowled. Sometimes Karen's teasing went too far.

After the meal Anthea carried the last stack of pans to Steve to be packed away.

"You need any help?"

She turned at the sound of John's voice. Shaking her head she put the pans on the top of a box. "All done now."

"Would you like to walk a ways up the beach with me? All day in the raft can test the wrong muscles."

Anthea didn't trust her voice. *Why do I let this guy do this to me?* she wondered. *I've never had any trouble discouraging men before.*

You don't want to discourage him, her conscience reminded her. She turned to face John, struck again by his vivid blue eyes. *They are the color of forget-me-nots,* she thought. "Sure, I'll walk with you."

There wasn't much of a path or very far they could go, but using different muscles did feel good. "Did you sleep well in the open last night?" she asked.

He laughed. "Needed sun glasses, the moon was so bright. Never saw so many stars even when Dad and I camped in the mountains."

"You're close to your dad."

"Yes," he admitted. "He used to be a coach and taught me to love sports and the outdoors."

"Is that why you write adventure stories for teens?"

He stopped to look at her. "How did you find out?"

"Is it a secret?" she asked.

He shook his head. "No. Just wondered how you knew. Do you have a kid brother who reads them?"

"No. My brother is only two years younger than I am. I have no idea what he reads. The high school boy paddling in the back today told me. Seems you are his kid brother's idol."

John's smile crinkled his eyes. "Glad to know someone enjoys them."

"How long have you written?"

"Since I could hold a pencil. My mom encouraged me. Now I'm addicted."

"Addicted, what do you mean?" Anthea looked at him in wonder.

"I can't not write," he told her, stopping as the path ended and they needed to turn back. "I decided to teach to support my habit."

"You must be a great teacher. I don't think my high school English teacher read anything but the classics, and I know she didn't write anything but nasty notes on my theme papers."

"You didn't get into Cornell's Vet school writing bad English papers." He reached to brush her hair back from her face.

"Where did you go to school?" Anthea asked, trying to hide how his touch made her feel.

"Nothing so prestigious as Ivy League. I took my degrees at Cortland State Teacher's College."

"Close to home," she remarked.

He nodded. "Dad had the accident in my senior year of high school. Mom needed me close by to help care for him."

"Can you talk about it? Can you tell me what happened?"

John sighed and looked out over the rushing river. "He coached high school baseball. He'd been to practice and drove home afterward. It was just getting dusk, so maybe the guy didn't see him. Anyway the other driver blew a stop sign and hit dad broadside. The car folded like a toy." He turned back to Anthea. "The other driver had a blood alcohol over the limit."

"Did he get hurt?"

John shook his head. "Shook up is all. My dad had to be cut out of the car. His back broke in the impact. He lost the use of his legs."

"He's lucky to be alive."

"You think so? Sometimes I wonder. A man as active as he had been strapped into a chair. What kind of a life is that?"

"Does he complain? Do you think he is sorry to be alive?"

He looked at her. "Those are questions I ask myself over and over. He fought his way back to a semblance of health. He taught sixth grade from a wheelchair until he retired."

"Sounds like he adjusted better than you did." Anthea touched his arm. "Don't you think God let him live for a reason? How many others has his courage impressed?"

"I don't know. He thinks God saved him for a purpose. I think God let him down when He didn't get my dad out of the way of a drunk driver."

"Look around you. Look at what God created here. It didn't happen in a hurry. Maybe you are expecting too much too soon for your father."

"You spoke of God's time in the boat today. You called it *kairos*."

"That's God's time, and it isn't like ours. God can see the end product when it is still a drop of water in the Rocky Mountains. He doesn't count how many days or how many drops of water it takes to create a Grand Canyon." She paused.

"How do your folks feel about the move to Arizona?" she asked to change the subject.

"They talked a lot about it. Came out here to visit on vacations and finally bought a place. You grew up here, didn't you?"

Anthea nodded. "Yes. My dad owns a sporting goods store in Flagstaff. I ran this river for the first time when I was eight years old."

"Wow! How many trips have you made?"

"This is my thirtieth." She grinned. "And it won't be my last."

"Did you travel with your parents, too?"

"Mom died when I was ten. I made the first trip with my dad, and later my brother came too."

"I'm sorry. I guess I am out of line to complain about my dad being crippled when you lost your mother."

She shrugged. "Why did a wonderful young woman have to get breast cancer? I can hear where your bitterness comes from. Where we are different is that I knew my mother was with the Lord. I couldn't ask her to come back to suffer more. Even as a little girl I sensed that."

"You have a lot more faith than I do." He stood to start back down the path. As Anthea rose, he bowed gallantly and offered her his arm.

Anthea grinned and laid her hand on his arm to walk back to camp. *I better be careful here,* she told herself. *This guy is getting too close to me. I'm not ready for romance.*

Chapter 2

R ick called his crew together before the conch
sounded to wake the camp. "Going to change
things around today. I want Ben, Petula, and
Anthea to take paddle rafts. I'll be guide on the fourth
one. That leaves Karen and Jeff on the oars. Steve will
keep rowing his big supply raft. Gus, you fill in where you
are needed."

"With whoever gets stuck with the non-paddlers,"
Karen commented.

"I've talked to Sue and convinced her to ride on one of
the oar boats. That means all of us work with no breaks
from rowing." Rick smiled. "Should help the situation."

"What about the husband, Bill?" Anthea asked.

Rick shrugged. "We'll see if he gets with the system
any better. Keep an eye on him in the rapids. We will get
into some better ones today." He glanced at his watch. "Go
blow your horn, Steve. Lets get this show on the river."

The rafters were getting used to the routine and had
their waterproof bags packed and piled on the riverbank,
ready to load, right after breakfast. Rick gathered them

together for more stories of Major John Wesley Powell, who first ran the river in the 1800s, while the rest of the crew packed the rafts.

Anthea watched John carry on an animated conversation with Rick when the story session ended. *One storyteller to another,* she thought. She felt a twinge of disappointment when she saw John follow Rick to his raft. *What did you expect?* she scolded herself. *The paying customers are told to change rafts to get to know others in the group. The man didn't make this trip to entertain you.*

She took her position at the back of the raft and tried to remember the names of the people going with her. *No Bill,* she thought with guilty relief. She noted that he had gone to Rick's raft. *Bet Rick suggested it so he could take care of him today,* Anthea thought.

The white-haired gentleman she had mistaken for a schoolteacher took the lead position in her raft. He told her some of the rivers he had run in the Pacific Northwest, so she knew he would do well in that position. When he told her he was a lawyer, she chuckled. *You sure missed that one by a mile,* she told herself. His son and daughter-in-law were also in law and spent their vacations rafting.

"Dad got me started at a young age," the son explained. "I met Beth on a raft trip in British Columbia. Turned out we both went to UCLA law school at the time."

"Romance on the river," his wife quipped.

The day went well. The rapids were a fun ride for all, and Anthea did not have the pressure of trying to guide a six-man raft with four paddlers. She did catch herself looking for Rick's raft to see John. *Got to stop this,* she scolded herself, going back to her running commentary on the geology and history of the Colorado River for those people in her raft.

In the afternoon they pulled into a huge cave. The winds and water had carved an amphitheater out of the bank of the river. "Sometimes there's a trip that brings along an orchestra to play in this setting," she told her fellow rafters.

"You bring a Frisbee?" Petula called to her.

"Ben will have one," she yelled back while making her raft secure to the riverbank.

"Is this a crew thing or can anyone join?" She felt the glow of hearing John's voice.

"If you think you can compete give it a try," she challenged him, running into the amphitheater.

Soon a group of the younger people had the plastic disk flying from one to the other. Rick stayed out of the game to answer questions from those exploring the area.

Taking a break to catch their breath, John and Anthea sat at the back of the cave and watched the others. "What did you think of the waterfall we saw this morning?" she asked him.

"Waterfall in the desert. Did Moses hit it with a stick?" he asked with a smile.

He does know the Bible, but I don't think he's a Christian, she thought. "Could be. You didn't get out to get pictures did you?"

"No. Rick told us those pretty green leaves were poison ivy." He smiled. "Bill tried to get close. You got any calamine lotion for later?"

"As a matter of fact I do. I'm the medic on the trip."

"You? Don't we have to have four feet to get medical attention from you?" he joked.

She laughed with him. "I used my EMT training to get a job on an ambulance to earn money for college. I worked a year between grad school and being accepted at Cornell." She turned to smile at him. "Have to admit my four-footed patients are easier to work on. They don't talk back."

"They only bite," he said with a grin.

"Haven't had a bad bite yet. Did get kicked by a horse."

"Ouch! I'll stick to dealing with unruly teenagers."

"Looks like Rick is getting people back to the boats. Are you enjoying your ride with him?"

"We've been discussing Powell. I'd read all I could find by and about him before making this trip. Rick has a fantastic knowledge. . . ." He reached to take Anthea's hand. "But I miss being with you."

She felt the blush but dared not voice her feelings of having him near. "We'll be stopping early tonight so we can hike to some Indian ruins. Maybe I'll see you then." She turned to run back to her raft.

"You can count on it," John called after her.

They did hike, but John stopped to take many pictures. "Will all this be part of a book?" Anthea asked him.

"Like cowboys and Indians?" He shook his head. "I'd like to write from the view point of the Indians who lived here."

"Sounds interesting to me. I've grown up hearing

stories of the Indians of this area."

"Good. I'll know who to contact for research."

"Anthea, will you follow the group down so we don't leave anyone up here?" Rick called.

"Sure." John and Anthea took their time getting back to the camp.

Karen raised her eyebrows when Anthea finally showed up to help prepare the evening meal. "Never saw you take an interest in a man before. Is the ice maiden finally thawing out?" she asked as Anthea joined her in setting out utensils.

"Can't I talk to a guy without it turning into a big romance?" Anthea growled.

"I don't know. You tell me," Karen retorted.

After their meal, people gathered on the beach instead of going off to their tents. "Rick loves to tell stories. This audience will get him started," Anthea whispered to John, sitting on a rock next to her.

"Did I tell you the story about the group who ran from a flood when the dam broke?" Rick asked.

"Told you so." Anthea nudged John in the ribs.

"I was on a trip when everyone had gone to bed for the night. In the darkest part of the night, one of the men woke the camp up screaming the dam had broken. The guy had us convinced. We ran over rocks and stickers in our nightshirts and bare feet to get to higher ground. After we all made it up the hill the guy came to and wondered why the panic. He looked pathetic. His eyes were round with wonder as he looked around. We went back to bed and made sure he got to his tent okay. At the end of the trip when his son picked him up, I asked him about his father. 'You mean he did it again?' the boy asked. Said that once in the dead of winter his dad had run through the house screaming 'fire'. Had all his family out in the snow in their pajamas before he woke up." Rick grinned at his audience. "Sure glad he isn't on this trip."

The other guides joined in with their stories. Ben claimed to have been awakened when a big horn sheep jumped over him in the night.

"Got stories to share?" John asked Anthea.

"Well there was the ring-tailed cat. They are smaller than a raccoon and very curious. I woke up with one playing with my long hair. I used to wear my hair down to my waist. After that I had it cut."

"I think we should put the tent up tonight," Beth told her husband.

Anthea saw the fear in Sue's eyes. "Don't worry, Sue. The cats don't bite, and a sheep hasn't ever missed and landed on anyone. You'll be okay." She turned to John. "I suppose all these tales will wind up in one of your books."

He shrugged. "Never know. You'll have to read them to find out."

"Didn't your father ever write about you?" Rick asked.

Anthea felt the blush. "I suppose so. His books are too technical for me to read."

"You told me your father owned a sporting goods store," John protested. "You didn't tell me he wrote books."

"She doesn't like to share the limelight with her famous father. Ever heard of Ken Hoyt?" Rick inquired.

"No," John admitted. "What does he write?"

"He is a professional kayaker. When he isn't teaching, he's writing guide books." Rick got up to answer a question from Steve.

"Or kayaking in South America," Anthea whispered.

"What about this store you told me about?" John asked her.

"Oh, he owns the store but has a good manager. Now my brother is learning the business to take it over when Glen decides to retire."

John put his hand on her arm. "I told you about my father. Can you talk about yours? I know your mother died young. When your dad went kayaking, who took care of you and your brother?"

"Aunt Edna and Uncle Tom." Anthea looked up while trying to blink back tears. "She's my mother's sister—never had kids of her own and took George and me in. Uncle Tom's a preacher," she added quietly.

"I could tell you had a strong faith. Sounds to me like your aunt and uncle gave you a lot more than a home."

She smiled weakly. "Yes they did. After Mother died, Dad kind of went off on his own. He loved us, but he loved the excitement of the rivers and the white water, too. I looked forward to our summer vacations when he would take us on trips. He used to guide on this river, and he got me started young."

She looked off into the distance as if seeing those years again. "By the time I was twelve, I could handle an oared boat. George started even younger. He qualified as a guide by the time he turned nineteen." She sighed.

"Couple of river rats."

"You make me feel guilty for having such stable parents. But I hear you about the summer vacations. Those trips into the mountains with my dad will always be precious memories."

"Does he know that?" she asked.

John blinked as if in surprise. "I think so. Many of the books I've written have been about our trips. But since his accident, I don't talk much about those times. Don't want him to feel bad about losing the use of his legs."

"Maybe he'd like to remember the good times you shared. Writing books for someone else to read isn't enough."

"You have a way of getting me to think, lady. You keep teaching the teacher. Do you do this to all the people who paddle your raft?"

Anthea shook her head. "I usually stay to myself and don't mingle with the clients any more than I have to. Actually, I like animals better than people."

John grinned and pulled on his beard. "Must be all this fur. You don't think of me as human."

"Oh, but I do," Anthea exclaimed before sitting back in horror of what she'd said. Her feelings boiled over in turmoil. Why did she let this man affect her so much?

Gently he touched her cheek with the palm of his hand. "It's okay, Anthea. Sometimes we can talk to people who are almost strangers more easily than we can talk to old friends. I'm hoping we will get to be old friends by the time this trip is ended."

Rick came back to where Anthea and John sat. "Looks

like the weather might change." He pointed to the clouds showing in the sky down river. "Those usually mean a storm within three days." He sat down next to John. "You get her to tell you about her father?"

"Yes, told me how he got her started on the Colorado."

"Gets in your blood. I make two or three trips a year."

John looked at Rick's wedding band. "Does your wife come with you?"

"Would you believe she's a doctor? Right now she's in Peru giving immunization shots to little kids." He smiled at John. "She married me knowing I was part river rat, and I love her for caring about kids who need her. Good marriage."

"I may write adventure, but this trip is teaching me how little I really know about how others live."

"Braving the rapids brings all kinds of people together. Oh, we get an occasional couple who never should have left civilization." He shrugged. "Who knows, maybe we will teach them something, too. Right now, I'm going to go climb in my raft and get some sleep."

"You sleep in the raft?" John asked in wonder.

"The dams up river let water out at different times. The farther down the river we go, the longer it takes the water to get to us. The theory is I will feel the raft start to float and wake up if the river rises."

"He's been known to sleep right through the water going down," Anthea warned. "Then we get up to rafts that are high and dry." She laughed teasingly.

"Nobody's perfect." Rick waved to them as he headed for his floating bed.

"I need to get some sleep too," Anthea said, getting to her feet.

John stood beside her and ran his fingers through her hair. "That ring-tailed cat had good taste."

Anthea stepped back. "I'll see you in the morning," she stammered turning to hide her emotions.

"I look forward to that," he said quietly, as she ran down the bank toward her campsite.

Chapter 3

Anthea hoped her glow of pleasure at seeing John early the next morning didn't show.

"Thought I could help out with breakfast," he offered.

Karen stretched before pointing to the pot of coffee on the large propane burner. "Help yourself. Are you good at cooking breakfast?"

Anthea cringed at Karen's words until she realized the girl had spoken seriously and not in fun as she usually did.

"I can pour a bowl of corn flakes without spilling," John offered.

"We have those, too, but how about flipping French toast?"

"Sure, why not?" John followed Karen to the grill being set up.

Anthea followed, more than a little miffed with the attention Karen showed John. "The batter is mixed. I'll cut bread for you," she offered before Karen could find a knife and start on the loaves of bread.

"The girls have you working, huh?" Rick asked as

he poured coffee.

"I volunteered," John told him as he tried moving the batter-soaked bread onto the hot griddle.

Rick shook his head. "Never offer to do women's work."

"Watch your mouth," Steve growled joining the group. "I make a living cooking, and it isn't just women's work."

Rick held up his hands in surrender. "Just trying to save the young man from grief."

"How're we doing, gang? Can I send this guy off to blow the conch? Put his hot air to work," Steve said with a grin in Rick's direction.

"I'm out of here. Sorry I interfered." Rick retreated toward the rafts on the riverbank.

John tossed another stack of French toast into a large metal bowl and put the cover back on.

Steve nodded in approval as he went to see that everything had been laid properly. Then he picked up the conch and blew the call to breakfast.

Anthea watched John continue to cook and serve as people came to fill their plates. She walked up behind him to thank him for his help. It must have startled him because he flipped the turner full of toast onto the ground.

"Now you're getting smart. Don't do a perfect job, or they'll expect it every time," Rick quipped, coming through the line to fill his plate.

Anthea dropped down to pick up the spilled bread. John stooped at the same time and their hands met. She swallowed down the thrill his touch sent through her. *This is crazy*, she told herself. *I'm getting shivers trying to pick up soggy French toast.*

"I made the mess. I should clean it up." Again John reached for the dirty toast.

"You're a guest, and I should be waiting on you," Anthea told him.

"Quit arguing and go back to cooking," Steve told John. "We have hungry people who need food."

Sheepishly, John wiped his hands and went back to the grill. Later he and Anthea took time to eat while others from the crew cleaned up and started packing up the kitchen area.

Sitting with her shoulder against his and a tin plate in her lap, Anthea told him, "You're a good cook."

"Anyone can dip bread in batter and toast it."

"But not everyone can bread it in dirt before they serve it." She grinned.

He banged his shoulder against hers. "If I weren't so hungry, I would drop this sticky syrup in your lap."

"You see if I let you in my kitchen again," she said in mock anger.

"Good. Rick says cooking is women's work. You can cook, can't you?"

Anthea smirked. "I am not going to tell you. You will have to come to dinner to find out for yourself."

"That's a date," John said firmly as he got up to take his plate to be washed.

When the rafts were packed and ready for the day, Rick tapped John on the shoulder. "I need a favor."

"Something you want rolled in dirt and fried on the grill?"

"I saw that." Rick smiled. "What I need is for you to keep an eye on Sue and Bill and go in the same raft with them. She said she didn't like it on the oared boat and wants to paddle today."

"Didn't like it! She sat up there like Cleopatra on the front of that boat."

Rick nodded his head. "I agree, but now she wants back in the boat with Bill. I've asked Gus to watch out for them, too."

"Okay. Glad to help out."

Gus motioned to John, who went to stand with the young swamper. "Looks like they are going with Anthea. Want me to take lead paddle today?"

"I don't care. You have a lot more experience than I do," John told him.

The men settled into the front seats after Bill and Sue fastened their packs and sat in the middle area. A professor and his wife were in the back. Gus whispered to John that he had been in a raft with them and they were strong paddlers.

"Going to need it," John mouthed back.

The oared boats took off first, and the paddle rafts followed.

"We're going through Crystal Rapids today. All of you will have to keep heads up and be ready to follow my commands," Anthea told her crew. "This is one of the bigger ones on this part of the river. It can be a fun run if we hit the waves right." She looked at Sue wiggling around on the middle seat. "Be sure to keep your feet in the straps. They're all that will hold you in the boat if you start to go over."

With a sigh, Anthea breathed a prayer and steered the boat into the current.

So far Rick's threat of a storm had not materialized. The sky remained blue with only wisps of clouds. Before long Bill was standing up with his ever-present camera, snapping pictures of the cliffs that rose higher as they went farther into the canyon.

"You like to swim?" the professor asked him.

Bill looked puzzled. "Not in this cold water."

"Then I suggest you sit down and pick up your paddle," the man said.

Anthea cringed inwardly. The professor had put her thoughts into words, but she worried how Bill would take them. Bill just smiled and kept on taking pictures. She thought it must have been five minutes before he sat down, put his camera in his pack, and finally picked up his paddle.

"Let's do a few practice commands before we get to Crystal," she suggested. She called out left and right turns and back paddle. Bill seemed to follow her directions. Sue never could remember which way to paddle for the turns. "Follow John, Sue. Paddle the same speed and direction he does, and you'll do fine," Anthea tried to encourage the young woman.

They could hear the roar before they saw the white water ahead. "This will be a fun ride," Anthea spoke with enthusiasm.

"Bill, I can't reach my pack, and I want a candy bar," Sue whined.

Anthea prayed, *Please God, help me keep these people safe.*

Bill moved to where he could open his wife's pack and gave her the candy bar.

"All forward," Anthea shouted holding her long paddle firmly to use it as a rudder. She could see Gus and John dig in to keep the power going. The professor and his wife did their best to keep up. Sue ate her candy bar. Bill straightened in his seat just as they hit the first waves. The raft dipped, and as it came back up, Bill went over the side.

Sue screamed and tried to stand up.

"Sit down and stay out of the way unless you want to go over too." John's firm words seemed to quell the girl and her fears.

Schoolteacher voice, Anthea thought as she glanced to make sure Sue was sitting down while she used her paddle to bring the raft close to Bill.

Gus reached over the side, grabbed the man's life vest, and pulled him into the boat.

Turning to check on Sue again, Anthea saw the woman start to stand up to get to her husband then look at John and sit back down. *Maybe I should have him shouting commands,* she thought.

"You all right?" Gus asked the dripping man.

Bill nodded his head. "It's cold."

"Get back up on your seat and brace your feet," Anthea told him as she signaled the waiting oar boat that they didn't need help. "The sun will warm you up."

"You might try paddling to get warm," the professor suggested with a note of sarcasm.

Sitting quiet, her candy bar forgotten, Sue picked up her paddle. Anthea watched her as she made sure her feet were secure in the straps on the bottom of the boat.

Bill looked around. "Thank you. I guess I didn't have my feet in the straps."

No one spoke. Bill picked up his paddle, and when Anthea gave the "all forward" command, he followed Gus's stroke and kept up a steady pace until they stopped for lunch.

Anthea saw Bill lie in the sun during the lunch break. *Good, he'll be dry and warm until we hit the next rapid.*

That afternoon they drifted in slow water with the hot sun beating down. Water guns came out of packs, and the battle began.

Anthea pulled out her secret weapon.

"Where did that come from?" John asked, seeing what appeared to be a modified boat pump.

"I keep it around to scare ravens out of camp," she said with a mock serious look.

"Let's paddle forward nice and easy," she instructed her paddlers. "I'll get us into range before Rick knows what hit him."

By the time the sun had started to drop down toward the edge of the cliffs above them, nearly everyone was as wet as Bill had been when he went over the side.

In the fun of the game, both Bill and Sue seemed to become part of the group. Anthea wondered about how the world works. *Here we have highly educated people playing like little children. We're all like one big family.*

When they camped for the night, she looked for John. *He must have gone farther up the hill to camp,* she thought when she didn't see him. She placed her own bedroll close to where the kitchen had been set up.

Steve whipped up one of his special desserts. He had an iron pot, which he put on coals and then put coals on top of the lid. The result was a perfectly baked pineapple upside-down cake. Anthea took her piece and found a rock to sit on.

"Is this place taken?"

She looked up with pleasure to see John. "Pull up a rock and join me."

"I've been sitting with Sue and Bill."

Anthea looked up in surprise. "Why?"

"I did yell at her pretty harshly. Didn't want any hard feelings."

"Thank you for yelling. We could have had both of them swimming." Anthea took a bite of cake. "So is she mad at you?"

"No. They do realize they haven't been the best crew members. I think Bill's bath in the cold water woke them up to the fact we need to work as a unit."

"Better late than never."

"I think they may have learned a lesson they will take home with them. Bill got to talking about his job, and it sounds like he's been doing his own thing there, too."

Anthea shook her head and put her plate on the ground in front of her. "These trips and the people fascinate me.

Like today when we had the water fight. A bunch of seemingly intelligent adults played like kids."

"Don't you think sometimes we take ourselves too seriously? Letting go and just having fun can be healthy."

"If you aren't responsible for the people who are acting crazy."

"You do a good job of keeping everyone in your boat safe. Bill was never in danger. And the water fight only brought fun and laughter. No danger there."

"I guess the Lord doesn't expect us to keep a sour face all the time."

"I don't think the Lord ever requires us to be unhappy. We bring it on ourselves," John told her with an expression she couldn't read.

"You talking religion to me?" Anthea voiced her wonder.

"Are you offended?"

"No, surprised. I didn't think you were a believer."

"I had a few fights with God when my father lost the use of his legs. I don't know how strong my faith is, but it is creeping back. This trip has helped."

"Really?" She turned to face him. "How?"

"You. You've made me look at things differently. I realize I may be more upset by my father's being a cripple than he is." He touched her hand. "I hope he gets to meet you. I have a feeling he is going to want to thank you for showing me my way back to the Lord."

Anthea dared not speak. She wasn't sure she could get a sound past the lump in her throat. "Maybe I can go see your folks sometime when I'm in Chandler."

"I hope you'll go there with me."

They looked up as Bill and Sue walked up to them. "We wanted you to know how much we have enjoyed being in the raft with you," Bill told her.

"Your stories about the area are fascinating," Sue added. "I'm going home and read more about the Grand Canyon now that I've seen it from the bottom up.

"Did you get over your swim today?" Anthea asked.

"Took a cold shock to wake me up." Bill grinned. "We took this whole thing as a lark until today when we both realized there is real danger in the river. We didn't want to bother you." He looked from Anthea to John. "But we do want you to know we appreciate your taking care of us in spite of ourselves."

"I will not even put a candy bar in my pack again. I promise to paddle 'til I get blisters," Sue offered.

"You don't have to do that," Anthea protested. "Besides, we have Gus and John trained to paddle enough for all of us."

The young couple laughed. "We hike out at Phantom Ranch, so we only have another day on the river. I'm grateful we wised up before we missed a chance to tell you what a great guide you are," Bill told Anthea. They turned to walk hand in hand toward their campsite.

John took Anthea's hand. "You prayed them through this didn't you?"

"I did not ask God to dump Bill in the river," she protested.

John laughed, still gripping her hand in his. "I didn't mean it unkindly. I watched you, and when we hit a rough spot or either Bill or Sue were acting unwisely, I could see the look on your face and knew you were praying."

She couldn't deny what he said so she didn't answer him at all.

"I'm not complaining, and I doubt they would either. You're special, and I think the Lord uses you to teach others to come to Him."

"Uncle Tom would like to hear that. He and Aunt Edna tried to teach George and me to set a good example. When you are practically preacher's kids, you have to mind your manners."

"One thing puzzles me. How did someone with your great faith and ability with people wind up wanting to be a doctor to dogs?"

"I told you, they don't talk back."

"They only bite." He put his hand lightly against her face. "You bring a whole new meaning to the phrase *lucky dog*."

"I plan to work on more than dogs," she whispered, trying to still her beating heart.

"You mean I have a chance? Here I thought I would have to go back to Ithaca and get a dog to attract your attention."

"You are crazy. How did we ever get on this conversation?"

He grinned. "I am only trying to understand you. I see a beautiful woman who knows more about the Colorado River than many professors of geology, future doctor of veterinary medicine, and a wonderful Christian."

"Anybody can be a Christian. I just happen to love the

Grand Canyon and animals, too."

"Could you find room in there for a high school English teacher?"

Her mouth went dry. "Maybe if you give me a little time to think about it," she answered quietly.

"We still have another week on the river. What can I do to impress you?"

"Just be yourself. I don't need to be impressed."

"I'll keep that in mind when I offer to cook French toast again." He chuckled.

Anthea stood up. "I won't be awake for breakfast if I don't get some sleep."

John looked up. "Stars are the windows of heaven. God sure left the light on for us tonight."

"My mother used to tell us that when we were little," she told him with wonder in her voice. "Aunt Edna would quote the Psalms where it says the Lord not only knows how many stars there are, He calls them by name."

They stood with their arms entwined, looking at the glittering sky above them. Finally Anthea slipped away from John. "I'll see you in the morning." She made her way to where she'd spread out her sleeping bag.

Chapter 4

Morning brought the bad weather Rick had forecast. The clouds hung low, hiding the tops of the cliffs. Anthea shivered as she rolled out into the brisk air and pulled a sweatshirt out of her pack.

"Doesn't look good," Karen commented, digging in her pack for warmer clothes.

"Supposed to hike this morning. Hope the rains hold off." Anthea pushed her belongings back into her waterproof bag and strapped it down, ready to be lashed to a raft.

Steve had been up before them and had coffee hot and steaming. Both girls wrapped their hands around their cups to warm them.

"Told you we were in for a change in the weather," Rick said cheerfully.

"You don't have to sound so happy about it," Karen growled.

"How many do we have leaving us at Phantom Ranch?" Anthea asked Rick.

"Only Sue and Bill. Gus will hike out with them. We

have three rafters and another swamper hiking in."

"Sue will never make the eight-mile trek to the top," Anthea predicted.

"Her husband thought of that. They have mules reserved to carry them up," Rick told her. "Did he survive his swim yesterday?"

"Made believers out of them. They both apologized to me last night. Said they didn't realize the dangers until he fell out of the raft," Anthea told her crew boss. "I think they will do fine now. At least they will try to follow directions."

Rick nodded. "Good. I'll still have Gus stick with them to help out where they lack the strength to paddle." He turned as he spotted Jeff pouring coffee. "Hey, Buddy, I need to talk to you."

"What's up, boss man?" Jeff stood with the two girls next to Rick.

"Going to hike today. You know the one that circles up around the top?"

Jeff nodded.

"How about if you lead? I'll send the girls up last to help anyone who gets stuck in the rocks." He patted Anthea on the back. "Our medic can pick up the pieces if anyone falls."

"I'll bring the duct tape," Karen offered with a grin.

Anthea poked her friend in the ribs. "Be good or I'll put it over your mouth."

Steve broke up the conversation by blowing the conch for breakfast.

Anthea sipped on her coffee, waiting until all the

clients had eaten before filling her plate. She didn't see John until he spoke from behind her.

"May I join you? I understand breakfast this morning comes without dirt. You have to add your own."

She turned to greet him. "I think I'll pass on the dirt today. If the weather stays like this, it may be mud pies for supper."

She followed him through the line, picking up a toasted bagel and fresh fruit.

"This food is great. Don't know how Steve packs so much in those boxes."

"We'll get more canned stuff by next week. The fresh vegetables and fruit only hold so long." She picked up a slice of melon and took a bite. She watched John eat scrambled eggs with salsa.

"We're going to go down river about a mile and beach the rafts while we hike today."

"Sounds good. Be a change to be out of the rafts for a while." He sipped his coffee. "Do you get to go, or did you get stuck staying with the rafts?"

She laughed. "Steve always volunteers for that job. Says it has taken him too long to build up his paunch to risk hiking and wearing it off."

"He is quite a character. Does he make many of these trips?"

Anthea shook her head and put her cup down. "He started out years ago as a paying customer. Kept coming back every year and doing more and more until the Colorado River Rafters offered him a free trip for all his work. He's a cook in San Francisco the rest of the year.

Takes his vacation to do one of these runs every summer."

John scraped his plate clean. "Sure glad I got on the trip he's cooking for."

Rick had gathered everyone around him to explain the plans for the day. Anthea went to help break down the kitchen area and pack everything back up. She saw John helping Gus carry bags and mats to the waiting rafts.

Sighing in disappointment, she saw the two men follow Sue and Bill into Karen's raft. *At least we will be able to hike together. Unless he finds Karen more interesting,* her mind nagged.

Everyone followed Jeff up the path. "You're sure this isn't a rough climb?" Lou asked.

"Not bad at all," Jeff reassured her.

Within one hundred feet, Lou stood at the bottom of a rock fall, looking up. "You've got to be kidding. You expect me to climb that?"

"You can do it," Jeff said confidently. "Just put your hands and feet where you see me put mine."

"Young man, you are two feet taller than I am, and my arms are not going to reach."

Anthea went to Lou and offered to guide the older woman up the rocks. "I'll be right behind you. If you fall, you land on me," she quipped.

"I'll go ahead and give you a hand up," John offered.

Anthea gave him a grateful look. Gradually the group made their way over the many rocks to the summit of the hill. Looking out over the broad expanse of dark vermillion-colored rocks, Lou told them, "It was worth the effort. Thanks for the help."

The path down the other side did not offer as many challenges except for being steep. "You went over the rocks like a mountain goat," John told Anthea.

"After a week without a shower, I probably smell like one, too."

He put an arm around her waist. "You smell good to me. Or is that because I'm so ripe myself?"

The two of them followed the group down, making sure no one else needed assistance. By the time everyone made it back to the rafts, it had started to rain. People dug through packs and put on rain gear while taking deep breaths of the pungent smell the rain brought to the desert.

"Smells like exotic spices," Lou told her rock-climbing guides.

There were no water fights that afternoon. Between the rapids and the rain, everyone felt wet and cold by the time they stopped for camp.

Anthea made her raft secure and went to help in the kitchen. Steve had water heating as soon as the propane stove could be lit. "Have hot water and instant soup, cocoa and tea right away," he called to the chilled people. Busy helping find the soup packets, Anthea looked up to see John putting up his tent. *Won't be sitting under the stars tonight,* she told herself.

Later she and Karen went to put up their own tent, and she returned in time to see John with a cup in his hand getting back into his tent. Disappointment filled her.

Anthea did not see John again until morning, when he came looking for breakfast. The weather had cleared, but the sun had not come over the cliffs to warm the air.

"So we get to Phantom Ranch today," John said as she refilled her coffee cup.

"Yes. We have three hiking out and four hiking in."

"Know any of them, or are you going to be trying to put names and faces together?"

She laughed. "You cured me of that game."

"So what's at Phantom Ranch?" he asked

"A telephone, if you want to call your girl friend." She regretted the words as soon as they left her lips.

John looked surprised but didn't answer. "I may call my mother to see if they are getting settled all right."

Anthea scolded herself over and over when John went to another raft to go down river. When they pulled into Phantom Ranch, she had chores to do for Rick to get ready for the next week. Anthea did not see John. *Serves you right if he does go call a girl friend,* she berated herself.

After Sue, Bill, and Gus were dropped off, the rafts were made secure farther down river. People wandered about, some to the small store a half-mile down the path. Anthea rejoined the group along with the four people who had hiked in. Jan and Jim shrugged off their big packs and introduced themselves. An older man carried a pack as large as those of the young couple. He introduced himself as Ed. The new swamper, Tony, looked like he could paddle a six-man raft by himself.

"We've got paddle power now," Rick declared, welcoming the new recruits. "Going to need it. This part of the river has some challenging rapids. We'll be going through Granite this afternoon. That's the official name.

The guides call it the Maytag. You'll feel like you're in a washing machine."

Anthea looked up in pleasure as John came to her side during Rick's explanation.

"Really that bad?" he whispered.

"Worse," she told him. "Why don't you go with Rick and get a really wild ride?"

"Why not with you? Afraid I won't follow directions?" he teased. He looked around the new group. "Got more people than we have places to paddle."

"We try to do that so people can take a rest and ride the oar boats. You could try that, too. Even take a turn trying to row one of them."

"Might be fun, but not in the rapids."

"Good idea."

"I'll take my chances with you this afternoon," he told her, picking up his daypack.

"Let's go," she called, starting for the rafts.

"I've always been up front. I want to try back here by you."

"Hey, we know that trick," Tony called from the lead paddle position. "You expect the guide to try and stay dry, so you sit next to her. Won't work this time."

Jim and Jan took the middle places. Pete, the young man on his graduation trip, sat opposite John. When Anthea learned they were all experienced river runners, she did only a few minor drills.

"How was the trip down?" John asked the new people.

"Hiked in snow for the first two miles."

"Snow! It was cold here but no snow," John exclaimed.

Jim laughed. "We were a few thousand feet higher than you. Hiked eight miles down."

"Not straight down," his wife corrected him. Then she grinned. "Even if it did feel that way at times."

"You pass any donkeys coming up?" Anthea asked.

"Only what they'd left behind. The path stinks," Tony complained.

John looked at Anthea. "Sue will just love that trip. Bill will never get her out of Manhattan again."

The group worked well together and was paddling full power when they hit the Granite Rapid. Water washed in on all sides. One wave hit hard on John's side of the raft, and he slid into the bottom of the boat.

"Deep enough to swim down there?" Anthea called to him as they came out of the white water.

"Thank God for self bailers!"

"I knew if I tried hard enough I could teach you to pray," she told him.

"It didn't take white water for you to convince me I needed to get my life in order," he said, getting back into position on the side of the raft.

"Great work, gang. We make a good team," Anthea told her crew.

"Do we get more like that one?" Jan asked.

"Gets wilder as we go down river," Anthea told her.

"Good, that's what we're here for," the young woman said, dipping her paddle in time to Tony, who sat in front of her.

By the time the group made camp that night, the six people in Anthea's raft had become good friends. Jan taught school and had heard of John Briggs, the author. "I'll have to take pictures to show my students." Then she looked at John's water-soaked beard and Aussie hat. "Then again, they will never believe it's the same guy on the book jacket."

After the evening meal, people joined together to talk. Anthea regretted not having John to herself, but these trips brought such a diverse group of people she enjoyed visiting with all of them.

The next day John told her he planned to take her advice and try an oar boat. "See if I can row straight."

"Who are you going with?"

"Jeff said I could go with him. We'll take turns, and when the going gets rough he'll take over."

"Have fun." Anthea went to her raft to get started down river. She watched John maneuver the pontoon-oared boat. *Not a bad job,* she told herself. *Must be paddling a canoe taught him something.*

The group stopped again to do some hiking. Anthea and John helped people up through the rocks. Lou came to them for help. The older woman stood by them, looking up the chimney she needed to climb, and declared, "I'll do it," with true defiance. She put her back on one side and her feet on the other and wiggled her way to the top, where she gave a cry of accomplishment.

Anthea went ahead of John and then reached down to grab her pack that he held up to her. They continued up the stream to where pools of warm water lay in the rock.

"I'm going to rinse off some of the dust," Anthea declared, sitting down in the middle of one pool. "No fair," she complained when John snapped her picture. "You'll show that to your friends, and they'll think guides do no work."

The two of them sat with their backs against one of the protruding rocks. Anthea opened her pack. "Do you have something to read?"

John nodded his head and pulled out a paperback novel.

"I'll share." She offered him a small New Testament. "I can't carry a big Bible in my pack, so Aunt Edna gave me this. Has the Psalms and Proverbs too."

He took the small, paper-bound book. "Good idea. Afraid I haven't been reading the big one I have at home very faithfully."

"Never too late to start," she said softly.

"No, I don't suppose it is. You've made me face a lot of things on this trip. Going back to Bible study will be a small step after the issues I've faced about my father's accident." He flipped through the pages. "I always liked the book of Acts." He smiled. "Men in action must appeal to me."

"I like to read the Psalms. Always find something there to match my mood."

"My mother says the Psalms are her favorite, too." He took Anthea's hand. "She's going to want to meet the woman who got me back to the Bible."

Anthea couldn't speak. Her mind tossed up bits and pieces like flotsam in the white water. *Meet his mother. Did that mean he wanted to see her after the trip? Where was this going?*

"Your parents are Christian?" she asked quietly.

He nodded. "Said it is what helped them deal with the changes Dad's accident brought to their lives." He squeezed the hand he still held. "Mom has been more than a little worried that I rejected the principles I'd been raised with. Oh, she's not pushy, but she has tried and tried to get me back to church. She is going to love you."

Anthea swallowed. "I look forward to meeting her." She tried to make the words sound sincere. *He'll think I'm being forward,* she worried, feeling the comfort of her hand in his.

"Time to head back." Rick's voice broke the spell. "We'll go back the high road," he called to Karen, who was to lead the way down.

"High road, is that going to be worse than those rocks we climbed?" Lou asked John and Anthea.

Anthea smiled to reassure the older woman. "The high road is a good path with no rocks to climb. It'll take us right back to the boats."

"I wish I'd known about it coming up," Lou scolded.

"Then you couldn't go home with pictures of your assent through the chimney," John told her. "I'm sure I got good shots of you."

"Not from the bottom, I hope," she quipped.

It didn't take long for the group to be back in the rafts and paddling down river once again. Anthea watched John row as much as she could and still keep her own raft in control. *He's getting good,* she thought. *Maybe he'll come back to work as a swamper next year.*

Don't get your hopes up, her conscience warned. *This ship board romance is going nowhere.*

Sighing, she followed Rick's lead until they pulled in for the night. Since she and Karen were on duty to prepare the evening meal, she didn't get to spend much time with John. After things had been cleared away, she found him writing in his journal.

"Got a plot for the next John Briggs adventure?"

He smiled and laid his notebook down. "Jeff says we hit some wild rapids tomorrow."

"Yes, we go through Hermit. I've been lucky and never tipped over a raft in it, but I have seen others go over."

"Don't think I'll volunteer to row through that one," he said.

"I've watched you row. You're getting the hang of it. Think you'd like to do this run again?"

"Depends on who my guide is," he told her, motioning for her to sit next to him. "Speaking of guides, will you give me a few more lessons in this?" He picked up her New Testament. "I've been away from the Bible for a while, and I need a refresher course."

Anthea felt the blood suffuse her face. *Is he teasing me?* she fretted. "I can loan it to you. You seem to remember your way around. I saw you open right to Acts."

"Maybe I need to read more than that. What do you suggest?"

She looked up at the sun setting behind the cliffs. The clouds were pink tendrils flowing behind. "Look up Psalm 19 and read the first verse."

" 'The heavens declare the glory of God, the skies proclaim the work of his hand.' " He followed her gaze. "Awesome. Don't know how I could have doubted the power and glory of God for a moment, let alone for years." He looked back at the woman beside him. "I owe you a lot."

"All I did was loan you the Book."

"And teach me to read it."

Chapter 5

Anthea, Jeff, and John sat together on the riverbank eating breakfast. "You going with me today?" Jeff asked John.

"Steve offered to let me row the supply boat. Think I can handle it?"

"You've done fine on the oared boat. Give Steve a break and see how the supply raft feels."

"What about Hermit Rapid? What is it like?" John asked.

"It's a series of seven waves. You go into it with as much power as you can so when you hit the waves you will go over the crest. Each wave gets higher, with the last one eighteen to twenty feet high. Five, six, and seven are a wild ride," Anthea answered him. "Have you ever dumped a raft in this one?" she asked Jeff.

He shook his head. "First time I ran the river, I fell out of the raft, but I've never been in a raft that's gone over."

"Does it happen often?" John asked in concern.

"No," Anthea and Jeff said together. "Usually just have people fall out," Anthea continued. "Actually this rafting is as safe as playing golf." She laughed at the look of doubt on John's face.

"I'm going to talk to Steve," John told them getting up. "If he won't take a risk on me, I'll be back," he told Jeff.

"You'll do fine," the young man replied, getting up to help break down the kitchen.

John did go with Steve. Anthea watched whenever she could, and he seemed to handle the big boat just fine. *Nice of him to give Steve a break,* she thought. There were a few clouds keeping the sun from beating down on them. "Perfect day," one of her paddlers commented.

"Sure is, and we'll be in some fun rapids right after lunch." She went on to explain the waves of the Hermit Rapid and tell her crew why she would need as much power as they could give her.

"We'll be ready for you," they assured her.

"That or we'll swim," her lead paddler added.

Steve spread out his usual array of meats, cheese, and vegetables along with various breads and spreads for lunch.

"Going to be hard to go back to PB and J after this," John told Anthea, biting into a well-stacked sandwich.

"Don't you cook?" she asked in surprise.

"If I'm working on a book, I sometimes even forget the peanut butter and jam. Guess I need a keeper."

"Don't look at me," she laughed. "I take care of animals, not authors."

His wistful look sent a shiver down her spine. "I'd hoped you might want the job."

A call from Rick sent Anthea to get directions from

her crew boss, and the conversation went no further.

Back on the river, the clouds moved in thicker, bringing a chill to the air. "Will we get more rain?" Anthea was asked.

"I don't think so. This probably indicates a storm up on top. Sun will be back to warm us up," she said cheerfully, silently praying she was right.

They lined up to make the run through Hermit with the two oared boats going through first. That would put Jeff and Ben below the rapids to help anyone in trouble coming through. Anthea took her raft through after Rick. Both made a good run. She steered into an eddy below the rapid to watch the others. Karen hit the seventh wave just off center. The wave washed over the left side of her raft, knocking all three paddlers on that side into the water. Anthea and her crew watched as the others in Karen's boat quickly pulled their crew members back into the raft.

With her eyes on Karen, Anthea didn't see Steve start into the rapid. When she looked back, he had just crested the fifth wave. "Doesn't look good," she muttered. "He doesn't have the power."

The raft crested the sixth wave. Then, as if in slow motion, the people below Hermit watched Steve's boat climb the seventh wave. Anthea saw John clinging to the front of the raft. They hit the curl of the seventh wave. Slowing, they followed the curve of the wave until the boat hung upside down.

Anthea held her breath. Other times in her many trips down the river she had seen rafts go upside down, but this time John was in the water. It seemed many moments before Steve's bald head bobbed up by the side of the overturned raft. She couldn't see John. Her mind went numb. Her heart pounded in her chest. *Where is he? What has happened?* In those seconds of not knowing, she realized how much John meant to her.

"Rick is signaling," her lead paddler called.

Anthea tore her gaze away from the accident to look to her boss. When she recognized his okay sign, she let her breath out and silently thanked God.

"What do we do now?" her paddlers asked.

"Rick has signaled that they will bring the supply boat to the side over there." She pointed across the river. "We're going to have to paddle hard to get there through the current running downstream."

"Let's go," her people shouted with paddles poised to obey her directions.

Anthea worked with them until they touched the rocks on the other side. "Rick will give instructions from here," she told her crew as she scrambled over the rocks to secure her boat and get to John. She could see him now. Water streamed from his wet hair. His Aussie hat hung from its strap down his back.

Thank You, God. He's okay, she prayed as she sprinted over the rocks to his side. Without thought, she grabbed him in a hug. "Are you all right?"

He hugged her back saying, "I am soaked. I'll get you wet."

She stepped back. "Are you cold?"

He grinned. "If I say yes, will you hug me again?"

Steve stood in the T-shirt and shorts he always wore,

with his hat dripping water down his back. "I'm cold, too, if you're handing out hugs."

"You scared me. I felt so helpless," she told the soggy men.

"I didn't have time to be scared," John told her. "Besides I knew you'd pray me through whatever happened."

She sighed. "I did try to do that."

"Okay, folks, listen up," Rick yelled. "We're going to get ropes under this raft and turn her back upright." He continued to shout orders to his crew to get throw bag ropes and start working them under the upside-down raft. When one rope hung up on something under the raft, Rick went under to set it straight.

"Great, now I've got to watch three of you for hypothermia," Anthea complained in mock anger.

"If you give out hugs, you'll have all the male passengers in the water," Rick teased, shaking some of the water out of his hair.

Anthea felt the blush stain her cheeks. Still she stood next to John. She could not bring herself to admit her feelings, but she continued to take comfort in his rescue.

"What happened?" Jeff asked John.

"Happened so fast I can't tell you. We went over. I fell in the water. Put my feet downstream like I'd been taught and came up close to Ben's oared boat and he pulled me in."

"I couldn't see you," Anthea said in a whisper.

"I'm sorry I scared you. Would think you've seen enough of these capsized rafts not to be frightened."

"You were never on one of them," she murmured.

He put an arm around her waist. "Thanks for caring." He pressed his lips against her forehead.

"Everyone grab on the ropes. If we all pull together we can get this baby back upright," Rick yelled.

People scrambled to get a foothold in the rocks and a handhold on the ropes. After several tries, the big supply raft came up on its side and finally bottom down, as it should be.

"Going to be soggy sandwiches the rest of the trip, Steve?" Jeff asked.

Steve shook his head. "If anything leaked, it will be the bread box." Then he looked around the group. "Some of you may wish you'd strapped your waterproof bags tighter if they're in this boat."

"You going to be okay to row?" Rick asked Steve quietly.

"I'll stay with him to help. If I'm rowing, I'll stay warm," John offered.

"We'll take turns so we both stay warm," Steve told Rick. "How far 'til we camp for tonight?"

"Depends if there is a group ahead of us. We'll take the first site that's big enough for us," Rick assured Steve. He looked at the clouds. "Don't think we'll get much rain out of those, but it is chilly. Let's get a move on."

Rick shouted orders to the others and soon had them all headed down river.

Anthea tried to keep an eye on Steve and John, but her place in line took her ahead of them. She had beached her boat and tied up for the night when Steve hit the river-bank. Jeff and Ben were there at once to take over. Anthea went to John. "You're shivering. Are you all right?"

"Steve rowed the last mile, and I got cold sitting on the front of the raft. I'll be okay in a minute."

Anthea saw Ben and Jeff unloading the supply boat. Tony, Karen, and the others were getting the waterproof packs and sleeping mats off the other rafts. Steve had grabbed his pack and headed up the bank to get into dry clothes. Spotting the tent bag, Anthea opened it and pulled out John's tent.

"Come on. Let's get this set up," she told him, noting how he still shivered. He followed her up the beach where others were setting up their camps. "This okay?" she asked, stopping at a fairly level spot.

"Fine," he chattered through clicking teeth. "I can get it up."

"Are you sure? I can go get your pack of clothes so you can get into something dry."

He nodded as he dumped the tent and poles out of their sack.

Anthea ran back to the boats to find John's sleeping bag and clothes. By the time she got back to him he had his tent up.

"I brought an extra pad," Pete in the next campsite told them. "Anything else I can do?" he asked the shivering John.

"No, thanks anyway."

Anthea tossed the pad into the tent and unrolled John's sleeping bag. "Oh, oh," she groaned. "Must have been in the boat that went over. This corner is damp."

John pointed to others who had sleeping bags lying on

the rocks to dry. "I'm not the only one."

"I'm going to open it up. You can put it over you and not be against the wet part. Use the liner from the bag to put over the mat. Here, I'll do it." She crawled into his tent with the sleeping bag.

She got his bed fixed and looked back out of the tent door. "You need to get out of those wet things. Lie down with the sleeping bag over you until you get warm." She crawled back out of his tent.

"Are you always this bossy?" he asked, still shaking with chills.

"Only with my patients. Now get in that tent and get warm."

"I think I'm being treated like a dog." He grinned back at her as he started to crawl into the tent. "And I like it."

"I'll go get you some hot chocolate."

"That sounds good. Thanks."

When Anthea checked on John half an hour later, he appeared to be asleep. *Good,* she thought. *He must finally be warm.* She went back to help prepare the evening meal, but her mind kept busy on more than making garlic bread. *What am I doing getting involved with a paying passenger? What am I doing getting involved with a man? This is not going to work. We live in two different worlds.* Her thoughts tormented her.

"Looks like the bread box held," Tony said, watching her toast garlic bread on the big grill.

"Saw a few people drying out sleeping bags, but all the food seems to be intact. Even the frozen stuff is all right."

"In that frigid water it probably froze more solid," Tony quipped, stealing a piece of bread. "Is John okay?"

"I think so. He got chilled riding the last mile on the front of the raft."

"He's a nice guy. I've enjoyed getting to know him."

"Me, too," she said quietly.

Anthea struggled with her thoughts. Each day she felt joy at seeing John. He continued to help with the rowing, but at meals they were together. In the evenings the group had bonded through their experiences of surviving the many rapids. Everyone sat together with coffee mugs, telling stories.

This isn't the real world, Anthea kept telling herself. *Off the river it will be different.* She watched and listened as the people from diverse backgrounds sat in the sand and laughed about getting dumped out of a white-water raft.

As usual, John sat next to her. She liked it when he would take her hand. He talked about hiking and camping with his father as a boy. He encouraged others to tell stories of their adventures.

"Are these going to wind up in one of your books?" she asked him one night.

He shrugged. "I'm always open to more ideas. Never sure what I will use and what I won't." He smiled. "My characters usually tell me what they want to do."

"Our time is getting short," she commented.

"Does it have to end when we are off the river?" He spoke softly.

"You'll be going back to New York."

"So will you."

"Not 'til the end of September when school starts."

"What will you do the rest of the summer? Are you going to guide another raft trip?"

She shook her head. "No. Wish I could but I have a job working in a small animal hospital."

"Guess I'm going to have to get a dog after all. Then I can make an appointment to see you."

"Do your parents have a dog?"

"Good idea. You'll have to meet Scotty." He smiled and looked across the river as if seeing the dog in his mind. When he turned back to her he smiled again. "When Dad retired, his students past and present gathered enough money to buy Dad a motorized scooter. He had the motorized wheelchair, but this scooter is road worthy. He put a basket on for Scotty, and they go everywhere. When I called Mom from Phantom Ranch, she said the only reason he comes home is to recharge the electric batteries. He has friends all over the complex where they live. Even started teaching a class at the recreation center in their park."

"Sounds like he will enjoy retirement. How about your mother?"

"Said she likes her job and has found a church in Mesa they like. Has wheelchair access for Dad." He took Anthea's hand in both of his. "Thanks to you, I can let go. I have been so angry that Dad had to lose the use of his legs, I didn't see how well he has adapted." He squeezed her hands. "You made me realize I have been the crippled one."

Anthea swallowed, trying not to show how much his words meant to her. *I can't let him know I love him,* she thought.

Before she could speak, Tony plopped down next to John. "Hey, how's the rowing? Looks to me like you could qualify as a swamper."

John dropped her hand to turn to Tony. "I haven't taken your job have I? Are you trying to be an apprentice like Jeff?"

Tony smirked. "No way. I have no desire to be a guide. I try to get on as a swamper to get a free trip. This has been great, being able to paddle nearly every day." He looked up at the rock formations looming up from the riverside. "I'm an engineer, and I come on these trips to look at the work of the Master Builder."

"Kind of like looking at the foundation of the world, isn't it?" John asked, pointing at the gray cliffs stained with the red from the layer above.

Tony nodded. "And I don't think God is finished yet." His voice held awe.

Jeff joined the group. "How does Lava Falls look this time of year?" he asked Anthea, sitting on a rock next to her.

"We'll have to scout it out from above. Will depend on how much water is coming from the dam."

"Lava Falls?" John questioned.

"Wildest rapid on this trip," Jeff told him.

John groaned. "Another Hermit?"

"Much worse," Tony told him. "I've taken an oared boat through before. Maybe you'd better paddle that day."

"It's the last real rapid before we take out," Anthea said wistfully.

"The woman is part water rat," Jeff teased. "Hates to leave the river."

She saw the look John gave her. Did he wonder what their relationship off river would be? She sighed. "Yes, I love the river." She tossed her hair back. "And I'll be back next year."

"The doctor will take a vacation?" Tony asked in mock horror.

"Practice will go to the dogs." Jeff laughed.

"You guys are awful." Anthea laughed with them.

"How do I apply to be a swamper?" John asked.

"You've been infected with river fever, too?" Tony asked.

"Know where I can find a good doctor?" he asked, hugging Anthea against him.

Anthea took the good-natured banter and laughed with the rest. Underneath she glowed with John's offer to run the river again.

"So when we hit this Lava Falls, will you let me in your raft?" John asked her.

"Only if you follow directions." She poked him in the ribs.

"You heard it, gentlemen. She will let me back in her boat."

The next to the last day of the trip, the boats were pulled up on the river bank while the crew and some of the paddlers hiked up the hill that overlooked the Lava Falls Rapid.

"We're going through that?" John asked in horror when he saw the boiling cauldron of water below.

"I'd like to take pictures. Could I stay here and come down on the last boat through?" Jim asked.

"You'd ride with me?" Steve asked.

"You've already done your turn in the water. Should be the safest boat through the rapids," Jim quipped. "I can take pictures of the rest of you."

"As long as you don't sell them to my children," Lou, the rock climber, stated. "One look at those, and they'd have me declared incompetent."

Spirits were high as people walked back down to the rafts. Tony clapped John on the back. "Good luck. You've got the best guide."

"In more ways than one," John replied.

"We're going to follow Rick's raft. There are rocks on the left, so we will try to hit the rapid right in the V-waves," Anthea told her crew.

She sat poised on the back of the raft. This would challenge her skills to see her passengers safely to the other side. She watched John brace his feet in the straps and look back to smile at her. He sat in the middle on her right side. He gave her a thumbs up as she gave the command, "All forward."

Coming into the boiling white water, she didn't see the rock on the right side. They bounced just off the center of the V-wave. The wave coming in from the left poured over them from five feet in the air. "Keep paddling," Anthea screamed above the roar. Before more than a couple people could dig in a paddle, the wave from the right side hit them from an even higher level. She gasped as she looked in John's spot and saw only his hat floating in the water. In seconds that seemed long minutes she saw that he still had the toes of one foot in the straps. Slowly she watched as he levered himself back in the raft. She maneuvered the raft until they floated in the river current below the Lava Falls Rapid.

Everyone proudly waved paddles in the air. "We made it!" they shouted.

"You did great," Anthea told them as she turned the raft so she could watch the others making their way through the rapids. Finally they saw Steve with Jim riding on the front of the supply boat go into the white water. They came out unscathed to join the others who cheered them heartily.

That night in camp was a celebration. "Took twenty-eight seconds to run Lava Falls," Rick told them.

"Felt like twenty-eight minutes," many agreed. The euphoria of making the 225-mile trip down the Colorado gave everyone a sense of accomplishment.

"Feels even better than winning a big case," one of the lawyers said.

"Is this the reason you keep coming back?" John asked Anthea, sitting with his arm around her.

"I guess I like the excitement and the good feeling of conquering the white water." She looked into his blue eyes. "How about you? How do you feel?"

"About you or about the river?" he asked with a look that sent a glow through her.

"Maybe we should start with the river," she answered meekly.

"I like the excitement. I'd like to do it again, but only if you are with me." He smiled. "That has been part of the excitement."

"Being on the river isn't the real world."

"No, but it doesn't mean we can't find our way in the real world. Out here, we've seen each other as we really are. Nothing artificial about survival."

"I want to believe that," she said quietly.

Chapter 6

Excitement ran high as everyone prepared to paddle to the take-out point.

"I'm going to stand in a hot shower for an hour," Jan exclaimed.

"Let's take the crew out to dinner," another suggested. "Where would be a good place to go, Anthea?"

"The crew will be going back to Flagstaff with the gear. It could be late before we get everything cleaned up and put away," Anthea explained.

"How late? We can wait for you."

"The paying passengers will go back by van. Going to take three to three and half-hours. You'll get back to the hotel around four."

"If we meet at seven, can you make it?"

Anthea smiled. "A meal at a real table sounds good. I'll talk to the rest of the crew and see if we can make it close to seven."

"Now give us a list of places that can hold a group this size," one of the passengers said. "I'll call and make reservations and leave the message with the hotel desk. People can call there for the details."

Anthea watched as John pulled a sheet of paper from his journal and handed it to her, along with a pen. She wrote down suggestions for the lady in charge.

"I'd prefer we had a dinner alone, but we'll make a date for that later," John told Anthea as the group dispersed and headed for the rafts.

"You going to row the last day?" she asked him.

"Tony said he'd help Steve. I'd like to go in your raft, if it's okay with you."

Anthea tried not to show her feelings. "I'd like that," she said quietly.

The rafts pulled into Diamond Creek just before noon. Everyone helped unload the gear. Passengers transferred their clothes from the waterproof bags provided by the tour to plastic bags in which they'd take them home. A large truck backed down the beach to be loaded with the rafts and supply boxes.

Anthea climbed into the back of the truck and packed the gear that was handed up to her.

"You need help up there?" John asked.

"It helps having you bring gear to the tailgate." She pointed to a covered area up the beach. "Don't you want to get some lunch?"

"Will you come with me?"

She shook her head. "I have to keep working."

"I'll go make you a sandwich. Would you like a soda with it?"

She smiled. "Yes, that would be great."

By the time John returned, the rafts were empty. Jeff and Ben were removing the supports, preparing to let the air out of the inflatable boats. "You must be about ready to leave. I will see you tonight won't I?" John asked Anthea with concern in his voice.

"I'll be there." She took the sandwich he handed her. "Might be late, but I promise to come."

"Good. We still have lots to talk about."

She looked up the beach. "The vans are loading up. You better get going."

"Until tonight," he called, running toward his ride to Flagstaff.

"I'm back," Anthea called, dropping her pack in her brother's hall several hours later.

"Hi," her sister-in-law greeted her. Suzie grinned. "I know the ritual. You head for the shower, and I dump your clothes in the washing machine."

"Not this bag. I left this in my car for when I got back."

"The clients taking you out to dinner?" Suzie asked.

Anthea nodded. "I have to call the hotel and find out where they decided."

"You mean you aren't going to try to get out of it?" Suzie asked in surprise.

"I kind of want to go," Anthea said, picking up her small suitcase. She didn't offer any other explanation in spite of Suzie's raised eyebrows. "I'm off to take a shower."

Later, wrapped in a towel, Anthea hunted through her suitcase. She threw a broomstick skirt of flowered print on the bed.

"Okay if I come in?" Suzie asked from the door.

"Sure." Anthea put a top next to the skirt.

"I've got one that would look great with that skirt. Let me run get it."

Moments later, Suzie burst in the room with a scoop-neck white top. She held it against the skirt. "See, it's perfect. It'll show off your tan," she enthused. She looked at the dresser. "Is that a curling iron? I didn't think you owned one."

"Oh, Suzie, don't tease."

"Tease! I've known you since high school, and you never primp." She stood back, hands on hips. "Confess, who is he?"

Anthea felt her face grow hot. "No one special," she muttered.

"If you're paying attention to what you're wearing and even going to curl your hair, he's special. Sit down and let me do your hair while you tell me."

"He teaches school in Ithaca. His parents just moved to Chandler."

"That's handy. A guy for all seasons." Suzie brushed Anthea's brown hair. "I'll just put a bit of curl in the ends so it falls soft on your shoulders. You'll be a knockout."

"He writes books, too." Anthea said quietly.

"What's he look like?"

Anthea shrugged. "Not much taller than I am. Brown, curly hair and a beard. Blue, blue eyes." Her voice took on a dreamy quality.

"Never thought I'd live to see the day. I hope he's good to you."

"Better than my brother?" Anthea teased. "Where is he anyway?"

"At the store. Working late again." Suzie combed through Anthea's hair, admiring her handy work.

"And where is Dad?"

"Teaching classes in Northern California. Said to tell you he'd be back before you left for school." Suzie looked at Anthea's face in the mirror. "You need some makeup."

"Never wear the stuff," Anthea protested.

"Do you own a lipstick?"

Anthea nodded her head. "It's in my suitcase."

"You get it out while I go get some mascara. Let's show this guy you are more than a river rat."

"Suzie, you fuss too much," Anthea scolded.

"You didn't tell me his name."

"John Briggs. It can't go anyplace. You know about meeting on the river. It isn't real out there. Back here in town, he won't be interested."

"Anthea Hoyt, I've been on the river. It's where people show their true selves. Nothing like survival to bring out the real person. If you cared about him there, you'll still care in town."

"But what about John?"

Suzie hugged her sister-in-law. "You look terrific, and I know you're even more beautiful on the inside. If this John doesn't know that, he doesn't deserve you. Now get going. You're late."

Anthea spotted John as soon as she walked into the restaurant. He and Rick were having an animated conversation until he looked up. He stood. It felt like slow motion as he walked to her. Taking her hands in his, he brushed her cheek with his lips. "You clean up real good, lady."

Anthea relaxed and smiled. She looked at his shining brown curly hair and neatly trimmed beard. The blue sport shirt brought out the blue in his eyes. "You even look like the guy on a book cover."

Hand in hand they walked to the table. Talk whirled around them, but they were unaware of it. "Do you fly out tomorrow?" she asked.

"No. I have a couple book signings at stores in Phoenix. I'll be around for a while longer. What about you? I know you work in an animal hospital, but you never told me where."

"Mesa. I'll stay with my aunt and uncle there.

"Wonderful." His face glowed. "I'm going to catch a bus to Phoenix tomorrow. I'll rent a car and go out to Chandler. When can I see you again?"

"You want a ride to Phoenix?" she asked.

He looked puzzled. "What do you mean?"

"I have my car at my brother's, and I'm heading back to Phoenix tomorrow. Mesa is just past the Phoenix airport, so I could drop you there and you can rent a car."

"I accept."

Rick pounded John on the back before he could say more. "You coming back next year?"

John put his arm around Anthea. "If I can get the right guide."

The party started to break up. People were back in the world and anxious to return to home and families.

Addresses were exchanged and promises of pictures abounded.

"I'll be out front of the hotel at seven," John told Anthea, giving her a hug as she left the restaurant.

"Have you had breakfast?" Anthea asked as John threw his gear in the trunk of her car the next morning.

"The hotel put out fruit and cereal. No dirt, though. Just didn't taste good." He shut the trunk and got into the car. "You want to stop someplace?"

"Not yet. Maybe down the road when I stop for gas we can get some coffee."

"Glad you know where you're going. Mom had trouble finding the hotel when they dropped me off."

"I grew up here. You probably know central New York a lot better than I do," Anthea said, making a turn onto Highway 17 south.

"So tell me about this clinic where you work."

"The vet who owns the place is getting ready to retire. He took me on while I was still in high school. Keeps telling me when I get my doctorate he will turn the place over to me."

"Is that what you want?"

Anthea shrugged. "Be great if I can figure out a way to finance the deal. I will have student loans to pay off, too." She glanced at John. "So what about you? Will you keep teaching in Ithaca?"

"For this year anyway, but I'm looking at other options."

"Thinking of writing full time?"

"No. Actually I'm thinking of moving here."

"Really?" Anthea looked surprised. "Just to be near your folks?"

John sighed. "It started out that way. I kept thinking they would need me with Dad's limitations. You've changed my way of looking at that—and so much more." He reached to touch her shoulder. "Now I want to move close to where you are."

Anthea felt her mouth go dry and her face go hot. She didn't try to answer.

John twisted in his seat to face her. "So when do you work, and how soon may I see you again?"

"I go back to the clinic on Monday. Usually get off work about six."

"How about you give me the address, and I'll pick you up for dinner."

"Don't you want to be with your parents?"

"I can see them when you are working. I'll be there on Monday at six."

Anthea tried to steer the conversation to safer ground. She joked about things they had done on the river. Before long she pulled into the Sky Harbor Airport.

John stood at the curb with his duffel bag and waved as Anthea pulled away.

Back with her aunt and uncle, Anthea tried not to think of John but found herself watching the clock on Monday afternoon. She held a puppy in her arms when she saw him come in the reception area.

"Is that for me?" he asked, petting the small dog.

"Afraid not. His little master would be heartbroken

not to get him back." She handed the dog to an assistant. "Will you please put him back in his kennel?" She turned to John. "I'll wash up and be right with you."

As she got into his rental, she said, "I have my car here."

"That's okay. I'll bring you back here after dinner. Where should we go?"

The time seemed to fly. She felt so natural being with John—sharing her thoughts and hearing his.

"My folks want to meet you," he said, taking her hands across the table. "Could you come out on Saturday?"

She nodded. "I don't have to work. You'll have to give me directions."

"I'll print them out and give them to you when I pick you up on Wednesday."

"I'm seeing you on Wednesday?" she asked in surprise.

"You're seeing me every day I can manage. I have to sign books tomorrow evening, and I promised to go to a youth center in the afternoon."

"You're getting to know this area. How do you like the heat of summer?"

"I stay in air conditioning like everyone else."

On Saturday, Anthea pulled into the gated community in Chandler and parked behind the rental car she recognized. John immediately came to escort her into the house.

His parents greeted her warmly. John Sr. introduced her to Scotty, who sat in his lap as he wheeled about the house. Scotty licked her hands and begged to be petted.

"Well, you have the approval of the boss of the house," Mrs. Briggs quipped. "Now why don't you two go have a swim? Dinner won't be ready for another hour."

Anthea and John walked to the community pool. "You seem to manage the heat of Phoenix in summer," she commented.

"Not so humid as New York. I hope you won't be upset, but Mom invited their new pastor and his wife to dinner. They are really taken with the pair and wanted me to get to know them," John apologized.

"Your parents are nice people. I'm sure she didn't mean anything by it."

"She is certainly delighted to have me back in church with them. I did enjoy the sermon on Sunday."

Anthea looked at him, pleased. "You went to church?"

"And it didn't fall down. The folks go to the early service. More people their age, they tell me."

After a leisurely swim, the couple sat in the shallow end of the pool, unwilling to let go of their moments together.

"When do you go back to New York?" Anthea asked.

"I have an open ticket. Don't have to leave for a while yet. I will have to go back before you do. High school starts before college."

"I'll miss you," she admitted softly.

"If I have my way, we won't be separated again."

She looked at him, afraid to ask what he meant.

He tilted her face toward his. "We were meant to be together forever." He pressed his lips to hers.

Anthea felt the glow fill her being. "Maybe we better go back. Your mother will wonder where we are."

Together they walked back to the Briggs' home. Anthea stopped dead in her tracks as she started in the door. John bumped into her.

"What are you doing here?" she exclaimed.

"We came to dinner. Why are you here? We thought you had a date."

Anthea turned to John. "I'd like you to meet my aunt and uncle," she said quietly.

"But that's the preacher I met on Sunday," John said, looking at the startled man beside his father. "How do you do, sir?" John offered his hand to the pastor.

"Well, we seem to have found some mutual friends," Mrs. Briggs said from the kitchen door. "Why don't you two get out of those wet suits and join us for dinner?"

John looked down at his swimwear and then at Uncle Tom. "I'm not dressed formally, but I would like to ask if I may marry your niece."

"You didn't ask me," Anthea protested, taking hold of John's arm.

"I have to get permission from the family first," John explained, putting an arm around her. "If she'll have me, I'd like you to perform the ceremony at Christmastime."

"Well, this is some celebration," Mr. Briggs boomed. He wheeled his chair to Anthea and took her hands. "I've always wanted a daughter, and now I am to have one."

Anthea leaned down to kiss his forehead. Soon everyone embraced one another and talked at once.

"Now will you two go get dressed before my dinner is ruined?" Mrs. Briggs scolded.

"Oh, I got your dress wet." Anthea looked at her aunt, laughed, and hugged her again. "I'll be right back."

"Edna, I'm Margaret," Mrs. Briggs greeted her guest.

"If we're going to plan a wedding while our youngsters are back in New York, we better be on a first-name basis."

Anthea giggled from the hall where John held her in an embrace. "We better get back there before they have all the details worked out," she told John, putting her face up to be kissed again.

MARILOU H. FLINKMAN

Marilou is very active in the Kairos Prison Ministry. This ecumenical program reaches out to those behind bars to lead them to Christ. The program is also instrumental in helping them make better choices and to turn over mistakes to the forgiving Father in heaven.

Marilou lives in Washington State with her best friend, who happens to be her husband. Now that her husband is retired, they spend much of their time traveling. Their six children are scattered with their own families throughout the northwestern states, including Alaska.

Sudden Showers

by Gail Sattler

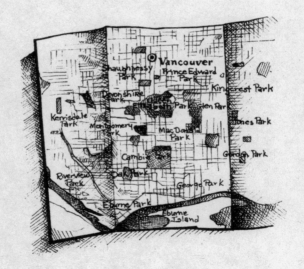

Chapter 1

Sharmane Winters leaned back on the park bench. Today was the first day of her summer vacation. Originally she had planned to drive up-country and explore the scenery, stopping for the night wherever she happened to be at suppertime. Unfortunately, her car now sat in her mechanic's lot awaiting a very expensive part which, upon its arrival, was going to eat up most of her vacation money and all of her one-week vacation.

Instead of sitting at home feeling sorry for herself, Sharmane intended to make the best of it. While she tried thinking of something to do that didn't involve her car, she grabbed a book and headed to the city park.

With birds chirping in the branches overhead and children screaming in the playground in the distance, Sharmane settled in and submerged herself in the lives of the characters. Totally engrossed as the plot thickened, she purposely ignored the darkening sky until a peal of thunder sounded in the distance, forcing her to pay attention.

Raindrops rustled the leaves as Sharmane raised her head to the thick clouds. A louder boom of thunder sounded as the patter of the rain increased to a steady drone and a flash of lightning lit the sky. Sharmane counted the seconds before the boom, trying to gauge how close the storm actually was.

The drizzle changed to a torrent. Sharmane abandoned the bench and huddled next to the trunk of the large oak in an attempt to keep dry until it passed. Since the sun had been shining brightly when she left, she had ignored the forecast and left her umbrella behind, a decision she now regretted.

Since she could no longer read, she fished through her purse for a scrap of paper to use as a bookmark but accidentally dropped the book. She picked it up and began to page through to find where she left off as more lightning flashed, followed by an immediate peal of thunder.

A large hand wrapped around her arm. "Come on!"

Sharmane screeched and yanked her arm away. A tall, wet man stood in front of her.

She hugged her purse to her chest, mentally preparing herself to hit him with it. "What are you doing?" she squeaked in a vain effort to sound calm, positive the stranger could hear the rapid hammering of her heart above the drone of the rain.

"Trying to get you out of here."

Sharmane backed up squarely against the tree, prepared to kick him if she had to, even though she doubted her soft sneakers would do much damage. Another bolt of lightning flashed, accompanied by a boom of thunder directly overhead. The stranger extended his hand, but she didn't take it.

He stood about ten inches taller than she did, and his wet clothing molded to his body emphasizing his height and the width of his broad shoulders, making the idea of opposing him almost laughable. If he wanted to, Sharmane had no doubt he could pick her up and throw her over his shoulder and carry her wherever he wanted, caveman style, with very little effort.

She concentrated on his face, hoping the unwavering eye contact would make him back off. That was a mistake. His eyes were a soft shade of sable brown, almost the same color as his hair, which lay stuck to his forehead. She wondered if when it was dry, his hair and eyes would be the same unique color. His lips were tightly drawn, making his lower lip protrude slightly, like a little boy pouting, except he was far too large and handsome for that.

"Don't you know that the most dangerous place in a lightning storm is under a tree? Do you want to become another statistic? We'll be safe inside one of the stores across the street."

As the force of the rain increased, Sharmane peeked out from under the protective cover of the tree. Lightning snaked directly overhead, lighting up the entire sky. As much as she hated to admit it, the man was right.

A shiver ran up her spine at the thought of getting soaked to the skin, but being wet in no way compared to being fried alive. Another bolt of lightning immediately followed by a peal of thunder helped Sharmane make up her mind in a hurry. "All right. Let's go."

This time, when he grabbed her hand, she didn't fight. She held on tight and ran with him across the soggy field, waited for two cars to go by before crossing the street, then dashed under the narrow awning of the row of stores. Sharmane gasped for breath and fiddled with her purse to bide some time while she recovered, hoping to avoid the embarrassment of being so winded after such a short run.

A shudder wracked her body from the top of her wet head to her freezing feet. Her socks were so wet that cold water squished between her toes, and a dribble of water snaked down her back. The only thing still dry was her book, safely zipped inside her leather purse.

The downpour splattered harshly on the pavement not sheltered by the narrow awning, falling so hard that the raindrops bounced before joining the growing stream in the gutter. Shivering again, she wrapped her arms around herself in an attempt to warm up.

Alex swiped a lock of dripping hair off his forehead as he studied the woman he had literally dragged out from under a tree. Her hair lay plastered to the top of her head, and her clothes were so wet everything stuck to her body in a way that appeared most uncomfortable.

He still could barely believe he was doing this, when he should have been at work.

Less than an hour ago, he'd stormed out of his office, much to the shock of his secretary, only meaning to go for a long walk. When he stepped outside, it briefly registered that the sky had darkened, because it had been sunny when he left for work, but he didn't care. He was so angry from yet another major corporate foul-up that he didn't feel the cold; at least he hadn't then.

In order to clear his mind and work the frustration out of his system, he meant to walk around the promenade at the perimeter of the park. Once didn't do it, and he was halfway through his second time around when it started to rain, which he found very fitting, considering his mood. And it wasn't just a little rain. In the blink of an eye the skies opened to a torrential downpour, sending everyone fleeing for cover. He had started to jog through the center of the park to get back to his dry, safe office. Then he saw the woman, who had been sitting on the bench on his first trip around the park, huddled under the tree still reading her book while lightning flashed directly overhead.

He couldn't, in good conscience, leave her there. Even if the lightning didn't hit that particular tree today, which being realistic, it probably wouldn't, he had only done the responsible thing. But he certainly hadn't meant to frighten her.

He looked at her again. The wet woman was pretty. She could probably stand to lose a few pounds, but so could he. He straightened his posture, his hand unconsciously resting on his stomach, and turned to face her.

Her blond hair hung in clumps at the moment, but when he first saw her it was fluffy and slightly curly at the ends and framed her face quite attractively. She had a pointy little chin, big blue eyes, and a pouty little mouth, which, when not fixed in a stubborn line, suited her pixie-like features.

A gust of wind caused them both to shiver at the same time.

Forcing a smile, he turned to the as yet unnamed

woman and cleared his throat in an attempt to compose himself.

"My name's Alex. I have an idea." Alex jerked his head to one side at the same time as he hitched his thumb over his shoulder. "Let's go in there and warm up with a hot cup of coffee. My treat."

For a moment, he thought she was going to refuse, but just as she opened her mouth someone opened the door, and the alluring aroma of fresh brewing coffee wafted out.

She glanced from side to side, eyed the crowd, and turned back to him. "Thank you," she mumbled then smiled weakly. "I'd appreciate that."

He smiled back and ushered the wet woman inside.

The hot coffee helped to ward off the chill somewhat. He sipped the coffee slowly, enjoying the liquid heat, knowing he should have been back at the office long ago, but he couldn't make himself move.

"So, do you often sit outside in the rain, Miss. . . ?" He let the word hang in the air as a smile tipped up the corners of his mouth and one eyebrow raised slightly.

Her cheeks flushed. "My name is Sharmane."

Alex's smile widened, and he nodded at the strange introduction.

"It was warm and sunny when I got there."

A rumble of thunder sounded in the distance, indicating the storm was passing as quickly as it had begun. "Yes, it sure came up fast."

"Not really. They predicted it on the forecast; I just ignored it."

They sipped the coffee in unison, then both stared into

their cups. It was almost like looking in a mirror. Alex couldn't think of a thing to say. He'd never lacked for conversation with a pretty woman before, and it didn't exactly do wonders for his ego.

"Feeling warmer now?" he finally asked.

"I guess so, except my feet are freezing because my socks are wet. And when my feet are cold, I'm cold all over."

Alex forced himself to smile when he really wanted to bury his face in his hands. He studied the bottom of his empty cup. "So take your socks off," he mumbled to no one in particular.

Her eyes opened wide as she stared at him. "What a great idea!"

Alex's ears heated up. He hadn't meant for her to hear that, nor could he believe she took him seriously.

With one quick gulp, she finished her coffee and thunked the cup down on the table. "Let's go outside, the rain stopped."

He followed her in silence. The second they got outside, she leaned against the building, pulled off one sneaker, then the sock, stuffed the sock into an outside pocket on her purse, slipped her bare foot back into the wet sneaker, and repeated the process. When both bare feet were again covered, she stood straight, beaming a smile from ear to ear. "That feels so much better. How about you? I'd imagine your socks are wet, too. Don't be shy."

The last thing he'd ever been called was shy, but he wasn't going to take off his socks, especially in front of a stranger or anyone else who happened to be walking by. He should have been at work, straightening out the mess with the quarterly budgets.

"Well, Alex, thanks for the coffee and for statistically saving my life today. I guess I should be going home now."

And he should have been back at work a long time ago. Being drenched by the sudden downpour then warming up by sharing a coffee with a pretty woman went a long way toward softening his foul mood. However, the words that came out of his mouth surprised him more than he surprised her.

"I've got nothing better to do. If you don't mind, I'd like to walk you home."

While she stood staring at him, he crooked his elbow and patted his arm to encourage her.

Hesitantly, she did tuck her hand inside, so he covered it with his other hand, patted it, and started to walk.

"I normally would have brought my car, but it's in the shop. I'm supposed to be on vacation this week. How about you?"

Visions of the mountains of papers and reports on his desk flashed through his mind. He couldn't remember it being any other way, from the time he started the company to present. He also couldn't remember the last time he'd had a vacation.

The stress was getting to him, and he knew it. What he'd done this morning was nothing short of certifiable. When the same budget report came back to him the third time with more errors, he'd lost it. Rather than say something he'd surely regret, he tossed off his suit jacket and left. His secretary tried to stop him, and the best he could do was shout on his way out the door that he'd be back some time that afternoon and to cancel his appointments. He'd never done anything so irresponsible in his life.

Instead of rushing back to do damage control, here he was walking in the opposite direction with a woman he'd just met.

He should have felt guilty, but he didn't. The work would still be there when he returned, whether it was in an hour, a day, or a week. He had competent staff, except for the latest fiasco. Terry knew how to run things in his absence. The company wouldn't fold just because he wasn't there.

Alex smiled as the weight of the world lifted from his shoulders. "I'm on vacation, too."

She sighed. "Well, it looks like you don't have any plans either. I mean, I did have plans, but without my car, everything kind of went out the window."

"Plans?"

She sighed again. "I'm stuck here in the city, but I'm not going to waste my time off. Instead of heading over to the island, I'm going to visit all the tourist spots I've never bothered to see because I live here, and do a bunch of stuff I've never done before, right in my own hometown. For the entire week, I'm going to do nothing but goof off."

Goof off? The idea held a certain appeal. Alex had traveled all over the world on business, but he'd never seen the attractions in his own backyard that people came from all over the world to see. Vancouver was one of the most beautiful places in the world, and he ignored it because he lived here.

"I don't have any plans either. I think I'm going to do the same."

She smiled, and his heart melted. "Well, maybe I'll see you some other time this week. Since my car is going to be really expensive to fix, I was planning on doing mostly stuff that's free or at least really cheap."

The thought of simple activities appealed to him. For a week, he could forget about being Alexander Brunnel the corporate executive and just be a regular guy, no stress, no worries.

"That sounds like a great idea. How about if I joined you? My car isn't in the shop; I wouldn't mind picking you up. We could go farther than walking, and it would be better than taking the bus."

"I don't know," she drawled. "We just met. I don't even know you."

"I could show you my driver's license and three major credit cards, and if that's not enough, I can supply references." He tried to give her his most engaging smile. "We'll be going to public places, you'll be safe."

She stopped in front of a small, older bungalow with neatly mown grass and a small flower bed beneath the front window. The house itself needed at least a coat of paint, and a few of the shingles were warped. "This is my house."

He tried not to cringe. It was nothing like what he was used to. The best he could come up with to describe it was the word "modest."

Alex escorted her to the door and waited for her to unlock it. "It's more fun to sightsee when you're not alone." He'd seen a lot of the world alone. At the time he hadn't thought about it, but perhaps that was why he didn't enjoy it as much as he thought he would.

"I suppose."

He grasped her hands then did his best to give Sharmane his most charming smile. "I would really love to goof off with you, and then when it's over, we can part as friends, no obligations, no hassles. How's that sound?"

She narrowed one eye and cocked her head. "I guess so. . . ."

"Great. I'll see you tomorrow morning."

Alex turned away and headed back to the office. He wasn't going to tie up any loose ends. He would simply pick up his suit jacket, tell Terry to look after things for the week, and leave.

He'd never goofed off in his life, and he couldn't remember ever looking forward to something more.

Chapter 2

Sharmane zipped her backpack shut at the exact second the doorbell rang.

A very different Alex stood in her doorway. Gone were the dress slacks, shirt, tie, and leather shoes, replaced by comfortably worn jeans, a T-shirt, and sneakers that had seen better days. Yesterday, she had thought it odd that he looked like he'd just stepped out of the office. Today, he looked like a man on vacation.

Last night, when she should have been sleeping, she'd lain awake staring at the ceiling and thinking about Alex. She had prayed long and hard, asking God if she was doing the right thing.

Again, she compared his appearance to yesterday. She wouldn't ask, but she wondered if he wasn't really on vacation after all. Perhaps he had been dressed so nicely because he was looking for work and had just finished an interview for a potential job. Being unemployed would explain why the idea of accompanying her on her cheap activities appealed to him so much and why he could do it with no advance preparation.

"Good morning, Sharmane. And what plans do we have for the day?"

"It looks like today will be sunny, so I thought we'd start by going to the Capilano Suspension Bridge. After that, I didn't want to make all the decisions, so I thought we could talk about what else we're going to do."

He smiled warmly. "That sounds great."

She followed him to his car, which was an older model economy car very similar to her own, except hers was newer and in much better shape. The condition of his car was almost questionable, but not wanting to be rude, she got in anyway and tucked her pack behind the seat. The interior was in worse shape than the exterior, but it was clean.

To her surprise, it started instantly and the motor purred like a finely tuned sports car.

He rested one hand on the stick shift and turned to her. "Believe it or not, I've never been to the suspension bridge. You might have to give me directions."

Sharmane pulled a map out of her backpack. "Me neither. But my neighbor went recently and she said it was packed with Japanese tourists, so I figured it would be a good place to start."

She watched as he fastened his seat belt. Even in profile, Alex was a very handsome man. And she had been right yesterday. When dry, his hair was exactly the same color as his eyes.

Rather than stare, she fixed her attention to the map. "It's funny, I've lived in Vancouver all my adult life, but I've never been to most of the popular tourist spots. I guess since I figure I can go anytime, that's why I haven't. So this week, that's what I want to do."

He nodded as he entered the traffic flow. "Same here."

Sharmane raised her head from the map. "I don't know anything about you."

When he turned to smile, her breath caught. It was almost like he practiced being distracting. His wide smile created the most attractive crinkles at the corners of his warm brown eyes, and his whole face shone. The man was movie-star handsome, and he likely knew it.

"There's not much about me to tell. I was raised in the suburbs of Vancouver, I came from a family of two boys and one girl, and we went to church every Sunday. I graduated from high school back in 1987, which makes me thirty-one years old. I've never been married, and my favorite color is blue."

Sharmane tried not to let her mouth gape open. "Church every Sunday?"

Briefly, he glanced at her then turned his attention back to his driving. "Yes. And I still do. Do you have a problem with that?"

"No. Not at all. I go to church every Sunday, too. Are you a Christian?" Her heart pounded, waiting for his reply.

"Yes, I am. I was born and raised in a Christian home and made my decision to follow Christ when I was in my teens. What about you?"

"I became a Christian as an adult."

"That's great. Praise the Lord." He glanced at her again and smiled, making her insides quiver, and turned his head forward as he drove. "So now you know all about me. Tell me about yourself, Sharmane."

She really didn't know much more about him than before, but she supposed she would find out more later. "I grew up in Kelowna then moved to Vancouver with my family in my teens. I'm twenty-nine, I've never been married either, and my favorite color is green."

He didn't volunteer any more personal information but instead changed the subject to the weather forecast, which was a determining factor for their choice of activities. Somehow they ended up discussing the news as they made their way through the city.

"I turn right after the bridge, right?"

She quickly paged through the map. "Yes. Right on Marine Drive, then north on Capilano Road." Sharmane looked up just in time to see the stone lions resting on their perches at the entrance to the Lions Gate Bridge.

"I hear they're talking again about budgeting to fix the existing bridge versus a new crossing."

The buzz of the tires humming on the metal grate set Sharmane's nerves on edge, and she forced herself to unclench her teeth. She didn't cross the Lions Gate Bridge often, because the sensation of almost slipping while driving on the grated bridge deck so high above the water always made her feel like she was going to throw up. She preferred to know there was good, solid concrete below her. The few times she ever crossed the Burrard Inlet, she tried to use the Second Narrows Bridge.

The green lighted arrow above the lane they were in changed to an amber X. The middle lane of the three-lane bridge was now switching direction to accommodate the traffic flow, and they were in that lane. Her guts wrenched. "Alex! They're closing the lane! Hurry!"

He had the nerve to chuckle. "Don't worry, we've got lots of time. Besides, it's monitored. They won't switch the other side to green until they've done a visual check that the lane is clear."

She tried to keep her voice from wavering, especially since Alex was unaffected. He changed lanes on the horrible metal surface without a hint of unease, and then they were back on cement roads and solid land. "I hate the Lions Gate Bridge," she grumbled.

The rest of the trip went without incident, and they soon arrived at the Capilano Canyon.

Sharmane slung the backpack over her shoulders, and they headed for the rope suspension bridge hanging over the ravine. The river churned and beat upon the rocks far, far below.

"This brochure says that it's 450 feet long, which is the world's longest suspension bridge, and that it's 230 feet above ground."

Alex simply nodded and they both looked down the length of the bridge, which seemed much longer when looking at it from the new perspective. The bridge swayed slightly with the movement and shifting weights. They stood back to watch the people venturing across.

Some people inched along cautiously, holding onto both sides of the rope railings at the same time as they walked in the exact center of the narrow bridge. A few hung onto the same side with both hands, but most walked relatively normally, using one hand to steady themselves as they walked slowly across. One rambunctious teenager stood in the center of the bridge halfway across and lifted both hands in the air while his friend snapped his picture.

When a lull in the flow of people crossing finally occurred, Alex's voice came from directly behind her, so close he was almost speaking in her ear. She didn't know he had been standing that close. "Well, are we going to do it, or not?"

Sharmane nodded. She grasped the rope railing tightly and took her first shaky step. The bridge shifted as she put her weight forward, and the unreasonable fear that the bridge would tip sent a surge of adrenaline coursing through her veins. Frantically, she grabbed the other side's railing as well and began to walk across slowly, guiding herself by hanging onto both sides at the same time, as countless others had done before her. She refused to think of the river below, and she kept her gaze fixed straight ahead, not down, not to the side. She didn't want to see the rushing water far below them as she crossed. At least on the Lions Gate Bridge, bad as it was, she was in a car.

Working her way forward slowly, guiding herself across by continuing to grasp both sides as she moved along, she gradually became used to the movement of the bridge as she walked and managed to loosen her grip as she progressed. Her heart pounded, and she still didn't look down.

Without letting go, she turned her head to speak over her shoulder at Alex. "This is fun!"

In a moment of bravery, she looked all the way behind herself to see that Alex was only holding onto one side.

He raised his chin slightly. "Don't look now, but someone is coming."

Sharmane froze in one place, still gripping both sides as she waited to see what would happen next.

"You've got to keep walking, Sharmane. You can do it."

She managed to let go long enough to let the other person past and then continued across once again using the rope railing on either side to guide her.

Finally, she was once more on solid ground.

"I fail to see why you wanted to come here if walking across the bridge was going to terrify you."

Sharmane laughed as a slight breeze rippled through her hair. She filled her lungs with the fresh, cool mountain air, tilted her head back, and shook it so her hair cascaded behind her as she reveled in her achievement. "It's the adventure. The accomplishment of overcoming fear. Doing something you've never done before. Wasn't that fun?"

He shrugged his shoulders. "If you say so."

"It was kind of like going on a roller coaster. Kind of scary but exhilarating at the same time."

"I suppose."

"Let's keep going. I want to go down the trail and find some animals to take pictures of. Did you bring a camera?"

"No, I didn't."

"I can make double prints for you, if you want. Think of it as paying you back for the coffee yesterday."

"Thank you, I'd appreciate it."

"You know, I was going to do this alone, but this is

so much more fun."

Alex nodded in response as they walked to the fenced observation area overlooking the canyon. He watched Sharmane shuck off her backpack, withdraw a small camera from one of the outside pouches, and start snapping a few pictures of the scenery. Like her house, the camera was modest and functional, just like the car he'd already heard so much about. He suspected everything she owned would fit into the same category.

"Okay, I've got a few pictures. Let's go do the trail."

The trail consisted of a mulched path wide enough for two people to walk side by side and lasted only a short fifteen to twenty minutes. They didn't see any wildlife except for birds and squirrels, but they stopped often to read the signs describing some of the plants and points of interest along the way. Very little was said, and being surrounded by trees, not people, had a profound effect on Alex.

The only noise was their footsteps in the mulch and the gurgling of the river in the distance. There was no need to rush, no need to keep an eye on the time, no need to hustle to his next appointment, and no need to worry that his messages were stacking up.

Sharmane was walking beside him, and unlike his business associates, his staff, the people at his church, even his friends, she didn't want anything from him. All she wanted was to walk beside him in the quiet and enjoy the scenery.

This was exactly what he needed, and for the first time in years, he was at peace. He didn't care if people wondered why he was walking around smiling for no apparent reason. He owed no one an explanation.

Too soon, they re-entered the clearing, and along with it, a crowd of people. For once, he didn't need his watch to tell him what time it was. His stomach told him it was lunchtime.

Small concession stands dotted the area, as well as a large number of tables, many of them still empty. He reached into his back pocket. "Can I get you something?"

Her hand on his arm stopped him. "You don't need to buy lunch. This is my treat; I brought enough for both of us. I thought it would be cheaper for you than buying something. Come on."

She led him to one of the tables on the edge of the grouping, plunked her backpack into the center of the table, and began unpacking an assortment of containers, as well as two juice boxes, onto the table.

Her words finally brought him out of his stupor. "If you'd like to give thanks for this, we can eat."

Alex couldn't believe it. She'd brought him lunch to save him money. Quickly, he bowed his head and folded his hands in his lap. "Dear Lord, thank You for this wonderful day and this getaway vacation to enjoy the beauty of Your creation. Thank You also for this food before us, Your continued blessings, and this day together. Amen."

"Amen." She slid a container of sandwiches toward him. "Dig in. I hope you like mustard."

Ignoring the crowd around them, he listened to Sharmane recapping some of the things they'd seen and done, at the same time enjoying the sound of her cheery voice and watching her animated expressions. But his mind was racing too much to respond.

All night long he'd tried to figure out what made him want to spend a week with this woman, and he hadn't come up with any answers. Now, he knew.

No one saw him as Alex Brunnel, the man. Instead, people only saw him as A. R. Brunnel, founder and owner of Arby Enterprises, Inc. People perceived him as one of the rich and famous set. He was rich, but he certainly wasn't famous, nor did he particularly like the lifestyle that went with it or the people who did. Because of it, though, people treated him differently than their other friends, and that included members of his church, where people should have known better.

Outside of his business he tried to lead an ordinary life, but people didn't share their ordinary daily happenings with him. If they weren't asking him to fund a project, they were asking if he could give someone they knew a job, or else they tried to impress him. He didn't want to be someone to be impressed. He wanted to be simply one of the guys.

Most of the single women he knew constantly flirted with him as a marriage prospect, compounded by their mothers frequently inviting him for a "casual" lunch or dinner, which was never casual when he got there. His own family was no better in their matchmaking attempts. And because of this, many of the other single men treated him with a cold respect to his face, but he could tell they were jealous. They didn't know what it was like to be pursued for only the wrong reasons.

He tried to be generous with his tithes and offerings and did his best to help those who needed it. Over time, though, the never-ending flow of people asking him for money or favors or trying to match him with their single daughters simply wore him down.

All he wanted was a simple friendship that had nothing to do with anything he owned or had achieved or what he could do for the other person.

And then he met Sharmane. After this week, she would never see him again, which was apparently fine with her. She had made him lunch, without expecting anything in return. It was such an ordinary thing for most people, but not for him.

It made him realize he needed more than a vacation from his work, he needed a vacation from his life. After the week was over he would be strengthened and refreshed, and he could go back to the rat race a new man. Until then, being with Sharmane was exactly what he needed. However, the only way to do this would be to not let her know who he really was. He couldn't take the chance that once she knew, she would become just like everyone else.

With Sharmane, he intended to be just Alex Brunnel, ordinary guy, and not A. R. Brunnel, walking wallet.

"Well, I guess that's about it for the Capilano Canyon. What do you want to do this afternoon?"

Alex blinked and concentrated on Sharmane's question. "I don't know. How about Stanley Park?"

"Sure, since we're so close. Let's go."

He helped gather the empty containers, and Sharmane again lifted her backpack to her shoulders. Now that he knew what had been in it, he felt guilty knowing she'd carried that weight all the time, just so they could have a cheap lunch. It made him appreciate her all the more.

She handed him her camera. "I want you to take a couple of pictures of me just so I can prove I did this. You wait here, and I'm going to stand by the entrance to the bridge. Take my picture so you get lots of scenery around me, and then I'm going to do the same as that kid did earlier. When I get to the middle, I'm going to wave. Then take my picture again. See you on the other side." That said, she jogged off in the direction of the bridge.

Alex found it strangely humbling to have someone give him orders. He suspected the time spent this week with Sharmane would provide many opportunities to experience things he wasn't used to.

He lifted Sharmane's camera to his eye to scan the area before she got there.

"Mr. Brunnel? Is that you?"

Alex didn't move, nor did he lower the camera in the hope that the speaker would think he was mistaken. He didn't look, but by the sound of the voice the next time, the speaker was closer. "Mr. Brunnel? What are you doing here?"

Alex tightened his grip on the camera then brought it down to his side. Everyone he knew should have been at work, and if not, this crowded tourist attraction should have been a safe hiding place. However, he hadn't calculated teenagers into the equation. Since it was summer holidays, they weren't in school.

One of his nephew's friends from the youth group

approached him, his girlfriend clinging to his arm.

Quickly, he scanned the area for Sharmane. Fortunately she was still heading toward the bridge, having been distracted by something along the way.

Alex nodded a greeting. "Kyle, Allyson. Hello."

"Where's Jason? I saw his car. But I didn't see yours."

There was a good reason for that. Yesterday, Sharmane had told him about her eight-year-old compact with some kind of transmission problem. If the expense of one repair was such a financial strain that it canceled her vacation, he didn't want to intimidate her by picking her up in his new car. Therefore, for the week, he'd traded his brand-new luxury car for his nephew's fifteen-year-old import.

Jason was thrilled with the trade, but Jason's father was not. However, Alex couldn't think of anyone else he could swap cars with on short notice and not need to explain why. His mechanic had agreed to do a tune-up and quick check, and then had ended up doing an all-nighter fixing every little thing wrong with Jason's car, which was quite an extensive list. Jason wouldn't recognize his own car when he got it back.

"Jason's not here. He had to work today, and he's got my car."

Kyle's blank expression told him that Kyle didn't understand what was going on, but fortunately he didn't ask for details. "Oh. Well. See you 'round, I guess."

They took their leave, giving Alex the chance to once again watch Sharmane.

He snapped a few pictures just as she arrived at the

entrance to the bridge and then positioned himself to get a good shot of her once she made it to the center. She waved bravely, and once he had a few more pictures, he pocketed the camera and joined her on the other side. Sharmane wanted to bypass the gift shop, but Alex insisted that he had to have one tacky souvenir of every place they went. He bought a small souvenir for Sharmane and she tried to protest, but he gave it to her anyway.

Alex didn't say much as he drove back across the Lions Gate Bridge and into Stanley Park.

"I know!" Sharmane chirped. "How about if we go around the Seawall? I've been to the Aquarium recently, but I've never actually been on the Seawall."

"Uh, me neither."

"It's five and a half miles around. Maybe we can rent in-line skates."

Alex knotted his brows. He'd never been on in-line skates in his life and doubted he could go five blocks without falling, never mind five miles. "I'd think I'd rather walk."

Chapter 3

Sharmane slipped her camera into her pocket. Alex hadn't said no, but he hadn't exactly been enthusiastic. Walking around the Seawall might not exactly be a "touristy" thing to do, but it was something she'd never done.

They started their walk at Brockton Point. First she took a picture of Alex standing at the railing overlooking the inlet, and then he took her picture as she ran to the water's edge to pick up a seashell. Then they began their journey around the perimeter of Stanley Park.

If she had been alone she wouldn't have gone on the Seawall because parts of it tended to be secluded. Being with a man who towered over her by nearly a foot made her feel safe. However, walking with Alex was as quiet as if she had been alone.

She wished she knew what was going on in his mind. At times he slowed his pace, looked out toward the water, inhaled deeply, and smiled as he exhaled. After awhile she couldn't stand the silence and found herself starting to babble. Alex didn't seem to mind. He agreed or disagreed with her comments and, to her surprise, encouraged her to keep yakking.

The tide was at midpoint when they arrived at the statue of the lady in the wetsuit. Sharmane snapped a picture of it. "Lots of people think she's a mermaid, but she's not, you know."

"I once read a little history blurb on her, but I can't remember the story."

"Me neither. I'll have to look it up when I get home."

As they continued on, Alex joined her in some small talk and a few jokes, as well as tossing suggestions for the rest of the week back and forth without coming to a firm decision.

The next point of interest was the dreaded Lions Gate Bridge. Despite Sharmane's apprehension of driving over it, being underneath the massive structure fascinated her. The thumps and clanks of the traffic on the metal surface increased in volume as they approached. Once directly beneath it they stopped to better see the magnitude of the construction from that viewpoint.

"I never expected it to be this noisy underneath. Aren't you going to take a picture of it?"

Sharmane pretended to shudder. "No way. I hate that bridge."

Alex laughed. It was a wonderful sound, deep and rich, and it warmed her heart. Sharmane found herself taking a picture of the stupid bridge not because she wanted to remember the bridge, but because the picture would remind her of Alex's laugh.

"There. I hope you're happy," she grumbled.

To her surprise, he stepped in front of her, grasping her hands over the top of the small camera. A smile lit his face, and he spoke so softly she barely heard him. "You know, I am happy. This is exactly what I needed. I want to thank you for including me in your plans."

She stared up at his face, mesmerized. She didn't know why, but Sharmane knew he wasn't joking. She had no idea why goofing off around town would mean so much to him, but she had to take his words at face value.

Small crinkles still highlighted the corners of his eyes. "Come on," he said. "Let's keep going."

To her surprise, he didn't completely drop her hands. He let go the hand holding her camera but kept her other hand still clasped within his. He smiled and began to walk as if it were natural for them to be holding hands.

Even though it shouldn't have, it felt right. He was easy to talk to. Before she realized what she was saying, she'd told him all about her job as office gofer and accounts payable clerk. They shared their favorite Bible verses, as well as discussed their respective churches. Sharmane found herself almost envying him his years growing up in an atmosphere where his family all attended the same church and worshiped together, since her family were not Christians.

As they passed Prospect Point and began their journey on the ocean side of the park, the air became cooler. By the time they reached Siwash Rock, the constant breeze off the ocean became downright cold, making her regret her choice of shorts instead of cotton pants.

When she could no longer suppress the chill, she

shivered. Alex stopped dead in his tracks, checked the goose bumps running up her bare arms and legs, and frowned. He began to rub her arms with his large and very warm hands, the friction warming her marginally.

"Why didn't you say you were cold? Let's change sides. Maybe I can block the wind."

She expected him to simply move to her other side, but he took his time to pick the camera out of her fingers and slip it into his pocket before he stepped to shelter her from the cold. Without hesitation, he grasped her other hand and continued walking at a slightly faster pace.

"Look over there." Alex pointed out to the ocean. "Can you see it? There's a seal."

"I think technically that's a sea lion, although I can't say I know what the difference is. I think I'll look it up when I get home, when I check out the story of the lady in the wetsuit."

He smiled again, and Sharmane felt something inside her stomach quiver. "Will you really?"

Sharmane swallowed past the frog in her throat. "Uh, yeah." Part of her wanted to take a picture of the animal, but a bigger part didn't want to let go of his hand. She tried to convince herself the only reason was that his hand was so warm.

Only a few brave souls were in the water when they reached the Third Beach, in comparison to the offshore beach near their starting point at the east side of the park, which had been crowded.

They kept walking and soon turned to a southeasterly direction with the wind at their backs. Away from the ocean the temperature continued to warm as they made their way inland and walked toward the Lost Lagoon.

Countless ducks, Canada geese, and majestic swans floated leisurely in the calm water. Along the shore of the small lake many swans sat atop nests surrounded on three sides by wire fences with the open side toward the water. Signs cautioned people not to bother the swans.

Sharmane pointed to a mother swan as they passed a nest. "It looks like soon there's going to be little swanlings swimming around."

He smiled that adorable smile again. "Swanlings?"

"You know. Baby swans. I don't know what they're called."

"Let me guess. Something else for you to look up, right?"

She returned his smile and nodded. "Right."

"I had no idea going on vacation would be so educational."

"I'm not going to comment."

Before she had to ask, Alex reached into his pocket and returned her camera. Unfortunately, in order to take any pictures, he had to release her hand and Sharmane missed the contact. Despite the beauty of the lagoon, she limited herself to three shots, and they continued on.

They followed the path to walk underneath West Georgia Street and approached the marina.

Sharmane sighed. "Look at all those yachts. You know, just one of them costs more than I make in a year. Also, I think you have to pay a huge membership fee to join these things. Have you ever wondered what it would be like to be so rich?"

Alex stiffened. This was the last thing he wanted to talk about with Sharmane. "It's not all it's cracked up to be," he mumbled. He knew exactly how much the membership here cost, because he knew people who moored their boats here.

"You know, the only time I've ever been on a boat is the ferry to Vancouver Island. That's where I was going to go, you know. I was going to drive all over Vancouver Island all week." She breathed a defeated little sigh that nearly broke his heart.

Alex could count the times he'd taken the ferry on one hand, even though he'd lived here his entire life. Every time he had to go to the island on business, he flew because the ferry took too long. "Why don't we do that tomorrow? We can take an early ferry out of Tswwassen, and I'll bet you'd like to see the flowers at the Butchart Gardens. We can spend the morning there, spend a little time in Victoria, drive to Nanaimo for dinner, then come home on the late ferry to Horseshoe Bay."

Her eyes widened, and her smile made his heart quicken. "That sounds great!"

While she was still lost in thought, Alex picked up her hand and led her onward. They were almost finished at the Seawall, and after all that walking he was starving and more than a little tired.

"I hope you don't mind if I take lots of pictures."

He grinned. He was beginning to wonder if that camera was permanently attached to her. "I think I expected that."

Her tiny hand squeezed his. "Thanks, Alex. That's going to be such fun."

Alex tightened his grip, not allowing her to let go as they headed for his nephew's car. He couldn't remember the last time he'd been able to enjoy the simplicity of holding a woman's hand without fear of complications. He couldn't help but like Sharmane, and surely she could see that. Yet, she didn't cling to him as other women did as soon as he let his guard down.

She insisted on stopping for a quick burger, and Alex didn't argue. Conversation flowed, and he'd never enjoyed a greasy burger and limp fries more.

Much too soon, they were standing at her front door. Sharmane reached inside her backpack and removed her wallet.

"How much do I owe you? Remember, you paid for my admission. And I want to pay for half the gas."

"Don't worry about it."

"And tomorrow there will be the cost of the ferry and even more gas. I want to give you the money now, in case it bruises your male ego for me to pay in front of you."

"Forget it."

She crossed her arms, still holding her wallet in one hand. "We agreed to each pay our own expenses, and I intend to do exactly that. And I'm going to pay for at least half of the gas since we're using your car. I know you weren't planning on doing this. I don't want to burden you with all the expense."

He bit his bottom lip to hold back his smile. The money she was talking about was pocket change to him.

"It's no burden, don't worry about it. I'm having a wonderful time."

Sharmane rested her hand on his forearm. Alex stared down at the point of contact. Her touch was gentle, and he was sure she only meant to emphasize her words, but his pulse jumped at her simple gesture.

"I mean it, Alex. I know you hadn't planned all this driving and stuff. I don't want it to be a big expense for you. I'm serious. Let me pay."

Alex didn't doubt that she meant it, and he was no longer smiling. "I don't want your money. All I want is your company."

She shook her head. "I know exactly how much gas your car takes, so don't try and fool me. I'm also paying for my own admissions and for half the ferry cost. If I don't pay for my share of this vacation, it ends today."

Alex felt like he'd just been punched in the gut. He couldn't believe this was happening to him, of all people. His words almost choked him, but he forced himself to say it. "All right. I'll let you know how much you owe me for the gas."

"Not just the gas. Everything."

He sucked in a deep breath and let it go. He didn't want her to pay a thing. Suddenly, he needed more than just an escape for himself; he wanted this to be the best vacation Sharmane ever had.

"Alex. . ."

He gritted his teeth. "Okay. I'll keep track of what everything costs, and you can pay me at the end of the week."

Her frown changed into a wide smile, and Alex never thought that losing a battle could feel so good.

"Okay, then I'll see you tomorrow. Good night." And the door closed.

For a few moments Alex remained standing, facing the closed door. He didn't think it would ever happen, but he thought he just might be falling in love.

Chapter 4

Alex checked the time as he rang Sharmane's doorbell. He still couldn't believe he was here. The sun had only just started to rise a few minutes ago. He should still have been in bed at this hour, yet he'd already been driving for an hour.

By taking an extra hot shower he'd managed to erase most of the stiffness from his legs, but he still regretted his suggestion of another day filled with more walking. If nothing else, this was a reminder to get some regular exercise rather than sit behind his desk all week long.

The door opened. "Cygnets!" Sharmane exclaimed.

Alex blinked. The words he expected to hear were "good morning," or even better would have been "good to see you." He glanced behind himself for something out of the ordinary, and seeing nothing, turned back to Sharmane.

She laughed at his blank expression. "Baby swans are called cygnets."

"That's nice. Are you ready to go?"

She nodded. "Yes. I have been waiting for you. I will

only be a minute."

Today she was dressed in jeans and a baggy pink T-shirt. Her blond hair was tied in a loose ponytail, and she looked fresh and alert, unlike how he felt. Rather than dwell on his own misery, he followed her inside.

Her house was small and functional yet had a homey and friendly atmosphere. Once in the kitchen, she picked up her backpack, giving him a bad feeling.

"I hope you haven't packed a lunch this time."

"But—"

He held up one hand. "Please, don't argue, I want to buy you lunch. Consider it my treat."

She opened her mouth, but before she could speak, Alex stiffened, crossed his arms, narrowed his eyes, and glared down at her. Sharmane's eyes widened, her mouth closed, and without a word, she laid the backpack on the table then returned a number of containers to the fridge.

"Thank you," he muttered.

She reached inside the backpack one more time. "Have you had breakfast?"

Alex pressed one hand into his stomach. Just the mention of food caused it to grumble. He'd given his housekeeper the week off, so he didn't have to face her questions every day, and he hadn't had time to fix himself something, so he'd left without eating. "No."

She pulled out a bag containing three muffins. "Me neither. We can eat these in the car while we're waiting in the ferry lineup."

He would give her that one, but only as a technicality. She ignored his lack of response. "I made coffee, and

I've got a spare travel mug you can borrow. Want some?"

"Yes, please," he mumbled.

She poured the coffee, transferred her wallet and camera from the backpack into her purse, and nearly shoved him out the door.

Sharmane tried to wipe the smile off her face as she made herself comfortable in Alex's car. For years she had wanted to tour Vancouver Island. Finally, she had saved up enough money to spend a week in motels and cover all the expenses comfortably. When her transmission blew, her dream crumbled, and she didn't know if she would ever get another opportunity. Alex's suggestion to catch the first ferry and do it in a day might have been pushing it, but this was exactly what she wanted to do. She'd miss the whale watching tour she wanted to attend, but this was the next best thing.

She gazed out the window and sighed. "Look, the sky is still a little pink from the sunrise."

He mumbled something she couldn't quite hear.

"Smile! It's going to be a gorgeous day!" She turned to face him, but he wasn't wearing anything close to a smile. "You're not a morning person, are you?"

"I'm not used to getting up before dawn," he mumbled again.

Sharmane patted herself on the back for the coffee she'd thought to make this morning, because he certainly could use it. After a few sips his mood improved, and soon he was behaving human again.

Since it was so early, they managed to avoid most of

the rush hour traffic. They arrived at the ferry dock in plenty of time to catch the first sailing and ate the muffins before they were directed onto the ferry.

Today they were both prepared for the cold. They donned their jackets and climbed the stairs to the upper deck to enjoy the morning ocean air. Conversation flowed easily as they walked through all areas of the ferry, and Alex even apologized for being such a grump. They refilled their coffee mugs at the cafeteria just before all passengers descended to the lower levels to prepare for docking at Victoria.

By the time they arrived at the Butchart Gardens, Sharmane was ready to burst at the seams. She couldn't wipe the smile off her face as they stood in the short line-up to enter, and she was in such a great mood she couldn't bring herself to protest as Alex paid her admission.

The beauty of the well laid out grounds and the myriad of color and fragrance was like nothing she had imagined. None of the tourist brochures served justice to the magnificence of the acres and acres of flowers from around the globe.

The wonder of God's creation was everywhere, from every delicate blossom to the selectively arranged boulders, from the carefully laid out rose garden to the area quarried out for the tall arching fountain, from the quaintly styled tea house and restaurant to the serenity of the fishes and turtles in the quiet pond surrounded by the large weeping trees.

Her favorite of all was the sunken Japanese Garden, and she shot an entire roll of film in that area alone.

Even though plants and flowers weren't exactly a "guy" thing, Alex very politely expressed his appreciation of the various sections. She appreciated the way he humored her by frequently offering to take a picture of her amongst the flowers, especially the roses, which were her favorites. Sharmane found herself laughing when he struck up a few silly poses standing among the pretty blossoms so she could take his picture.

Despite wanting to stay longer, Sharmane didn't want to push her luck. Only because he made her promise, she bit her tongue when he treated her to lunch at the tea-room. Following that, they walked one last time through the Japanese Gardens and headed for the exit. However, instead of going to the gate, Alex went to the gift shop.

"Alex, I—"

He wagged one finger in the air. "I told you, I want to buy a tacky souvenir of every place we go, and you agreed."

She nodded and sighed. She would have three rolls of pictures to remind her of this very special day, but a small souvenir probably wouldn't hurt.

The vast selection of things to buy astounded her. The gift shop held everything from seed packets to posters to jewelry and china to clothing. They browsed through every item the store held, and Sharmane enjoyed every minute of it. For the longest time, she adored a thin gold watch with a picture of a rose on the face and rhinestones all around instead of numbers. Since she already had a perfectly good watch, Sharmane selected a T-shirt with a rose on it instead, and Alex bought a key chain and a pot holder he claimed was for his mother.

Before they left, Sharmane made a short detour to the ladies room, and they left for their next destination, Victoria's famed Inner Harbor area. Because he had humored her at the Butchart Gardens, she pretended to enjoy the antique car museum in downtown Victoria, but they both enjoyed the wax museum. They walked into the Empress Hotel to check out the grand old building, and she couldn't help but be impressed by the harpist in one of the elegant dining rooms.

By mid-afternoon, they were back in the car and on the highway headed for Nanaimo. The countryside was beautiful and mostly undisturbed, and taking into account all the sights of the day, Sharmane couldn't remember ever having enjoyed herself more. The sky started to cloud over, which made the long drive ahead of them more comfortable without the sun blaring down on them.

"That was wonderful, especially the gardens. Thank you so much for doing this."

"Don't mention it. It was nice."

"Nice? What kind of lame word is 'nice'?"

He laughed, making Sharmane's insides turned to jelly.

"The flowers were *nice*, but I liked the frogs best."

Sharmane couldn't hold back her smile, so she swatted him in the arm. "Since we got lots of pictures of you, I'll have doubles made up. Don't you have a camera?"

His smile disappeared in the blink of an eye, and his attention turned completely to the road in front of them. "Yes, I have a camera, it's just—I think you'd probably take better pictures than me."

"You just lack confidence. It's not hard to take good

pictures, but it is an art. You have to have a critical eye and a little imagination. I took a course once. You know, the kind for serious hobbyists. It was a lot of fun, and I learned a lot."

Apparently, he also had an interest in photography as a hobby, because he was able to share some good tips on lighting and perspective, making her wonder how he possibly could have thought she would take better pictures.

Throughout the three-hour drive, she was both surprised and delighted to share all their common interests and then amiably agree to disagree on others.

She couldn't help but like him, but she tempered her thoughts with the knowledge that despite all the time they'd spent together in the last three days, she really didn't know much about him.

Every time she talked to him he divulged many personal details about his likes and dislikes, his preferences, and his interests. However, she didn't know anything about his life. Every time the conversation drifted to his job, his family, his friends, or anything else that would have told her specific information he became evasive; and he did it in such a way that the conversation was over by the time she realized he hadn't told her what she wanted to know.

She still didn't know what he did for a living or if he even had a job, nor did she know where he lived or which church he went to, even though she'd been more than open in telling him those same details about herself.

At first she had tried not to think about it, but the more he sidestepped her hints, then her direct questions, she began to suspect he was doing it on purpose, and she wished she knew why. If he was embarrassed because he was unemployed, she thought she'd been more than clear that it didn't matter to her. Last night, she'd wanted to call him and discuss their plans for the day, but she'd lost the cell phone number he had given her. When she tried to look his number up in the phone book, the only A. Brunnel listed was an address in an area where only the very wealthy lived.

By the time they arrived at Nanaimo they were starving, so they picked the first restaurant they saw, which was a Chinese buffet. As was becoming common, they talked until they lost track of time, then ran laughing to the car, because neither of them could remember when the last ferry sailed.

Fortunately, they caught it, and Sharmane considered it one more adventure to make the trip across the Strait of Georgia in the dark.

The night had turned cold, and Alex was glad he'd remembered to bring a jacket, because that allowed them to stand on the upper deck to enjoy the quiet of the water in the silence of the dark night. Unfortunately the sky was black, the heavy cloud cover completely obliterating the moon and stars. The glory of God's universe above them would have been the perfect end to a perfect day.

Despite countless marathon sessions with his business, he couldn't ever remember being so tired, but this was a good tired. For two days they'd done nothing but walk and sightsee, and despite knowing how stiff he was going to be tomorrow, he knew he'd never regret it. He closed his eyes and inhaled a deep breath of the cool ocean air. A particularly cold gust caused them both to shiver, but he didn't want to go inside. Without speaking, he gently rested his hands on Sharmane's shoulders and guided her to stand with her back nestled into him so they could stand together for warmth. He kept one hand on her shoulder and covered her hand holding the railing with his.

She was so short he could comfortably rest his chin on the top of her head. She didn't protest, and except for the odd strand of hair blowing up to tickle his face, nothing moved except the air around them and the gentle vibration and slight rocking of the moving ferry.

If he could make time stand still, this would be the moment. Already, he had to acknowledge how much he would miss her when their time together was up.

He had never been the sentimental type, but he was accumulating a host of souvenirs so that he would never forget this short week.

Deep down inside, he had to know that Sharmane would not easily forget him. He had more or less tagged along on her dream, but she had created his. He knew she had plenty of photos with him in them, but he wanted to be more than a fond reminder relegated to an old box of vacation memories. He wanted her to think of him often, because he knew he would think of her every day.

During the few minutes they had not been together at the gift shop at the Butchart Gardens, he'd bought the watch she'd been so enamored with.

The woman had elegant taste. When he paid for the

watch, he confirmed what he suspected when she first looked at it. What she assumed were rhinestones adorning the watch were really diamonds. No doubt when she saw it out of the display case she would realize that, and knowing Sharmane, she would also question his ability to pay for it. As much as he battled with it, he knew that when their vacation was over his conscience would not let them separate without telling her who he really was. Once she knew, she wouldn't question the expense. Also, once she knew, he doubted she would ever want to see him again because of his deceit.

Alex squeezed his eyes shut and pressed himself closer to Sharmane. He couldn't lie to himself; he was deceiving her. He prayed God would forgive him, but he didn't want to take the chance that when he told her the truth, everything would change. Sunday he would confess, but until then, as difficult as it was, he would continue to keep his secrets.

He knew she was starting to wonder what it was he was hiding, and so far he'd been able to circumvent her questions, but he didn't know how long he would be able to keep it up and still remain credible.

He bowed his head and nuzzled his face into her hair, wondering if this would be the only time he'd be able to hold her like this, using the cold for an excuse. In not being completely honest with her, he was forfeiting his right to do what he most wanted, and that was to court her properly.

"Did you feel that? It's starting to rain."

Alex raised his head, and a drop of rain landed on his forehead. "It's just a drop or two. It might stop." He prayed for it to stop. He didn't want the moment to be broken.

The drizzle increased. She moved, forcing him to release her. "It's not. We'd better go inside."

The mood inside was nothing like the early morning trip. Most people were sitting quietly, the outer decks on all levels were all but deserted, and with the exception of the noise of the ferry's engine, all was quiet.

Sharmane sat in one of the padded seats beside the window, so Alex lowered himself beside her. It was good to get his weight off his feet, but he would have preferred to be outside in the cool air to stay alert.

"So where do you think we should go tomorrow?"

Alex fought to hold back a yawn. "Is there anything we can do that we won't have to walk all day? I'm positive we walked twice as much today as we did yesterday."

Her eyebrows scrunched, and she squeezed her lips together in such a way that her mouth tilted. "I don't know. I doubt it. Let me think." Her blond hair hung in a straggly mess around her face, and she swiped one hand through it to push it back.

He forced himself to look away. The urge to kiss her was almost overwhelming. Instead, he pressed himself into the soft seat, stretched his weary legs out in front of him, and draped one arm behind her along the back of the chair.

Outside, the rain increased to a steady drone. Every once in a while, the wind splattered a gust of rain against the window. Inside the ferry's sitting area, all was warm and dry.

"It's probably going to rain all day, so we'll have to

pick something indoors."

"Sounds like a good idea."

"You're probably all flowered out, so I guess you don't want to go to Queen Elizabeth Park to see the conservatory where all the flowers are."

"You got that right."

If he couldn't kiss her, then he had to touch her. Alex brushed his fingers along her shoulder, and when she didn't seem to mind he pulled her just a little closer. She took him up on his hint and rested her head on his shoulder.

"What about the art gallery?"

There weren't many places that attracted tourists where he would see some of the upper crust people he knew, but the art gallery would surely be one of them, and therefore, he refused to go there. "Nope. Too boring."

"I guess going up the gondola and taking a hike on Grouse Mountain is out. You wouldn't count the long drive as being inside, would you?"

He rested his head against the side of hers, smiling to himself at the softness of her hair. "Nope."

"I have a coupon for skydiving at that place in Matsqui. You don't have to walk, you just kind of fall."

He let his eyes drift shut. "You're joking, right?" he mumbled.

Sharmane chuckled. She had been joking, but she knew someone who had tried skydiving once. An instructor went down with the person to make sure the parachute opened properly and all went well. She didn't really want to do such a dangerous thing, but she had to ask, just to see his reaction—which was exactly as she expected.

"Yes, I'm joking. Besides, I don't think they do parachuting in the rain. We could go to the Vancouver Aquarium at Stanley Park. That's indoors. But it means walking."

"Uh-uh."

Sharmane felt his head press into the top of hers a little more. She could see that he was tired, after all, for two days they had done nothing but walk, but she really couldn't think of anything touristy that involved sitting. For a few minutes, she tried to think of something to do that didn't involve too much walking.

"How about the Pacific Space Center? They have lots of features to sit for. I hear the laser show is great."

She waited, but there was no response. Sharmane was about to lift her head when she heard Alex's soft snore.

Chapter 5

Alex pocketed the tickets, led Sharmane to one of the rear cars, and stood behind her as she climbed the two stairs.

She turned her head back over her shoulder and smiled so sweetly he nearly stumbled. "I've never been on a real train. Taking the Royal Hudson was such a great idea!"

"It came to me in a moment of genius."

She rolled her eyes and harrumphed, and they stepped into the car to select their seats. Alex motioned Sharmane to take the window seat, and they waited for all the passengers to board.

She was being so polite about it, but he still felt stupid about last night. The last thing he remembered was discussing suggestions for the remainder of their vacation, and the next thing he knew Sharmane was shaking him, saying that they were about to dock.

The hour-long drive between her house and his was taking its toll. In addition to the late hours, all the driving, the lack of sleep, and two days of solid walking, the motion of the ferry had finished him off. He couldn't remember the last time he'd been so embarrassed. But, Sharmane had been so gracious about it he felt another piece of his heart melting away in her grasp, and she didn't even know it. He wished he could explain that because of the distance between her house and his, he'd only had four hours sleep that night, but he couldn't without admitting that he lived in the exclusive British Properties area of West Vancouver.

He stared out the window as he spoke. "I'm really sorry about last night." The words having been said, he returned his attention to her face.

"Don't worry about it. I guess I'm used to more activity than you are. I do a lot of running around at work, it's a very busy office, and I'm constantly doing errands and running back and forth to the stockroom all day."

She looked him straight in the eye and he knew what she expected him to say. He cleared his throat. "I'm used to sitting a lot."

She sighed, and her disappointment pierced his soul. Evading her questions was taking its toll; the guilt was getting to him, but there wasn't any other way. When he did come clean, she would hate him for it. He couldn't allow that to happen until he had spent all the time with her he could. After their excursion today, there were only three days left of their time together, but that was only if they counted Sunday, which he wasn't sure she did.

The porter, dressed in a classic uniform, walked down the aisle checking tickets, and the train pulled out of the station at the reasonable time of 10 A.M. Today, the sun had been up before he was. And also today, the only walking they would do would be for an hour in Squamish. After that, they would climb aboard the *MV Britannia* for a cruise returning to Vancouver's Harbor Cruises Marina, where they would be bused back to the train station to collect the car and go home, unless they made other plans for the evening.

Sharmane patted her purse. "Did you bring your camera today? I brought extra film."

He smiled, not wanting to think of how many rolls she'd already taken. "I'm going to leave all the photography up to you."

Her return smile did strange things to his stomach; things that had nothing to do with the swaying of the train as it lumbered down the track.

"I've never been to Squamish before. I'll bet they have a section of town specially made up for the tourists to have lunch. That will be so much fun. And I'm so excited about taking the cruise back. I don't even care if it's still raining." She patted her purse again. "This time I brought my fold-up umbrella. I don't want to get caught in the rain again." She proceeded to dig a pile of brochures out of her purse and began to flip through them. "I got these while you were paying for the tickets. It says that King George rode the Royal Hudson number 2860 in 1939. It was restored in 1974, and now it's the only antique steam engine in main line service in North America today."

He looked down at her purse. He could never figure out the hidden depths of a woman's purse, and he didn't figure this was the time to find out. "This is a vacation, not a fact-finding mission. Can't you just enjoy the ride?"

"But I am enjoying the ride."

Alex couldn't stop himself. He reached for her hand and gave it a gentle squeeze. "Me, too." Without letting go, he switched his attention to the mountain scenery on one side, and the Queen Charlotte Channel on the other as they rode toward the town of Squamish. The contrast between the mountain on one side and the water on the other would have made a marvelous picture. He let his mind wander to one day renting a helicopter with Sharmane and flying over the channel to get a picture of the old black train on the track on the mountainside in what was probably a breathtaking scenic shot.

Sharmane looked down at their joined hands and felt the heat creeping up her cheeks. He'd been more than clear that he didn't want to let go, and she didn't protest. She was enjoying more than just the ride.

Her original plans of driving around alone could in no way compare to what she was now experiencing. She'd never before felt so close to another person, most especially not a man. More than the simple pleasure of not being alone, it even went beyond sharing a good time with a friend. Sharmane in no way believed in love at first sight, but even knowing how short a time it had been since they met, she wondered if she could possibly be falling for a man she really didn't know.

He was kind and gentle, generous to a fault, they shared many common interests, but other than basic personality traits, what she knew about him could fit in a thimble.

Considering the questionable condition of his car in

comparison to the way it ran, she thought he could be a mechanic, but he admitted to sitting most of the time, and a mechanic wouldn't do that. She suspected he wasn't unemployed as she originally assumed, but still, she couldn't be sure because every time she brought up anything even remotely hinting at what he did for a living, he very efficiently skirted the issue. Likewise, details of his home, including the location and if it was a small apartment or a castle fit for a king were also vague.

Another thing that confused her was that so far everything they had done was relatively inexpensive, as far as tourist spots went. However, she had sneaked a peek at the prices for the different packages for today's excursion, and he had chosen the most expensive options, and then insisted that it was his treat, telling her in no uncertain terms that for once, she was not to argue.

The change in his demeanor had caught her off guard. She had seen a brief glimpse of it when he insisted she not pack a lunch before their excursion to Vancouver Island. But today at the train station, when she had actually started to argue with him, the change had shocked her. Instead of the carefree and gentle Alex she was used to, in an instant he became a man she didn't want to cross, a man whose authority was not to be questioned. She wasn't the only one to notice. Even the clerk at the ticket counter treated him differently than the other people buying tickets. But when he tucked his wallet into the pocket of his jeans and turned around, all was the same again, as if nothing had happened.

She didn't understand it, and she didn't know what

to think. All she knew was that she'd never enjoyed herself so much.

"I think you wanted to discuss what we were going to do tomorrow and Saturday."

Sharmane blinked, shaken out of her musings. "Uh, yes. The forecast is bright and sunny for both days."

He smiled, and Sharmane's foolish heart fluttered.

"How about something that's supposed to be the ultimate in relaxing. Ever been fishing?"

"Fishing?"

He nodded. "You know. You sit in a boat in the middle of a lake, put a worm on a hook, toss it into the water, and pull out a fish."

"I've never been fishing before. I don't know what to do, and I don't have a fishing rod or anything."

"Me neither. But my brother and his son go fishing all the time. It sounds pretty easy, and they seem to have a good time. I can find out their favorite spot, and I'll bet I could even borrow all their fishing equipment and their boat. It's one of those six-seater types."

Sharmane's breath caught and her whole body stiffened. "Really? You can borrow a boat? A real boat? They wouldn't mind?"

"Stan's been telling me for years I should give it a try, so I think he'd welcome the opportunity to give it to me."

"Wow. . .a boat. . ."

"It's not a big deal. We're going on a boat today for the return trip."

She waved her free hand in the air, which also served to remind her that he was still holding onto her left hand.

"That's different. That's a big cruise ship with a restaurant and hundreds of people on it, a whole crew and a captain and everything. I think it would be fun to go on a little boat, just the two of us."

He patted her hand. "Then it's settled. Today, we'll be pampered, and tomorrow, we'll be lazy."

And they were pampered. They had a lovely brunch in the train's parlor car and then returned to their seats to chat while they enjoyed the beauty of the scenery on their trip through the mountains.

By the time the arrived at the Squamish station, the rain had stopped.

As soon as they left the passenger car, they walked alongside the train so Sharmane could take a few pictures of the grand old engine. Even though it wasn't moving, steam still puffed out the smokestack. She made sure to take a picture of the front of the glossy black engine, highlighting the big shiny numbers.

During their leisurely stroll in Squamish, even though neither of them was hungry, they stopped at the cutest little bistro for coffee and dessert. As usual, they got lost in conversation, and again had to run all the way to where the *MV Britannia* was docked.

Once aboard, Sharmane imagined what it must have been like aboard the *Titanic* as they sailed along, the wind in her hair and the ocean breeze in her face, only she could always see the shore, and this boat wasn't going to sink. Mid-afternoon, they had a meal of baked salmon unlike any Sharmane had ever experienced and then spent the rest of the trip on the outside deck.

As they neared Lion's Bay, they passed the ferry coming out of the Horseshoe Bay terminal on its way to Nanaimo, and the people on both boats waved at each other in passing. While exploring the cruise ship, Sharmane discovered that while nowhere near the size of an ocean liner, the *MV Britannia's* capacity was five hundred people, which she considered absolutely huge.

An air-conditioned tour bus returned them to the rail station, but rather than drive through rush hour traffic, Alex insisted on stopping for dinner. She was surprised that she could eat anything, considering all she'd eaten in the course of their day, but told herself that such a vacation could only happen once in a lifetime.

Too soon, they were standing on her doorstep. After Alex made sure there were no intruders inside, he stepped close to her and rested his fingers on her cheek, making Sharmane's heartbeat quicken.

"I'd really like to invite myself in, but I have to be at my brother's house before it gets too late, so I can get all that fishing stuff and make sure everything is okay with the boat."

His fingers moved slightly, and his thumb drifted to her chin. Sharmane struggled to breathe. Holding hands, which should have been merely an affectionate gesture, had set her insides aflutter, but now his simple touch turned her knees to jelly. She forced herself to clear her throat so she could speak. "Do you want to phone him first?"

He stepped closer. Her heart started to pound. "No, I'll call him on my cell; I don't want to get to his house too late, they all have to get up for work in the morning. I'll be back to pick you up at nine o'clock."

She could feel a slight pressure as he tipped up her chin. Part of her had been waiting for this moment, but part of her didn't want it. As much as she liked him, she didn't know anything about him.

Her eyes drifted shut anyway. His lips brushed hers briefly instead of the longer kiss she'd expected and had come to realize she wanted. He stepped back leaving her feeling strangely disappointed.

"See you tomorrow, Sharmane."

Chapter 6

Sharmane gasped as Alex pulled up in front of her house. There sat a white pickup which emphasized the perfection of the sleek candy-apple red speedboat behind it. She dashed out of the house leaving the door wide open and was standing beside the boat before Alex fully exited the truck.

She ran her fingers on the smooth finish. She'd never seen a boat like this up close, much less ridden in one. "Your brother let you *borrow* this?"

He grinned in response. "Pretty nice, huh?"

"This isn't for fishing. This is a speedboat."

"He fishes from it. But I think they water-ski mostly."

"Water-ski?" She pulled her hand back as quickly as if the boat were red-hot.

He grinned. "Don't worry, I didn't bring the skis. I didn't think it would be a good idea to try something like that without having someone experienced along. I only brought the fishing stuff."

Sharmane let her hand drop to her side. "Oh. Okay."

He opened the passenger door, where she could see a

small tackle box, a net, and two broken-down fishing rods stuffed behind the seat. "Get your stuff, and let's get going."

"I packed a lunch, and this time I hope you're not going to argue with me."

He laughed again, spreading warmth from Sharmane's heart to the tips of her toes. "I knew you would. Thank you."

She dashed into the house and returned with her backpack and camera, and they were on their way.

Sharmane carefully read his brother's handwritten directions to the Pitt River, where after much tribulation, Alex managed to back the trailer into the water and set the boat afloat. Soon everything they needed was stowed, and they were gliding north on their way to Pitt Lake, which was only accessible by boat.

The wind pushed Sharmane's hair back as she leaned slightly over the side, where her face wasn't sheltered by the small windshield. "This is so different than the ocean. It's so fresh and clean."

"Stan says this is a tidal lake. Except for it being fresh water, it's almost like the ocean. Except it's inland."

Sharmane laughed. "Those things make it not like the ocean at all."

The waterway widened, and Alex steered the boat into the center. The sparkling glossy red speedboat seemed drastically out of place in the pristine natural setting. The water was glassy smooth, so still that Sharmane could see perfect reflections of the blue sky and fluffy clouds above. Trees and boulders lined the shore, the varying shades of green also reflected in the water so perfectly it was like looking in a mirror, except for a slight ripple of the lake's surface. She snapped a couple pictures, knowing she could never completely capture the undefiled beauty on film.

Sharmane inhaled deeply, fully enjoying the scent of the water mingled with the pure woodsy scent of the trees.

The boat slowed, gradually drifting to a stop. "This seems like as good a spot as any."

She almost didn't feel right about being here, it was so perfect, but she could see other boats floating around closer to the shore. Another motorboat appeared briefly in the distance, turned around, and sped away, fading into the distance of the long lake. "How do you tell which spots are best for fishing?"

He shrugged his shoulders. "I don't know."

"Are we supposed to just let the boat float, or are we supposed to be driving slowly? Or is there an anchor or something?"

"I don't know that either."

"Much good you are. And when we catch our fish, do you have any idea what to do with it?"

He raised one finger in the air. "Yes. Stan says it's catch and release-only here. You have to let it go."

Her smile dropped. "Let it go? What's the point of fishing then?"

Again, he shrugged his shoulders. "It's a sport. The challenge of human versus fish. I have no intention of cutting open a fish and scooping out its innards, do you?"

Sharmane shuddered at the thought. "Catch and release will be fine."

Alex patted his shirt pocket. "Stan said we catch it, scoop it into the net, take the hook out of its mouth, pat it, and let it go. I've got the fishing licenses right here. Let's get started."

He pulled two white beat-up hats out from under the seat and plunked one on her head then the other on his. "These are Stan and Jason's fishing hats. Necessary equipment, they say."

Before she could think of a reply, he slotted the two fishing rods together, opened the tackle box, then pulled out a folded up piece of paper. "They told me that we can use either lures or flies to fish, depending on what kind of fish we want to catch."

"You mean we get a choice?"

He held up a shiny metal thing with a multi-edged hook dangling from it. "According to Stan, this kind of thing," he shook it for emphasis, "is a type of lure called a Wobbler."

Sharmane examined it. "What kind of fish does it catch?"

"I don't know. But I think he said you catch salmon and trout with flies." He opened the second slot and picked up a long skinny thing made with pink and white feathers fastened to a single hook. "This is a fly. There's a bunch of different kinds here. There's a Hootchie, a Rolled Muddler, a Doc Spratley, and that one is called a Woolly-something-or-other. He told me a few more, but I didn't write them all down."

"Oh, those are too cute to get all wet and let a fish put one in its mouth. What about those?" She pointed to the third drawer.

"These are called spinners." He held one up. "If I

remember correctly, this one is called a Dragonfly, but Stan spoke so fast, I don't remember the other names. It was hard enough to write down the names of the flies."

"What's the difference?"

He opened his mouth at the same time as he shrugged his shoulders.

Sharmane lifted her palms toward him to silence him. "Let me guess, you don't know."

"You guessed right." He started to fasten the pretty pink fly to one of the lines. "I think you should use the pink one. It looks like something a woman should use. I'll use this green one."

"If your brother does so much fishing and even has a boat, how come you don't go with him?"

"No time. It's not something I did as a boy, either. My family went to church on Sunday, not fishing. Stan and Jason tend to go Saturdays, but they don't go as often as they used to, now that Jason's seventeen."

Sharmane did a little mental calculating on the age of Alex's brother. "You must be the youngest, and Stan is the oldest right?"

"Uh-huh," he mumbled, sticking his tongue out the corner of his mouth as he threaded the line through the hole to fasten the pretty green feathered thing to the other line. He waved one hand in the air and grinned. "Ladies first."

"I don't know what to do."

"Put your thumb on the reel, release the catch, hold the rod over your shoulder, and cast. I'll wait for you to do it first."

"Thanks a lot," she muttered.

Doing exactly as instructed, Sharmane rested the rod on her shoulder then moved it slightly with every count, readying herself to cast it out. "One. . . Two. . . Thr—"

"Wait! Stop! You've hooked me!"

Sharmane dropped the rod to the boat floor with a clatter. The sight of Alex holding the hook on his shoulder made her feel faint at what she'd done. "Alex! I'm sorry! Where's the first aid kit!"

He shook his head. "You just got my shirt, not me. Can you pull it out so it doesn't rip?"

She couldn't stop her fingers from trembling, but she did manage to work the hook out of the fabric without leaving a hole. "I'm so sorry."

"Don't worry about it. Try again. This time, I'll stand farther away."

"I don't think this was such a good idea."

"Nonsense. No damage was done."

This time she stood at the back of the boat, while Alex stood in the front. She swung the rod with all her might and let the line go.

Alex peered down over the side of the boat. "I think you're supposed to cast the flies as far as you can over the surface of the water and drag it in, not send it straight down."

"I told you I'd never done this before." She reeled it in then laid her rod down. "Your turn."

Alex made a great show of patting his hat, sitting straight and tall, and squaring his shoulders. Sharmane didn't know why he was trying so hard to look superior, when the silly hat totally negated his efforts.

He cleared his throat and cast. Sharmane watched it go almost straight up and then fall straight down about eight feet off the side of the boat. "You didn't do any better than I did."

He reeled it in. "We'll get the hang of this. This is supposed to be relaxing."

After a number of attempts, their casting improved and soon they were able to cast out a fair distance. They tried casting out at the same time off opposite sides of the boat but kept clashing rods, so they decided to take turns casting from the same side. Besides, Sharmane was in no rush to get a fish. They would only be letting it go.

Alex took his turn to cast. "I cast mine farther than you did."

"Did not."

"Did too."

"Sez who?"

"Bet I catch the first fish."

"Bet you don't."

"Even if I don't, mine will be bigger."

"No way." Sharmane laid her rod on the bottom of the boat and leaned over the side. She slapped the water, splashing a few drops on him. "Take that!"

"Hey! No fair!" He finished reeling in his empty fly and then turned with a grin that Sharmane didn't want to interpret. "Your turn," he said, a little too sweetly.

"I think it's time we had lunch, don't you think?"

"Coward."

She held out a container and smiled back sweetly.

"With or without mustard?"

He accepted it but didn't open it. He dipped one hand over the side, scooped out a palm full of water, and threw it at her.

"Hey!" Sharmane grabbed the net, dipped it in the water, then wiggled it over his head so droplets splashed all over him.

Alex dipped his hat over the side of the boat and then tossed the water at her, but Sharmane saw it coming and ducked, only getting hit by a few stray drops.

"Stop it, Alex, you're rocking the boat too much!"

"I can swim."

She opened her mouth to retort, but the words left her. Alex had plopped the limp, wet hat back on his head. A few drops of water trickled down his cheek, and he sat completely still, grinning like an idiot, waiting.

Sharmane had never seen him like this, but from the brilliance of his smile and the simple joy in his face, it struck her that he needed to goof around more often.

All week long, since she couldn't figure out what he wasn't telling her, she tried to understand why. Up until now, he'd been reserved, almost formal, despite the casual activities they'd chosen.

Now, she finally put her finger on it. Alex was that one person who was lonely in a crowd, although she didn't know why. Perhaps she would never know the reason for his secrets, but they no longer mattered. If by goofing around together she had helped him find whatever he was looking for, she thanked God she could help her Christian brother.

When they first agreed to spend the week together, it had been Alex's suggestion that at the end of the week, they part as friends, along with the unspoken statement that they would never see each other again. If he needed this week to sort out his private dilemmas, then that was the way it would be. It was a week she would never forget, and she had to be thankful for the company. This vacation had turned into more fun than she ever could have realized.

"Never mind. I surrender. Now let's eat lunch and catch a fish."

She wasn't surprised when Alex reached for her hands as they prayed over their sandwiches. What did surprise her was that she realized when their vacation was over, she would miss him.

After their lunch was finished, Alex cast his fly while Sharmane stuffed the empty containers into her backpack.

Alex went stiff. "I caught something!"

Sharmane dropped the backpack. His line was tight and the fishing rod curved with tension as he struggled to reel in a fighting fish. Up until now, she'd considered fishing boring, but now her heart was pounding and she had to restrain herself from shouting to cheer him on as he pitted his limited skill against the fish.

She grabbed the net and leaned to the side of the boat, ready to scoop it up.

To her shock, he braced his feet wide apart and stood. The boat rocked perilously.

"What are you doing! Sit down!"

"I can't! I have to pull it in!" He pulled the rod over

his shoulder, winding furiously, making the boat rock even worse.

Sharmane frantically grabbed onto the side of the boat, leaning to the side in an attempt to counterbalance Alex as he leaned his weight backward against the pull of the fish. "You don't have to do anything!" she yelled. "We're only going to let it go anyway."

He leaned forward and yanked again. "It's the principle of the thing."

"I refuse to drown because of a principle!"

One final yank and the fish cleared the water. The thing was well over a foot long and thrashed so hard she didn't know how she was going to fit it in the net. Alex staggered back, then landed on his behind on the seat, making the boat rock even worse. Sharmane fumbled for the net and tried to capture the wriggling fish, but because of the fish's struggles and the motion of the boat, she couldn't get it in the net. Finally, Alex let the fish drop to the floor, so she dropped the net and clambered to subdue it with her hands.

"Yuck! It's slimy!"

Alex dropped his rod and also attempted to still the fish. "Of course it's slimy. It's a fish."

Together they pinned the squirming fish to the floor.

"I don't think it's good for it to be out of the water," Sharmane ground out between her teeth.

Alex nodded so fast the soggy hat fell off. "You hold it still, and I'll get the hook out if its mouth. Ready?"

Sharmane did her best to wrap both hands around it while Alex used the pliers from his brother's tackle box to pry the hook out of the fish's mouth as best as he could.

"Don't hurt it! Look, it's got a hole in its chin." She couldn't believe the burn of tears starting in the back of her eyes in sympathy for a dumb fish as she rose to her knees to start the process of putting the poor injured thing back in the water.

"Wait. I haven't patted it yet."

She lifted her head, about to tell him her thoughts on that, but the second she made eye contact, she saw Alex holding her camera with a napkin.

"Smile!"

"Now just a—"

The click of the camera silenced her. He touched the wiggling fish's head. "There. I patted it. Now put it back."

As gently as she could manage the thrashing fish, she bent over the side and nearly had the fish into the water when she heard another click.

"You didn't just take a picture of my rear—"

He grinned defiantly. "I want this one for my collection. I'll call it, 'Returning To the Wild.' Maybe I should enter it in a photography contest. I'd probably win."

The fish landed in the water with a splash. Rather than watch it swim away, Sharmane turned toward Alex about to tell him what she thought of his photography skills, but he took one look at her and burst out laughing.

Sharmane pressed her lips together and lunged for him, making the boat shift with the sudden movement. Sharmane felt herself about to fall, so she grabbed the front of his shirt to steady herself before she fell overboard. The combination of the rocking boat and abrupt motion caused both of them to drop to their knees.

The strong scent of the fish from her hands, which were entangled in his shirt, wafted between them. She stared at the way she was holding his shirt, unable to believe what she had done. He looked down too, but all he did was laugh.

She gave him a gentle shake. "What's gotten into you?"

Alex opened his mouth to speak, but no words came out. He didn't have an answer. All he could think of was how they were, how he only had to move a couple of inches, and he was in the perfect position to kiss her.

He didn't want to touch her with his slimy hands, and he couldn't drop her camera, so he relaxed his body, and her firm grip naturally drew them closer, although he was sure that was not her intent.

Before she could realize what he was doing, he tilted his head and claimed her mouth with his own, kissing her the way he had wanted to for days. And with his kiss, he gave her the last piece of his heart.

Gradually, they separated. He tried to analyze her dazed expression; hoping and praying what was happening to her was even a fraction of what was happening to him. If there had been any doubt before, he now knew for sure that he had fallen in love.

Her voice came out in a raspy whisper. "I think that's enough fishing. We should go home."

Chapter 7

Alex knocked on Sharmane's door and waited. Today felt different than yesterday. It was Saturday, but it wasn't simply that there hadn't been the usual rush hour traffic to contend with. The week was over and the weekend had begun, a reminder that Monday loomed closer.

He still hadn't pieced together what happened yesterday. After they'd both collected their wits they'd given up on fishing and instead had taken the boat around the lake a few times, taking turns driving. Since they both stunk like fish, rather than going out to a restaurant Sharmane had invited him to her house for dinner. It wasn't the same as the countless times he'd been invited to the home of a single woman. The good china had not been set out, no one had taken pains to dress up. The meal was ordinary and dessert was not rich or fancy—only store-bought cookies. Best of all, after dinner they'd both put their feet up on the coffee table and watched television with no hidden agendas.

It had felt relaxed and domestic. And he'd liked it.

Unfortunately, he was forced to leave earlier than he wanted because he had to return the boat.

The door opened.

Alex cleared his throat and stiffened. "So what are our plans for today?"

"I have to go to the mall."

"The mall? You can go to the mall any day."

She patted her purse. "I have to drop off all my film at the one-hour photo place, because this is the last day of our vacation and I promised I'd give you copies. Tomorrow is back to normal with church and stuff, and Monday is back to work."

Alex felt like he'd just been punched in the gut. He knew it was coming, but now that the last day had come, he wasn't ready. Just in case, he'd brought along the watch to give to her, but hearing her say it only proved how much he didn't want it to happen.

He forced himself to smile. "If we must go shopping, let's do tourist shopping. Let's go to Robson Street."

Her eyes lit up, and he felt somewhat better. "That sounds like a great idea!"

"And you can leave your camera at home today, right?"

She grinned. "Only if you insist."

The Robson Street shopping area of downtown Vancouver was everything their fishing trip wasn't. It was crowded, noisy, busy with sights and sounds, and smelled with everything from scented soap to exotic foods to mingled perfumes from the crowd to car exhaust. People talked and laughed, babies cried, traffic rumbled, music drifted from a few open doors, and nothing was still.

She wanted to go into every store, and Alex didn't mind. He held onto her hand from the moment they left the car and wouldn't let go, claiming he didn't want to get separated in the crowd. Together they checked out the wide variety of the specialty shops and checked everything the trendy area had to offer—every imaginable souvenir, holograms, naturally scented soaps, jade carvings and jewelry, and countless handmade crafts.

At the photo store, Alex couldn't believe his eyes at the number of rolls of film she emptied out of her purse, and she wasn't the least bit embarrassed about it.

They stopped for lunch at a sidewalk café and treated themselves to frozen yogurt with waffle cones so fresh they were still slightly warm.

Alex made sure to buy a few souvenirs, but every purchase was bittersweet, because he knew everything would remind him of today, their last day together, and how it would end. Very soon, he would have to tell her who he was. And she would hate him for it.

She wanted to stop for an early dinner, and Alex didn't want to do or say anything to spoil the day. Once seated inside the restaurant, she pulled out all the photos and divided them evenly, since she'd gotten doubles of everything. They laughed at many of them, and others made him feel reminiscent, even though it had only been a few days.

Too soon, she gathered all her purchases and photos and checked her watch. "They said my car would be ready at six, so we'd better go. If you don't mind, can you drop me off at the auto shop? Then you don't have to worry about driving me home."

Alex opened his mouth but no words came out. This was it. It was over.

"We'd better hurry. I don't want them to close before we get there."

He had no choice but to follow.

Sharmane wondered if she'd said or done something wrong, because Alex was silent most of the trip. In a way, even though it was strange, she preferred the silence. For their last few minutes together, it seemed right. The finality of their vacation being over left her with such an overwhelming sadness she didn't know if she could talk without breaking into tears.

She didn't know if it was good or bad when they pulled into the parking lot at the repair shop. Rather than draw out a long good-bye, Sharmane opened the car door before he turned off the ignition and held out the envelope that she had prepared last night.

"This is for you."

His eyebrows knotted as he accepted it.

"Promise me you won't open it until you get home."

"But—"

"Promise me. Please."

"Uh, okay, I promise."

"And thanks for everything, Alex. It's been a great week. Bye!" With that, Sharmane turned and dashed toward the building before she did or said something she would regret.

"Wait! Sharmane!"

She didn't stop. It was painful enough to say good-bye; she couldn't allow it to drag out.

She barely managed to compose herself to face the mechanic. While he searched for the work order, Sharmane watched Alex's car meld into the traffic and disappear. He didn't know it, but he'd taken a piece of her heart with him. No matter what he was hiding, even if it was that he was a convicted felon, she couldn't deny it. The final parting stab in her heart told her what she hadn't wanted to admit. She was more than halfway in love with him, and now, he was gone without ever knowing it.

Having her car back was a hollow victory. Once Sharmane arrived home, she felt restless when she should have felt good with her life back to normal. Where once she had anticipated browsing at leisure through the scores of photographs, she couldn't look at them. Instead, she sat on the couch holding a scented soap she had bought today and thought of how Alex had teased her about why she wanted to smell like a watermelon.

She'd lived by herself for years, but because Alex was never coming back, she'd never felt so lonely.

The unexpected rap of a knock on her door made her suddenly grateful for whoever was stopping by for an unscheduled visit.

Her heart nearly stopped when she opened the door. It was Alex.

"I have something for you." He reached into his pocket.

Sharmane should have felt it coming. She had kept track of the amount of gas and expenses they'd incurred and tucked the cash into an envelope, then given it to him at the last minute on purpose. In a way, it was cowardly, but she had thought it would work, except here he was about to try to return it.

"Please, Alex. Don't do this. Don't spoil what was a wonderful vacation by having it end on an argument."

"We can talk about that later." He fumbled in his pocket and pulled out a small bag. "I was saving this for our last day together, but you ran off before I could give it to you."

Her heart pounded. She recognized the Butchart Gardens logo. At the same time that she didn't want a gift from him, she was thrilled that he had. Her hands shook when she pulled out the watch she'd been drooling over. For one of the few times in her life, she was almost speechless. Tears burned the backs of her eyes. "Oh, Alex," she mumbled, trying to speak past the tightness in her throat. "I don't know what to say. Thank you."

"Then don't say anything. I'm glad you like it."

He stepped closer to take off her old watch and fasten the new one onto her wrist. The rose pictured was beautiful, and the stones shone even more than they did in the artificial light of the store. Rather than give the neighbors a show of what was happening on her doorstep, she was about to invite him in, but the sparkle of the watch stopped her.

She tilted it to catch the sunlight. The light played into a rainbow of brilliant colors with the cut of the stones, and the beauty of it stopped all other thoughts. Suddenly, a sinking feeling settled into the pit of her stomach. The rhinestones shone too much, meaning they weren't rhinestones, they were diamonds, and therefore, the watch was worth far more than she originally thought.

The second she looked up, he cringed, confirming her suspicion. She opened her mouth to speak, but his words cut her off.

"I know what you're going to say." He rested his fingers on her arm. "I want you to have it."

"But—"

He reached into his back pocket and pulled out the envelope she'd given him. "And I'm giving this back. Sharmane, I can't accept this."

Her head started to spin. She couldn't allow this sudden show of male ego to override common sense. She pointed to the street, toward his car. The money they were talking about had to be at least three car payments on his. . .

Her arm drifted back down to her side and Sharmane blinked, but the sight before her didn't change. The car parked in front of her house, the only car in the vicinity, was a very new, shiny foreign luxury car. She didn't know what it was, only that it was well beyond her lifestyle. "Where's your car?"

"That was my nephew's car. We traded cars for the week. I have mine back now."

She stared at the car then back at him. "That car costs more money than I make in a year."

"If I can afford the car, I can certainly afford the watch."

"And here I've been insisting on paying for my half of the gas and stuff. Is there anything else I should know that's going to make me feel even more stupid?"

"Sharmane, I—"

The phone rang inside the house, but Sharmane ignored it. "How dare you lie to me."

"I didn't lie. I just didn't tell you the truth."

She rested her fists on her hips. "And there's a difference?"

"Well, technically. . ."

The phone continued to ring.

"Aren't you going to answer that?"

"The answering machine will get it. Talk."

"I might have misled you a little."

She looked at the car again. "A little? I think you have some explaining to do."

He dragged one palm down his face. "You know the Arby Building, where we met?"

Sharmane blinked. She remembered it well. It was the high-rise office tower next to the park. "Of course. I was worried that you didn't have a job, but you work for Arby, don't you? And it must be a pretty good job, too."

He squeezed his eyes shut. "It's a little more complicated than that. I actually—"

The phone stopped ringing. Her recorded voice delivered a cheery message, followed by Barry's. "Hey, Sharmane! Where are you? I'm calling to remind you that Frank and Darlene's party is tonight, and it's not too late to change your mind. You can wear that little red number I got you last week. And that perfume in the green bottle. Call me before seven if you can make it. Bye."

Sharmane opened her mouth to continue, but Alex

stepped forward, forcing her to step back into the house. He shut the door abruptly and crossed his arms. "Who was that? Apparently I'm not the only one to be keeping secrets here."

"Secrets? You want to talk about secrets? Look who's talking! What do you do that you can afford a car like that?"

He crossed his arms over his chest. "I don't just work for Arby Enterprises. I own it."

"Own it? You told me your name is Alex Brunnel. Or is it?"

"I haven't lied to you, although I have been guilty of omission. My full name is Alexander R. Brunnel. I was going to register the name for the business license as ARB Enterprises, but Jason started calling it Arby to tease me, and it kind of stuck."

She stared at him while his words sank in. The owner of Arby Enterprises would be wealthy beyond her wildest imagination. A millionaire.

Sharmane shook her head and backed up another step. "No. This can't be happening."

"Who was that on the phone? How is your boyfriend going to feel about you being out with another man all week? Talk about breaking trust. You led me to believe you were single."

"Boyfriend? That was Barry, my brother, with another matchmaking attempt! And what gives you the right to talk about trust? You led me to believe you were unemployed, but nothing could be further from the truth. How could I ever believe a thing you say? Get out."

Before her eyes, his face turned to stone. In an instant, he turned and stomped out. The slam of the door echoed in the silent house.

Sharmane buried her face in her hands and pressed her forehead into the back of the closed door. "Dear Lord," she mumbled, "please help me. Was I right to be so angry? Is it possible to fall in love with someone you barely know, and then find you don't know them at all? Why do I feel so empty inside? I don't know what to pray for, but I trust You and whatever You choose to show me."

A knock sounded on the door. She wasn't going to answer it, but whoever it was knocked again then rang the doorbell.

Sharmane rubbed her eyes to make herself presentable then opened the door.

Alex stood in the doorway, water dripping down his face, his wet hair plastered to his head, his clothes drenched.

"It's raining. May I come in?"

Sure enough, the rain pelted down behind him. Just like the day they'd met, a sudden shower had come out of nowhere.

She nodded.

"Can we talk?"

She nodded again and led him to the couch.

As they sat, he cleared his throat and reached for her hands, holding them gently while he spoke.

"I couldn't let it end like this," he said, his voice low and quiet. "I have to explain. I can only say I was being selfish. When we first met, running away for a week was exactly what I thought I needed, but I worried that when you found out about me, everything would change. I justified trading the car so you wouldn't feel intimidated. I wanted you to think of me just as an ordinary man, so I started to lead you to believe things that were not true. As the week progressed, I wanted to tell you the truth, but by then, everything had spiraled out of control. And then I didn't want to take the chance that something like this would happen. That you'd hate me, and it would be over."

She couldn't comment. She couldn't speak. She could barely think. A gentle squeeze of her hands made her throat tighten, further inhibiting her from speaking.

"I was starting to fall in love with you, Sharmane. And I was hoping that you could feel even a little of the same toward me."

All she could do was stare at their joined hands. Everything he did and said indicated sincerity, but she really didn't know, because she didn't know who Alex really was.

"I'm dying here. Please say something."

"I don't know what to say. I thought I was starting to get to know you, but I really don't know you at all."

"But you do. For the first time since I can remember, I could relax and not care about who was watching or that anyone wanted anything from me. I didn't have to worry about people pretending to like me or that I wouldn't like them. When you threw me out, I stood there beside the car, kicking myself for what I'd done. And when the rain started, it seemed so fitting. I just laid my head on the roof of the car and prayed for God to give me the strength to talk to you again."

She nodded, but didn't speak. She, too, had prayed for strength.

"What I'd really like is for us to get to know each other better. Let me show you who Alex Brunnel really is. I didn't believe in love at first sight but it's happened, and I'm hoping the same has happened to you. I hope it won't be all that long, that with God's blessings, we'll soon be married. I love you, Sharmane."

She wanted to protest, but she couldn't. Even though she couldn't justify his deception, she could understand why he'd done what he had.

"I think I love you, too, but this has all happened so fast. I need more time."

His eyes closed for a few seconds, and she could both see and feel him relax at the same time.

"Can we start by attending church together tomorrow morning?"

Sharmane smiled. "I don't know if I'm ready to meet your family, but I'd like it if you could come to church with me, and after that, I was going to meet my brother. Do you want to tell him he doesn't need to play match-maker any more?"

Sharmane ran her fingers through Alex's wet hair, and his large hands cupped her face. "Yes, I'll show him you've found Mr. Right." And his kiss ended his reply.

GAIL SATTLER

Gail Sattler lives in a suburb of Vancouver, BC, with her husband and three sons, where a vacation really is only an hour away. Living amongst the beauty of God's creation so near the mountains and the ocean makes it easy to be a hometown tour guide for friends and family, despite an abundance of rain, and she feels truly blessed to live there. She often writes on her back deck where she can see the mountains, which is a great inspiration to compose love stories that are only possible with God in that happy ending. Gail has also written a number of novels for the Barbour Publishing's **Heartsong Presents** line. You are invited to visit Gail's web site at http://www.gailsattler.com.

A Letter to Our Readers

Dear Readers:

In order that we might better contribute to your reading enjoyment, we would appreciate your taking a few minutes to respond to the following questions. When completed, please return to the following: Fiction Editor, Barbour Publishing, Inc., P.O. Box 719, Uhrichsville, OH 44683.

1. Did you enjoy reading *Summer Getaways*?
   ❏ Very much, I would like to see more books like this.
   ❏ Moderately—I would have enjoyed it more if _____
   _____
   _____

2. What influenced your decision to purchase this book?
   (Check those that apply.)
   ❏ Cover   ❏ Back cover copy   ❏ Title   ❏ Price
   ❏ Friends   ❏ Publicity   ❏ Other _____

3. Which story was your favorite?
   ❏ *Spring in Paris*   ❏ *River Runners*
   ❏ *Wall of Stone*   ❏ *Sudden Showers*

4. Please check your age range:
   ❏ Under 18   ❏ 18–24   ❏ 25–34
   ❏ 35–45   ❏ 46–55   ❏ Over 55 _____

5. How many hours per week do you read? _____

Name _____

Occupation _____

Address _____

City _____ State _____ Zip _____

If you enjoyed

Summer Getaways

then read:

Summer Dreams

Summer Breezes by Veda Boyd Jones.
À la Mode by Yvonne Lehman.
King of Hearts by Tracie Peterson.
No Groom for the Wedding by Kathleen Yapp.

HEARTSONG
PRESENTS

If you love Christian romance...

$10.⁹⁹

You'll love Heartsong Presents' inspiring and faith-filled romances by today's very best Christian authors...DiAnn Mills, Wanda E. Brunstetter, and Yvonne Lehman, to mention a few!

When you join Heartsong Presents, you'll enjoy 4 brand-new mass market, 176-page books—two contemporary and two historical—that will build you up in your faith when you discover God's role in every relationship you read about!

Imagine...four new romances every four weeks—with men and women like you who long to meet the one God has chosen as the love of their lives...all for the low price of $10.99 postpaid.

Mass Market 176 Pages

To join, simply visit www.heartsong presents.com or complete the coupon below and mail it to the address provided.

YES! Sign me up for Heartsong!

NEW MEMBERSHIPS WILL BE SHIPPED IMMEDIATELY!
Send no money now. We'll bill you only $10.99 post-paid with your first shipment of four books. Or for faster action, call 1-740-922-7280.

NAME _____

ADDRESS _____

CITY _____STATE_____ ZIP_____

MAIL TO: HEARTSONG PRESENTS, P.O. Box 721, Uhrichsville, Ohio 44683
or sign–up at **WWW.HEARTSONGPRESENTS.COM**

ADPG05